M000291017

*To Pau~ ...
Enjoy!.*

GARDEN GIRL

Renny deGroot.

RENNY DEGROOT

Copyright © 2021 Renny deGroot

ISBN 978-0-9936947-6-9

All Rights Reserved. No part of this publication may be reproduced, stored in a retrieval system, or transmitted, in any form or in any means – by electronic, mechanical, photocopying, recording or otherwise – without prior written permission.

Toadhollow Publishing 7509 Cavan Rd Bewdley, Ontario K0L 1E0

Contact Renny at: http://www.rennydegroot.com

ALSO BY RENNY DEGROOT

<u>FICTION:</u>
Family Business
After Paris
Torn Asunder

<u>NON-FICTION:</u>
32 Signal Regiment: Royal Canadian Signal Corps – A History

This is a work of fiction. Although set in the beautiful island of Cape Breton, Nova Scotia, Canada, the names, characters, businesses, events and incidents are the products of the author's imagination. Any resemblance to actual persons, living or dead, or actual events is purely coincidental. The story is not intended to represent the actual methods and practices of the Cape Breton Regional Police Service.

Dedicated to the people of Nova Scotia—the province of my birth and always in my heart.

PROLOGUE
AUGUST 17TH, 2009

SARAH TURNED AWAY. HER heart pounded with the joy of it all. The words she had just spoken were still in her mouth: "It's my decision and honestly, I just don't care about your opinion anymore."

She smiled as half a dozen crows rose from the fence rail, cawing noisily in fear as the shadow of a mighty bald eagle soared above, his eye no doubt trained on his scurrying victims below. Sarah took a deep breath, enjoying the early evening breeze that carried the sound of wailing seagulls and the smell of decaying seaweed. In the distance, the sun sparkled on the choppy waters between her vantage point on Cape Breton and the mainland of Nova Scotia. Sarah was so focussed on the happy view of her future, set against the backdrop of this beloved spot, that she didn't hear the soft sound of a length of two-by- four lumber being hefted. She didn't see the shadow as it was swung.

In one instant she felt happier than in all of her nineteen-year life, and in the next she was in blinding pain as the weapon crushed her skull. She cried out in shock, but the sound was short-lived on her dying lips.

CHAPTER 1

MAY 2019

VANESSA HUNT SCRUBBED AT the bacon grill-pan absent-mindedly while she looked out the kitchen window. The barren tree in front of her house was filled with crows cawing amongst themselves while a nuthatch pecked for insects lurking under the dead bark. The grey ocean heaved and rolled in the distance as a bleak backdrop to the dead tree.

Vanessa drained the water from the sink and spoke aloud. "Sorry, birds. Enjoy your last morning on that tree. I promise to put up a feeder when the tree is gone."

She dried her hands and hung the towel neatly on the handle of the cupboard below the sink. She gave the kitchen one last glance and felt a warm glow.

She nodded to herself. *I love this place. The inside is perfect after three years of renovations and now it's high time to start on the outside.*

Vanessa glanced at the round face of the wall clock hanging above the fridge. *Where is that fella? I love Nova Scotia, but they sure work to their own schedules here. If this was back home in Ontario and a contractor was running half an hour late, I'd tear a strip off him.*

She put on her blue parka and light blue gloves. She tended towards wearing blues and greens, knowing they looked good on her. Those colours brought out her sea-green eyes and contrasted with her ash blond shoulder-length hair. The smattering of freckles across her nose and cheeks weren't as obvious as they once were, now hidden in laugh creases. Vanessa wasn't a vain woman but believed that even retired women in their mid-fifties should make an effort to look after themselves.

She went out through the bright butter-yellow painted mud-room to the side yard. Even here, sheltered by the house, the wind was fierce, coming off St. George's Bay. She looked in vain for any sign of tulips poking up yet. She heard the crows screaming as they lifted into the air. *Ah, he must be here.*

Vanessa hastened to the front of the house where a rusty black pickup truck stopped with a puff of diesel fumes and the ticking of a cooling engine. The backhoe on the trailer seemed very large for the job at hand.

Vanessa waited while the man hitched up his work pants before stretching out her hand to shake his. "You must be Joe."

The heavy-set man nodded and gestured with his thumb to the younger version of himself who climbed out of the passenger side. "This is Mike."

Vanessa nodded. "Hi, Mike."

"Hiya."

Joe stepped into the overgrown flower bed and slapped the tree. "This is her?"

Vanessa nodded. "Yes. I need that removed completely, including the roots as much as possible, and then," she paced out an oval "I want this dug out so I can put in a little pond. I'm thinking ten feet long by five feet wide and five feet deep."

"Hmm."

Vanessa looked at the backhoe. "Isn't that machine too big for this job?"

3

"Nope. I can do anything, big or small, with this baby."

"Well, that's terrific. Shall I leave you to it?"

"What do you want done with the wood?"

"Could you chunk it up for me and just leave it off to the side there? Not the roots, obviously."

He smiled a gap-toothed smile. "Sounds good. We'll get this tree out and cut up then and it'll just about be time for a cup of tea."

Vanessa nodded. "I'll be ready."

She went back into the house, revelling in the warmth of the wood-burning stove in the living room. She didn't want to stand at the kitchen window obviously staring so she went up to the spare bedroom of the one and a half storey century home and perched on the edge of the bed. From here she had a perfect view of the work below.

The speed with which the two men got to work amazed Vanessa. They rolled the backhoe off the trailer, and fastened a heavy chain around the trunk with the other end attached to the machine. It wasn't a huge tree, and before Vanessa could have imagined it, the tree was pulled out and lay on the lawn. Mike took a chainsaw from the truck and sliced through the limbs while Joe manoeuvred the backhoe into position to dig out the pond. With the first scoop of the bucket everything came to a stop. Joe waved at Mike to catch his attention, and the chainsaw whined to a stop. Joe lowered the bucket again, gently resting it on the ground while Mike stood gaping.

Vanessa frowned. What are they looking at? She stood pressed against the window. *Oh, my God. Are those...oh my God, they are. They're bones. Human bones?*

CHAPTER 2

DETECTIVE GORDIE MACLEAN FUMBLED inside his jacket to pull out his phone. His Great Pyrenees dog pricked her ears at the sound and stopped to sit at his feet while he answered the call.

MacLean pushed his mop of silver hair out of his eyes and glanced at the display. "Damn." He looked down at the dog. "Do I really need to answer this?" She cocked her head and watched him. He sighed and then pressed the phone to his ear. He cupped his hand around his mouth to reduce the wind noise. "Hey, Boss."

The distant sound of Sergeant Arsenault came through. "Where are you, MacLean?"

"Close to home. Just out with Taz for the morning constitutional."

"We've got a report of bones dug up in a garden up near Port Mulroy, so that's your patch."

MacLean nodded even though no one other than his dog could see him. "Right. It's probably nothing. Probably a pet cemetery."

"The homeowner insists the bones are human."

MacLean rolled his eyes at Taz, who wagged her tail. "Let me get back to the house and I'll call you back. You can give me the details then."

MacLean slid the phone back into his inside pocket. "Sorry girl, short walk today. Fancy going for a drive?"

Taz wagged her tail some more and gazed up at him, her golden-brown eyes looking surprisingly like MacLean's own eyes.

Gordie MacLean enjoyed working on his own and loved living alone. At fifty-three years old he knew that his head of thick silver-white hair made him look older but didn't worry about it. He loved country music and still smoked, although occasionally considered quitting. All Gordie needed was Taz for company and he was content. This corner of Cape Breton Island was usually quiet. Most of his work involved domestics and the odd sexual assault. The Major Crimes Unit of the Cape Breton Regional Police Service, of which he was a part, was headquartered in Sydney which was an hour and a half away. He worked on his own, going to the office for meetings and to process evidence. Murders were part of the responsibilities of the MCU but he had never been the lead on one. That was city stuff. Most of his patch was rural and small towns where people generally got along.

MacLean spent ten minutes following the coastal trail back to where he had left his Santa Fe. He popped open the back and Taz leaped in. He drove back to his house on Shannon Road, parked beside the white bungalow and opened the back for the dog to jump out.

MacLean punched the speed dial number on his home phone for his Staff Sergeant, John Arsenault. "OK, I'm here with pen in hand. Give me the info."

"It's just before Port Mulroy off Route 19. The house is on Parish Lane. The first house, municipal number 2 Parish Lane. If you get to the church, you've missed it."

"OK. I can picture the area. I'm on my way now."

"The homeowner is Vanessa Hunt."

"Does she sound hysterical?"

"Not at all."

"Right. I'll let you know when I pull out the dog-collar."

MacLean heard Arsenault chuckle as he disconnected. MacLean looked at the phone in his hand. He didn't often hear laughter coming from Arsenault.

MacLean looked at his dog. "You'll have to stay in the car while I check it out. Can't have you digging up the rest of some long-lost relative, right?"

The dog's white feathery tail waved, and she trotted to the door.

MacLean and Taz went back out to the car, the dog settling down on the blanket he always kept in the back for her. The back seat was permanently folded down to give the dog lots of space. Gordie MacLean never had more than one passenger in the car. His sister and mother lived in Halifax and his father was long dead, for which Gordie regularly gave thanks.

MacLean took his time, enjoying the springtime drive. It took him forty minutes to find the exact house since he went past it the first time. He turned around in the church parking lot and drove back the few minutes to Parish Lane. A row of cedar trees sheltered the driveway from the main road, so the backhoe wasn't obvious until he turned into the lane.

MacLean opened a rear door and poured water into Taz's water dish from the four-litre bottle he kept in the back. "Have a nap, girl."

He slammed the door and walked towards the backhoe. A woman came out of the house followed by two men dressed in work clothes.

MacLean pulled out his business card and handed it to the woman. She was a good inch taller than his five foot eight inches. He liked that she walked erect with good posture. "Mrs. Hunt?"

She shook her head. "Ms. Hunt. Better still, please call me Vanessa."

He nodded. "Vanessa, I'm Detective Gordie MacLean." He turned to the older of the two men with Vanessa. "And you are?"

"I'm Joe Curry and this is my son, Mike. I own the equipment." Joe kept his hands stuffed into his pockets.

MacLean turned back to Vanessa. "So, what seems to be the problem here?"

She gestured for him to follow her. He walked across the lawn to where the partially amputated tree lay. They stepped through piles of dead branches to the edge of the pit with its lumps of freshly exposed soil shining wetly. Vanessa pointed to the bucket of the digger. There, in its teeth, a long bone sat wedged. Part of an arm, or maybe a leg. It was a long time since MacLean had done his forensics course.

MacLean frowned. "Jesus."

Vanessa touched MacLean's arm. "And look down there."

He followed her pointing hand to examine the excavated hole. He saw more bones, most strikingly, the skull. No question about it. A human skull. "Right, let's get back further. I'll have to call the Forensic Identification team. This is going to take a while, so let's go in the house and I can take your statements."

Joe made a face. "How long is a while? I have another job scheduled for tomorrow and planned on taking the backhoe there this afternoon."

MacLean shook his head. "That may still happen, but we aren't moving the bones until the forensics team has taken their photos. Sorry. You folks go on in and I'll just go back to the car to call it in."

Taz lifted her head hopefully when MacLean got back in the car. He dialled his sergeant and then stroked the dog's big head as she rested it on his shoulder. "I shouldn't have brought you along, big girl. Sorry, you'll have a long day stuck in the car now."

His boss answered.. "MacLean? Who are you talking to?"

"The dog. Listen. It's the real thing. We've got a set of bones here, one of which is stuck in the teeth of the digger."

"Christ."

"I'm guessing the forensics team will want to do all the photos themselves. Or do you want me to just take them with my phone? The guy who owns the machine is keen to get going with it."

"No, no. Don't move anything. There could be forensics on the machine aside from the bone itself. Damn it all, Doyle picked a great time to be off with a heart attack." Doyle was MacLean's colleague in MCU. MacLean heard the sigh from Sergeant Arsenault. "Well, there's no help for it. You'll have to take the lead."

"That's what I figured. I'll tape the scene and take their statements and we'll all just hang out here then."

"Right. I'll get the team over there as soon as possible. MacLean, don't screw this up."

MacLean gritted his teeth. "I'm not in the habit of screwing things up."

"No, but you've had nothing this big before." Arsenault hung up without saying goodbye.

MacLean leaned over and pulled his crime scene kit bag onto the passenger seat. He took out a roll of yellow tape and climbed out of the car. He walked back to where the dead tree lay and started there, tying an end to a limb pointing up like an accusing finger. From there he went around marking off a wide circle with the tape, tying it to bushes, a patio table, a tree and then back to the dead tree again. He tossed the roll of tape back into his car and then went to the house. Vanessa must have been watching because she met him at the door, holding it open to allow him to pass her as he stepped inside. He smelled perfume, but not something overpowering. Something musky and warm.

He took off his brown leather hiking boots, grateful that his socks were in good shape, and followed her into the living room.

Vanessa gestured to an oversized armchair under a tall window giving a view over the side yard. "Please make yourself comfortable, Detective."

MacLean sat down and looked around the room. "This is really nice. You must have done a lot of work here."

Vanessa held up the teapot. "Tea? I'm afraid I don't drink coffee so tea's your only option."

"Yes, please. Just milk."

Mike took the opportunity to lean forward and take a cookie from the plate on the pine coffee table. He slid back to his place on the sofa, father and son looking even more alike in their shared discomfort sitting side by side in this stranger's home.

Vanessa set the steaming mug on the small round table beside MacLean's chair.

MacLean took a sip and set it back down. "Perfect, thank you."

She smiled a genuine-looking smile. "So, tell us, what happens now?"

MacLean flipped open his notebook and pulled a pen from his breast pocket. "Now you'll all tell me everything you can about this place and how you came to discover the bones. Let's start with you. How long have you owned this property?"

Vanessa sat back in the spindle-backed rocking chair. "It will be three years on May first. I bought it from the Diocesan Council. I understand that the property belonged to a woman who once served as a housekeeper for the church. It had been in her family since it was built more than a hundred years ago, but she died without family and so she left it to the church."

"Right. Do you know the name of that woman?"

Joe chipped in. "It was Mary Ryan. I used to come to this house when I was a child because Mary did the communion classes here."

Vanessa clapped her hands. "Oh, how wonderful. So, you know what the house looked like before I had it renovated."

"Wouldn't recognize it now. It's like a different house." With those comments Joe leaned in and took the last cookie from the plate before sinking back into the sofa again. His son's forehead creased slightly at the sight of the cookie in his father's hand.

MacLean made a note. "Mary Ryan. Any idea when she died, Joe?"

"Nope."

"OK, go ahead Vanessa. You bought it three years ago, but you didn't do any gardening until now?" MacLean realized his question sounded like a rebuke. "I mean, you didn't do any real digging in that area until now?"

"No. I've spent most of my time and money doing up the inside first. I've planted a few bulbs, but that's it. This is the summer for tackling the landscaping and that dead tree was first on the list."

MacLean thought about what other information she may have. "Did anyone ever show much interest in your plans for the landscaping? Neighbours stopping by, that sort of thing?"

"Nothing that really strikes me as odd. The community has been very welcoming and of course very curious about the changes I've made inside, so certainly people have stopped in over the past couple of years." Vanessa ticked off names on her fingers. "Barb and Bill MacIsaac from the next house up along Parish Lane, various contractors, Horace from down the lane on the other side of Route 19. He sometimes brings me fresh fish. The local priest, Father John, of course." Vanessa smiled. "He's had little luck with me, I'm afraid, but I go to church at Christmas so that gives him the hope that keeps him coming back, I suppose."

"But no one with a particular interest in your outside plans?"

Vanessa shook her head. "I'm afraid not." She smiled then and very quietly murmured, "A murder."

MacLean frowned and caught the eye of Joe, whose mouth fell open. Even Mike, who seemed, a moment ago, on the verge of falling asleep, seemed to shock into wakefulness.

MacLean's voice was cool. *Is she some kind of ghoul?* "I think you're getting ahead of yourself there, Vanessa. We have no idea if this is a murder or not. The bones may have been there for the past hundred years and been part of an original family plot or something."

Vanessa flushed a bright red. "Oh, heavens. I didn't mean that at all. It's just that every morning the crows gathered in that dead tree and shouted at me. They were the only ones who seemed to take a great interest in what was happening to that space."

MacLean frowned even deeper.

Vanessa shrugged. "A group of crows is called 'a murder'."

Before MacLean could respond, Joe said, "Really? I thought a bunch of birds was a flock. Always a flock."

MacLean didn't want to admit that he thought the same thing. "No, different birds have different names for a group. For crows it's a murder."

Joe turned to his son. "Did you know that?"

"I think I heard it somewhere before."

Joe rolled his eyes at his son.

MacLean nodded to Vanessa. "I think that's everything for you right now. If you think of anything to add, please let me know."

He turned his attention to Joe and Mike. He took their full names, phone numbers and addresses. Then he began questioning them in detail. "Joe, you were here before. Did you ever notice anything odd about that part of the property before?"

Joe shook his head. "Like what?"

"Like, was there ever a small cross there or something else that might indicate it was a burial spot?"

"No. I was a kid when I was here. I noticed nothing other than what time it was and wishing I could leave as quick as possible."

"You haven't been here since then? That was..." MacLean took a guess "somewhere around forty years ago?"

Joe nodded. "Something like that."

"Mike, what about you? Did you take your communion classes here as well?"

"No, we had ours in the church basement."

"Have you ever been here for any other reason?"

"Nope."

"So, Joe, tell me about this morning."

"We got here this morning and after a quick chat with Ms. Hunt just to confirm what we were doing, we got down to it. Took the tree down in no time. It was pretty much ready to fall anyway, and then while Mike started chunking up the tree, I got ready to dig out the pond. We should have been done and gone by now." Joe's mouth turned down as he considered his blown schedule.

"Did you see anything before you raised the bone in the bucket?"

"Not really. I was just focussed on digging in the right place. I was going to drop the earth at one end of the hole like Ms. Hunt asked me to, so that's all I was thinking about."

"Until you saw the bone."

"Right. Until I saw the bone. Even then, at first, I thought it was just a white piece of wood. It took a minute to realize what it was, but as soon as I did, I just lowered the bucket again and stopped."

"You did the right thing. If you had dropped the load, you might have destroyed some evidence."

Joe nodded and looked pleased.

MacLean prompted him. "And then?"

"I stopped the machine and called for Mike to come take a look." Joe looked at his son, who nodded.

Joe continued, "We stood there staring at this bone and then I looked down in the hole and saw a pile of bones. And then Ms. Hunt came out and we all just looked until Ms. Hunt said not to touch anything, and she'd call the police."

MacLean stopped writing. "Anything else you can think of? What about you, Mike? Anything to add?"

"Nope."

MacLean closed his notebook. "All right. That should do for now."

Joe brightened. "Does that mean we can go?"

MacLean nodded. "You can take your truck and trailer, but not the backhoe until the forensics team has finished with it."

Joe and Mike stood. "Will you call me to let me know when I can pick it up?"

"I will. Thank you for your patience. I'm guessing you can get it tomorrow."

"Will we be able to finish the job tomorrow?"

"Oh, no. That will be awhile. You'll have to reschedule that with Ms. Hunt. She can contact you about that."

Joe sighed. "Right, then. Let's go, Mike."

MacLean stood as well. "I'll walk out with you." He took his jacket from the hook in the mudroom, pulled on his boots and walked to the truck with the two men and as they manoeuvred the truck and trailer out of the drive, pulled out his pack of cigarettes and lit one. Gordie drew deeply, enjoying the first deep drag as it filled his lungs, but when he started coughing the simple pleasure was reduced. He walked over to his vehicle and opened the back, sitting on the edge of the cargo area while Taz nuzzled his neck.

"Sorry, girl. I had no idea this was going to take so long." He glanced at his watch. "No time to take you home and come back. The gang should be here any time now."

MacLean started as Vanessa came around and stood in front of him. He felt himself grow warm, as he realized she must have heard him talking to his dog.

Vanessa's eyes widened as Taz stood up. "What an enormous dog. What's his name?"

"*Her* name is Taz. I don't notice her size anymore. She's 110 pounds, so I suppose most people would agree with you."

"May I pat her?"

"Oh, yes. She's very friendly."

Vanessa stretched in to scratch under Taz's chin.

MacLean nodded. "That's good. Most people automatically try to pat the top of the dog's head, but that makes her tilt her head back. It's more of a threat than what you just did. That way she can smell you as your hand approaches and it's not threatening. Her breed is all about protection, so she's probably warier than some dogs."

Taz wagged her tail and poked her nose into Vanessa's hand.

MacLean smiled at the dog. "Sure, Taz. Make me a liar. After me saying you're wary." He pinched the end of his cigarette butt and tucked it into the packet. Years of training ensured he didn't add anything to a crime scene.

Vanessa grinned. "She's gorgeous. Please do let her come into the house. I'm sure she's bored with sitting here all this time."

"I couldn't do that. Your house is too tidy for the likes of Taz. She's a walking shed machine."

"That doesn't matter. I love dogs and keep thinking I should get one of my own but somehow with the move here from Ontario and then all the work in the house, the time hasn't been right yet. Please, do come in with her."

"Are you sure?"

"Absolutely."

"All right. That's very kind. I'll just walk her down the lane for a minute and then we'll come in."

"May I walk with you? If you're making calls or whatever I understand, and I'll go back in."

"No, it's fine."

They walked to the end of her driveway and then turned right, up the lane away from the shore. Taz walked along in the grass, sniffing contentedly at all the new smells.

MacLean picked up on something she had said. "So, you came here from Ontario."

"Yes."

"What brought you here?"

"I inherited some money from my mother. Enough to take early retirement from teaching, and I decided that a whole new life was in order. I had nothing keeping me in Ontario and I've been here to Nova Scotia on holiday before and decided I'd take the leap."

"Are you glad you did?"

"Definitely. The pace of life is so different here. I'm a poet and it suits me. The sea within walking distance, nature all around me, and friendly people. What's not to like?"

"Did you come from a city in Ontario?"

She nodded. "Toronto."

They reached a bend in the lane and without consultation they turned to go back. They were on a shallow rise which gave a spectacular view of the ocean below. A large tanker chugged through the strait.

MacLean gave Vanessa one last chance to change her mind about letting Taz inside. "She's got wet feet now. She'll be fine in the car."

Vanessa shook her head and led the way through the mudroom door. "Please, bring her in."

The dog went straight to the wood stove and lay down in front of it with a sigh. Vanessa smiled at MacLean and he nodded. Any person who liked his dog was a decent person in MacLean's book.

They chatted about the house and area for a few minutes, and then MacLean saw the forensics van turn into the driveway.

MacLean stood up. "Please stay here. I'll take the team through what we have."

Taz opened her eyes and MacLean put up his hand to stop her from following him. He went out to the yard to meet with the team.

CHAPTER 3

THE TWO MEN AND one woman from the forensics team were suiting up in their white Scene of Crime overalls. MacLean resisted the urge for another cigarette and went over to their van. "Hi, guys."

The team leader, a tall thin man wearing black-rimmed glasses, named John Allan nodded. "MacLean."

"When you're ready, I'll show you what we've got."

Allan finished slipping the white booties over his shoes. "Right. Lead on."

MacLean led the way up to the yellow tape. From their viewpoint outside the tape, the bone was clearly visible, hanging from the teeth of the digger. "There you have it."

MacLean held the tape up to allow Allan and the two other forensic technicians to duck underneath. He stayed on his side of the tape and watched as the three white-clad specialists inched towards the digger and the raw earth of the pit. MacLean spoke as they fanned out to approach the pit from three different angles. He gave them the highlights of what he knew so far. It was a short summary and when finished, he stopped talking. No one needed chatter while they were concentrating on looking for evidence.

MacLean stood watching for a few moments and then went back to his car. He leaned against the hood and had a cigarette, nipping it again when he got to the end. He called out to Allan. "I'll just go inside and update the homeowner."

He tapped on the door and went inside without waiting for a response. Taz stood up and stretched before coming over to poke at him. MacLean rested his hand on her head, and she sat down by his feet.

Vanessa stood by the window, watching. "I suppose they'll be awhile."

MacLean nodded. "I'm afraid so. They'll take all their photos. They'll search for any bits of fabric or other debris that may have been lifted out of the site by the digger. After that, they'll really get down to it and dig their way down to the area around the bones. Once they've brushed away all the dirt, exposing everything they feel is relevant, and after taking photos, they'll remove the bones to take them back to the lab."

Vanessa sighed. "It's not the way I imagined getting the pond dug out."

"No. I guess not. I'm going to leave them to it and I'm going to head down to headquarters to brief my sergeant."

Vanessa raised her eyebrows. "Oh. Somehow I thought we were in this together and that you would stay around until things were back to normal."

MacLean shook his head. "'Fraid not."

She nodded. "I suppose that would be a waste of police time."

MacLean smiled. "I can get started on a few things while Detective Allan and his team are doing their thing."

"Of course."

He wasn't sure why he was reluctant to leave. "I'll drop around tomorrow to let you know where things stand."

The worried look on Vanessa's face brightened. "I'd appreciate that. Thank you."

MacLean turned towards the door. "Come on, Taz."

"Detective MacLean?"

He turned back to Vanessa "Yes?"

"What's Taz short for?"

He laughed and looked down at the dog. "When she was a pup, she was like a Tasmanian Devil, tearing around the place."

"Ah. She's changed now."

"Thank God."

He and his dog walked to the edge of the tape. MacLean knew he didn't need to restrain Taz. She wouldn't cross the line unless he told her to. "Allan? I'm heading down to HQ now. You've got my number if anything develops that you think I need to know."

Allan waved and then carried on talking to the team as the two forensic identification technicians crouched over the hole, taking photographs.

***

It was a little out of the way to drop Taz off at home, but MacLean knew from experience that Sergeant Arsenault frowned on having her in the office. She tended to leave a cloud of white dog hair behind wherever she went, and Arsenault was a bit of a stickler for tidiness and following the rules.

"Sorry, dear girl. You've had enough excitement for one day. You're on house arrest for the rest of the day, and maybe evening."

MacLean saw in the rear-view mirror that she lifted her head when he spoke. Her right ear stood straight up, while the other, the one edged in grey, flopped down, giving her a quizzical expression.

"Don't worry. I'll get Shirley from next door to come in and give you some dinner."

Taz lay down, muzzle on her front paws.

"Yes, I know you like that, anyway. She always gives you more than you should get."

MacLean turned into his driveway and he and the dog went into the house. He filled her water dish and made himself a cheese sandwich to eat on the drive to Sydney. He called the neighbour to leave a message asking her to come over later to feed Taz.

"Right, then. I'm off."

He gave Taz one more pat on the head and half a dog cookie. There was a dog flap in the kitchen door that led out to a fenced-in backyard, so Taz would be fine until he came home again, whenever that might be.

He got in the car with his sandwich beside him on the passenger seat. He'd swing by and get a coffee at Tim Horton's on his way through Saint Peter's.

He called through to his sergeant as he drove. "Hey, Sergeant. MacLean here. The team's in place, so I'm on my way down to HQ now. I thought I'd start with missing persons to see what we might be looking at."

"Does it look fresh?"

"No, it's been there for quite some time. I'm guessing years."

"Like, a lot of years? Old family, graveyard, maybe?"

"Hard to say, but there were no markers or anything, so that seems unlikely."

"OK. We'll talk when you get here. MacLean?"

"Yeah?"

"You don't have the damn dog with you, do you?"

MacLean snapped. "No."

"Good." The phone disengaged.

***

It was after six o'clock when the F.I. team got back to HQ with the bones and delivered them to the lab. Allan came through to MacLean's cubicle and sat in the spare chair.

MacLean tipped his own chair back and folded his hands behind his head. "What can you tell me?"

"It wasn't very deep. It's amazing the corpse hasn't appeared before now."

"Hmm. That could suggest the burial was done in a hurry."

Allan shrugged. "Possibly."

"Any thoughts on gender?"

"Female. Based on the quick look I took, I'd say youngish. Late teens to early twenties. The sternum isn't fused to the clavicle yet. We'll do a proper look tomorrow, so don't take it as gospel."

"That's helpful. Even if the age changes, I can eliminate any missing persons for male. That's a start, anyway."

Allan stood. "I'll have a proper report tomorrow on likely race and age, but I figured you'd want to at least know the sex as soon as possible."

"Were there any artifacts like clothing or jewellery? Or I.D.?" he added hopefully.

"Some pieces of fabric and buttons. Not much else."

"I wonder how long she's been down there."

"I'll probably get you a better idea on that in the next day or two. We've taken soil samples to help with the aging."

"OK, thanks, John. Appreciate it."

Allan walked away, and MacLean spent ten minutes updating his notes. He reviewed them and then went down the hall to Sergeant Arsenault's office. The door was open, so he tapped and walked in.

Sergeant Arsenault was a muscular man, showing evidence of hours spent with weights in the gym. His dark moustache was always perfectly trimmed, as was his regulation length, side parted hair.

MacLean had a moment to notice how tight Arsenault's sleeves were around his bulging biceps. *I wonder if he has the shirts tailored to fit that way.*

Arsenault set his pen down on the desk. "Well, what do we know so far?"

MacLean glanced at one of the two chairs facing the desk and then looked back at his sergeant.

Arsenault waved his hand at the chair. "All right, sit down."

MacLean flipped open his notebook, even though there wasn't enough information there for him to need his notes, took his time studying the pages and then spoke in his usual, slow, easygoing voice. He sensed Arsenault wanted to snap his fingers and say something like 'pick up the pace, man.' MacLean had heard him do that to others, but he refused to be rushed.

When MacLean finished reviewing what he knew as a fact, Arsenault picked up his pen and tapped it on the desk. "So, a young female. Do you have any hits from missing persons that could be a match?"

MacLean nodded. "Three, maybe four, depending on confirmation of age."

"Don't get ahead of yourself and contact any of the families yet. We want to get the confirmation of age first. Maybe dental records will help us."

MacLean closed his book. "I'll wait to find out how long the bones have been there before knowing if I've got a full set of possibles."

Arsenault nodded. "Of course. That makes sense."

"Don't worry, Sarge." MacLean saw the flush of irritation on Arsenault's face at his use of this short form for the rank he'd risen to so quickly in his career.

MacLean continued. "I know this is the first time I'm lead for an unexplained death, but I've been involved in enough cases to know the procedure. Take it step by step. Tomorrow I'll be in the lab with the team and as soon as they know anything about the when and how, I'll figure out where we go."

"Yes, all right. Just keep me posted." Arsenault went back to the report he had been reviewing and MacLean knew he'd been dismissed.

MacLean called Allan, who had already left the building. "John, I meant to ask if the fellow who owns the backhoe can fetch it tomorrow. He's keen to get on with his work."

"Yes, we've processed it. We will be going back to the site to do a wider dig, but we're pretty confident that there's nothing else to be found there, so don't let him start working on the site."

"No, not to worry. I've explained to the homeowner that the work would have to be rescheduled. At the moment, I just want to release the equipment."

"Go ahead."

MacLean called Joe Curry and gave him the good news, and then he called Vanessa Hunt.

"Ms. Hunt? This is Detective MacLean."

"I thought we had graduated to you calling me Vanessa."

MacLean smiled. "Vanessa, then. I just wanted to let you know that I've called Joe Curry to let him know that he can come and get the backhoe tomorrow."

"I'm sure he was happy about that."

"Yes, I'd say he was."

"Thank you for letting me know. I understand from Detective Allan that they'll be coming back here to do more digging?"

"That's right. Two people will be back tomorrow, but they seem confident that there won't be any other surprises there."

"One was enough."

"Yes, I'm sure."

"So, you won't be coming back tomorrow?"

"No. I have plenty to be getting on with here, but if I have any updates that I can share with you, I'll let you know."

Vanessa seemed as though she wanted to make the conversation stretch on. "You work long hours. How does poor Taz manage?"

"I have a very good neighbour who helps out."

"Ah. If ever the neighbour isn't available, and you need someone to look after her, I'd be happy to pitch in."

MacLean frowned. "That's very kind. I'll keep it in mind. You have a good evening now. I hope you aren't too upset by today's drama."

"Thank you for your concern, Detective. I'll be fine. Take care."

"Yeah. Bye, now."

MacLean thought about the conversation. *Is she just lonely? Seems very friendly for someone who's just gone through the experience she's had today.* He shook his head and put her out of his mind as he set up the briefing room for the morning.

Along one side wall of the small room were two eight-foot tables that were used for any number of purposes, ranging from holding pizza boxes to crime scene evidence to papers for collating. At the front of the room there was a large wall monitor hooked up to a computer which was used to display PowerPoint presentations and beside that, a whiteboard. A small wooden table sat under the whiteboard, holding markers, magnets and sticky notes. In the corner, a group of flags stood proudly. The red and white Canadian flag, the predominantly blue and white provincial flag, and the mainly green and yellow Cape Breton Regional Municipality flag added a splash of colour to the otherwise drab room. Having eyes only for what he'd need for the briefing, he set everything up with chairs in rows facing the whiteboard, checked that the markers worked, and a brush was available. Tomorrow they'd assign him at least one detective to help run down leads.

Satisfied with the arrangements, he put on his jacket. Time for the long drive home. Gordie MacLean wasn't normally a person who got wound up about work, but he knew that Arsenault would be happy to use this as an excuse to shuffle him off to an early retirement. *I won't give him a reason. I don't have his sharp style, but I know what I'm doing.*

I hope.

CHAPTER 4

MACLEAN WAS BACK IN the office before eight o'clock the next morning. He was a morning person, so didn't mind the early start. He'd taken the time for a short walk with Taz and then left her settling in for a sleep on her bed in the corner of the kitchen.

Allan had sent him some photographs from the scene which MacLean enlarged and printed off. He posted these on the whiteboard with magnets. At 8:30 they assembled the team in the boardroom ready for the briefing. Staff Sergeant Arsenault started by introducing the case since he had taken the initial call. Then he turned it over to MacLean.

MacLean went through what had taken place at the site, pointing to the photos of the bone in the digger and then the exposed bones in the pit. The last photo was of the bones laid out on the table in the lab.

"Anything you can tell us so far about the remains, Allan?"

Allan took MacLean's place at the front of the room. "Based on the pelvis opening, the high forehead and diminished brow, we identified the remains as female. Linda, our Forensic Anthropologist, had an initial look. and she puts the age somewhere between eighteen and twenty-one."

One of the newer detectives in the Major Crimes Unit, Detective Albright, raised her hand. Slim with short glossy chestnut hair and high cheekbones, she had a petite exotic look to her which contrasted with the husky men in the room.

Allan nodded.

"How accurate is the aging? Is that something we can count on, or do you need to run more tests?"

Allan turned and pointed to the photograph of the bones on the table. "It should be quite accurate. You can see here that the sternum is fused to the clavicle. That, together with the fact that the wrist bones are fused, along with some other key fusions means that she's definitely at least eighteen and most likely as old as twenty-one."

Albright made a note in her book. "Thank you."

Allan continued. "Today we'll work on determining race and how long she's been in the ground and of course, cause of death."

MacLean took over again. "I did some preliminary searches of open missing persons cases for Cape Breton, but of course we have no way of knowing if she's even from around here. She may have been a tourist or a student. When we find out her race, we can narrow things down a bit more, but just going with what we know now we've got four possibilities from here on the Island."

Sergeant Arsenault stood up. "Right now, we'll consider this a crime until we know differently. Albright, effective immediately you're assigned to work with Detective MacLean." He turned to MacLean. "If you need more people, we'll look at it, but as you know, we're stretched, so do your best with Albright."

MacLean frowned to make it appear that he was upset at not having more help. *Sounds good to me. No one telling me what to do and why I'm doing everything wrong.*

The meeting broke up, and Albright followed MacLean to his desk. "OK. What would you like me to do?"

"I'm ready for a coffee. What about you?"

"I could use a tea."

She followed him out to his car, and he drove across Grand Lake Road to Mayflower Mall. He parked, and they made their way inside to the Tim Horton's.

MacLean pulled out his wallet and looked at the young woman beside him. Like him, she wore casual, comfortable clothes. Her dark pants with a blue turtleneck sweater gave her a tidy appearance.

"I'm buying. What'll it be, Detective Albright?"

"A steeped tea, and please, call me Roxanne."

They got their order, and MacLean led the way to a corner table. "Well, Roxanne, I'm Gordie. Welcome to our little team."

She smiled. "Thanks. I know I'm new, and some people think I'm too young, but I'm keen to learn."

He tipped his cup against hers. "That's good enough for me. Whereabouts do you live?"

"Big Pond."

"Nice. Near the water?"

"Yes. I live with my Nana."

He raised his eyebrows.

"She's eighty-five and although she's in great shape, still drives and, whatnot, she likes having someone in the house, and I like being with her."

"Sounds like a good arrangement."

They chatted about where she lived compared to where he did. They both loved being near the water to go for walks, or in her case, for a run.

He stood. "Ready to go back? I'd like to see how they're making out with identifying the race of Garden Girl."

"Is that what we're calling her?"

"For the moment. Until we know who she was."

Roxanne drained the last of her tea and dropped the paper cup in the blue bin on the way out. MacLean still had half of his drink and he took it with him.

He lit a cigarette as soon as they stepped outside and smoked it as they sauntered to the car. He unlocked the car so she could get in, and he leaned against the driver side door for a moment to finish the cigarette.

He got in and glanced over to the girl. "Thank you for not giving me grief about the smoking."

She shrugged. "You're a grown-up. I guess you know what you're doing."

He nodded. *I like her. This might work out.*

They dropped their jackets off on the back of their chairs and then MacLean led the way to the lab where the bones were laid out on the stainless-steel table.

Allan looked up when they came in the room. "We've only been at it for an hour. I hope you're not looking for more already."

MacLean smiled. "Don't get into a knot. I thought it would be good for both of us to watch and learn as you do your magic on our Garden Girl."

Allan dipped his head. "OK. Most of you guys just want the bottom line. You don't want to see how we get there."

"I'm not most guys."

Allan nodded. "Fair enough."

"So, take us through what you're doing, please."

Allan gestured MacLean and Albright to come closer, and the three of them huddled over the skull. "See here? The eye orbitals are oval."

MacLean frowned. "You mean they don't always look like that?"

Allan straightened and walked over to his large screen computer. They followed him over and watched as he clicked on a few files and then leaned in as he displayed three photos on the screen.

Allan pointed to the first. "These are more circular than Garden

Girl. This is typical of Mongoloid. And this," he pointed to the second photo. "See how these almost look squared? That's typical of Negroid."

MacLean shook his head. "Huh. I see it now." He looked at his partner. "Did you know about these differences?"

Albright frowned. "I took a forensics course in university and remember that there were differences, but to be honest, I wouldn't have been able to tell you now what they were. It's fascinating to see it actually live."

MacLean raised one eyebrow.

She blushed. "So to speak."

Allan remained seated behind the computer. "There are other differences besides the eye orbitals." He pointed to the nasal cavity in the two photos. "See here on the Mongoloid skull the small, round cavity?"

MacLean nodded.

"And here on the Negroid skull? See how it's much wider?"

"Huh."

Allan rose. "Now let's look at Garden Girl."

They went back and huddled over the skull.

Allan pointed. "Her nasal cavity is long and narrow. Typical of Caucasoid. The combination of the eye orbitals, the nasal cavity and the flat cranium, I can tell you that Garden Girl was Caucasian."

Albright nodded. "She's white."

Allan lifted a finger. "Not necessarily."

Albright and MacLean looked at each other.

Allan shook his head. "Even using those labels are old school and are only somewhat useful for narrowing down the field. Only DNA testing will give you a definitive answer about ancestry, but these generalities should help with identification. Just because she's Caucasoid, doesn't mean she's white. She could be South Asian or something else that fits the Caucasian profile."

MacLean nodded. "Well, it gives us a starting point. Now we can go through and start calling for dental records. Hopefully, we'll be able to put a proper name to her before much longer."

Allan nodded. "We'll do some measurements of her femur and humerus and get you her height. That might help as well."

"Anything you can give us will help."

MacLean assigned Albright to start calling around to get the dental records. Knowing that she was not Negroid took one person off the list.

Albright looked at the three remaining files. "Let's hope it's one of your three."

MacLean put on his computer glasses. They were old, black-framed reading glasses that were no longer strong enough for actual reading, but perfect for hours in front of the computer. He pulled up the file with the crime scene photos and slowly clicked through them. He studied the positioning of the bones. One of the arms appeared as though it had been resting on the rib cage. *I wonder if the other arm had been resting like that too before being ripped up by the digger. Were you positioned carefully? Arms folded in prayer, or was it just coincidence? Were you dumped in without any thought other than getting the job done as fast as possible?*

By late afternoon Albright had provided the emailed dental records to the forensics team. MacLean's phone rang. "Allan. What do you know?"

Albright looked up.

MacLean nodded, listening. "Right. Great work. Thanks to your team for getting this done so quickly."

MacLean hung up and looked at his partner. "We've got her. We know who she is."

CHAPTER 5

MACLEAN FELT THE URGE to move. He stood and walked over to Albright's desk. "It was one of the three. Her name is Sarah Campbell."

Albright rifled through the manila file folders on her desk and pulled out the correct one. She opened the file and read from the missing person's document. "Sarah Lynn Campbell, nineteen years old. Shoulder length auburn hair. Five feet eight inches. No scars. No broken bones."

MacLean took the photo from her. It was a colour photo of a smiling girl wearing a high school graduation gown, simply adorned with a small gold cross on a chain and delicate gold hoop earrings. She had a typical Celtic look with thick wavy burnished hair, pale skin and a smattering of freckles across her nose. He walked down the hall and posted the photo on the whiteboard, carefully positioning the magnets on the edges. He took the black marker and wrote her name above the picture. Sarah Lynn Campbell. He nodded. *No more Garden Girl.*

MacLean went back to Albright. "Go on. What else does the report say?"

"Date of birth thirteenth of March 1990. Last seen on the afternoon of the seventeenth of August 2009 leaving the Super Save Grocery in Port Mulroy after completing her shift as cashier. She was wearing a short, flowered sundress and red sandals."

MacLean went to his computer and scrolled through the crime scene photos. "They found sandals in the grave." He clicked through a few more shots until he came to one focussed on the fragments of fabric. Years of being in the earth didn't help, but even now the flower pattern was clear.

He took the missing persons file from Albright. "I'll let Sarge know we've got the I.D. Meanwhile, you can pull out the information on next of kin. We'll have to do the notification and hopefully get something of hers for a DNA comparison."

MacLean rapped his knuckle on the door frame of Sergeant Arsenault's office and stepped inside when his boss waved him in.

Arsenault leaned back in his leather chair. "Well?"

MacLean sat down uninvited and opened the file on his knees. "We've got an I.D. Of course, we'll have to wait for DNA comparison to be a hundred percent sure, but, well, we're sure."

Arsenault nodded. "OK, and?"

"And her name is Sarah Lynn Campbell. Nineteen years old."

"From where?"

"Port Mulroy."

"Your patch."

"Yes."

"Ever hear of her before this?"

"No. She's been missing since 2009. I was with Arson then."

Arsenault grunted. "Hmph."

MacLean mentally shook his head. *You figure I should be familiar with every cold case just because it's in my patch?*

"So, what's the plan?"

"Detective Albright is pulling out the next of kin info and we'll head out there now to make the tentative notification. From here we start asking questions. See where it leads us."

Arsenault sighed. "All right. Keep me posted."

MacLean stood up. He sensed Arsenault was again cursing the absent Doyle for being off with his heart attack. He left the room saying nothing further. *Go ahead and worry. There's nothing Doyle could do that Albright and I won't do. I will find out who stole the life of that beautiful girl, no matter how long it takes. I'm coming for you, buddy, whoever you are.*

***

The parents, William and Alice Campbell, lived in Creignish. MacLean telephoned before they left to check if someone would be home. Despite Alice's tearful questions, MacLean simply told her they had information that they wanted to discuss and left it at that.

He had a quick smoke before climbing into his car. Albright drove her own car as far as Big Pond so that MacLean wouldn't have as far to go to drop her off after they finished with the parents. He considered going on his own but decided that wouldn't be right. Albright needed to learn this, and the mother might prefer a sympathetic woman there, anyway.

MacLean wasn't used to spending so much time with other people so enjoyed the half hour drive on his own. He tuned the satellite radio to the 70s folk music station and hummed along with the songs he knew. When he pulled into the driveway behind Albright's car, he admired the big two-storey white house with green shutters. The front curtain twitched and then the door opened before Albright reached the front porch. *Nana.*

Albright went into the house but instead of following her in, the white-haired woman with funky blue-rimmed glasses came down to MacLean's car.

He rolled down the window, and she stuck her hand in through it. He twisted around to face the window and took her thin hand in his. "You must be Roxanne's Nana."

"And you must be her new partner, Detective MacLean."

He smiled. "Gordie."

"And I'm Helen. Do you want to come in for a cup of tea?"

Before he could turn her down, Albright came back out of the house and hurried to the car. "Nana, I told you we couldn't stay. We have to go. I'm not sure what time I'll be back, so don't wait supper for me."

"All right. I just thought I'd offer."

MacLean smiled up at Helen. "Another time. I have a feeling we'll be seeing more of each other."

She rested her hand on his shoulder. "I'll count on it." She stepped back and gave a jaunty wave before turning to go back up to the house.

He wound the window up and started the car.

His partner sighed. "Sorry about that. I just had to make a quick pit stop. I thought she'd come back in the house with me, but she's very sociable."

MacLean headed off along Highway 4. "No worries. She seems feisty."

"Oh, she is that all right."

He glanced over. "You can't fool me. You treasure her."

She grinned. "Yeah, I guess I do."

She turned up the radio, and they drove without further conversation. Gordie liked that. He didn't want to talk all the time.

It was late afternoon by the time they found the house of William and Alice Campbell. The two-storey house was old, and the board and batten siding grey and weathered. Once-white railings on the veranda were now a peeling, dirty ivory colour. Their wooden screen door squealed in protest when he pulled it open to rap on the front door.

A woman with shaggy grey hair who might have been anywhere

between fifty and sixty opened the door. She pushed a strand of limp hair behind her ear. "Whatever you're selling, we don't want any."

"Mrs. Campbell?"

Her eyes narrowed. "Yes."

MacLean pulled his identification from his inside pocket and held it up for her. "I'm Detective MacLean and this is Detective Albright. May we come in?"

Mrs. Campbell bit her bottom lip. "Oh, God. Sorry." She turned, and they followed her into the house. She led them into a long room which served as a living room and dining room.

She gestured to the brown sofa as she fell into one of the two leatherette recliners. "Sit down."

MacLean continued to stand while Albright perched on the edge of the couch. "Is your husband at home, Mrs. Campbell?"

"No. He probably stopped in at the Legion on the way home from work."

"Would you like to call him?"

She shook her head. "He's useless, anyway. Just tell me. It's about Sarah. What is it? What have you found?"

He sat down then as well. "I'm afraid we have some bad news."

"Well?"

"There was a body found yesterday. Well, just bones actually."

Tears slid down Alice Campbell's cheeks. "Oh my God." She crossed herself.

He went on, his voice soft and slow. "We believe it's Sarah."

She shook her head then. "How can you know if it's just bones? They all look alike, don't they?" Her voice was high pitched, completely different from the tired voice with which she had greeted them at the door.

"We've compared Sarah's dental records and we feel quite confident that it's her, I'm afraid."

Alice Campbell pulled a tissue from the sleeve of her cardigan and dabbed at her eyes and then blew her nose.

MacLean nodded at Albright, who stood up. She touched Mrs. Campbell on the shoulder. "I'll get some tea, shall I? Or would you prefer coffee?"

The older woman shook her head. "I don't drink coffee." She pointed down the hall. "Kitchen's down there."

Albright nodded. "I'll find it."

MacLean rested his arms on his knees as he leaned towards Mrs. Campbell. "May I call you Alice?"

She nodded.

"Alice, we'll need to compare the DNA just to be sure of the identification. Would you still have an old hairbrush or toothbrush of Sarah's that I could take away with me?"

"Yes, everything is just as it was. I thought she might come back. Well, for a while I did, and then I guess I knew she wouldn't come back, but still I just left her room with everything as it was."

"I understand."

She seemed to have shrunk down into the big chair. "Sometimes I lie on her bed. Just, you know..." Her voice trailed off.

"Just so you can feel her presence. Yes, I understand."

She nodded.

"Alice, I'll want to ask you some questions about when Sarah disappeared. It would be helpful if your husband was here to help fill in the gaps. Perhaps you should call him."

She nodded. "All right. I will." She pulled herself out of the chair and walked over to the television where the handset of a cordless phone rested. She pushed one of the speed-dial numbers. Her voice had lost its note of hysteria now, and she sounded almost catatonic.

"Bill, you need to come home. The police are here." She listened for a moment. "No, no. It's nothing to do with the neighbours. It's about Sarah." Her voice broke. "They found her, Bill. She's dead."

She listened for another few seconds and then pushed the button to disengage. "He's coming. It's just down the road. He'll be here in a few minutes."

"Maybe while we're waiting, we could go up to Sarah's room together and you can find something with her DNA on it. Are you up to that?"

She nodded, seeming to be glad for something to do. She led the way to the staircase by the front door and he followed her up to the second level. The typical small landing with three bedrooms and a bathroom awaited. Only one door was closed, the other two revealed unmade beds. It appeared that Mr. and Mrs. Campbell each had their own room.

Alice opened the door and went to the dressing table. On a white lace doily, a brush and comb lay neatly waiting for someone to come and use them.

MacLean pulled out latex gloves from his pocket, slid his hands into them and then picked up the brush. There were dark hairs clumped into the bristles. "Has anyone else used this brush?"

Alice shook her head. "Not as far as I know. Sarah was fussy. I don't think she'd let her friends use her brush, and certainly neither Bill nor I have used it."

MacLean held the brush carefully so as not to smudge the prints. He had paper evidence bags downstairs and now took a quick look around the room. "Let's go back down, but Detective Albright and I will want to search the room later. Will that be all right with you?"

She nodded.

"Do you know if Sarah had a diary?"

"Not that I ever found."

He suspected she had already gone through the room with a fine-tooth comb in search of a clue about her daughter's disappearance.

Albright called up the stairs. "Tea's ready whenever you are."

MacLean led the way back down the stairs. He stopped at his jacket, which hung on a wooden pedestal coat rack to pull out a paper bag from his large flap pocket. He dropped the brush in and sealed it, folding the top of the bag over the small brush before tucking the package back into the jacket pocket.

He went into the living room where Alice had slumped back into the large chair with a mug of tea. She wrapped her hands around the mug as if she were very cold. The bright yellow and black mug with 'The Coast' inscribed across it contrasted with her pale fingers, as though the blood had drained from her hands.

Albright nodded to the pot of tea and then looked at MacLean. "Want a cup?"

"Sure. Sounds good."

He was halfway through the tea when the door banged open. Alice started and blinked at MacLean as if she had forgotten that she wasn't alone.

Bill Campbell kicked off his tan leather work boots in the direction of the coat stand but came into the living room, still wearing a yellow raincoat and green baseball cap. He had an untidy grey beard and moustache which made him look older than the mid-to- late fifties that MacLean believed Sarah's father to be.

MacLean and Albright both pulled out their identification and stood to greet the man. Campbell glanced at each identification, and then pulled off his raincoat, tossing it over the back of a dining room chair, leaving his ball cap on. He pulled out another chair from the table and turned it to face the living room.

MacLean glanced at Alice. She didn't seem surprised that her husband wouldn't bring the chair close to her.

Bill Campbell sat down and crossed his arms over his chest. "So, tell me then."

MacLean sat at the end of the couch closest to Bill. He could smell the man. The fumes of beer, clothes in need of laundering and unwashed body odours hung in the air. MacLean gritted his teeth. That smell always made his stomach churn. He pointed to the teapot. "Can Detective Albright pour you some tea?"

Campbell frowned. "No. Just get it over with."

MacLean nodded. "We believe we have found the remains of your daughter."

"Believe? Not sure?"

"I now have Sarah's hairbrush, which we will use to confirm the DNA, but we are quite confident it's her. I'm very sorry."

Alice sniffled again as tears trailed down her cheeks.

Her husband didn't look at her. "Where?"

"Not far outside Port Mulroy. In the garden of a house on Parish Lane in Newtown."

"Right."

MacLean looked at Alice now. "Do you, do either of you, know anyone on Parish Lane? Would you have any idea how she would come to be there?"

Alice shook her head.

MacLean looked at Bill. "What about you, Bill? May I call you Bill?"

Campbell shrugged. "It's my name. And no. I never knew anyone there and have no idea why she'd be there." He paused before continuing. "So, has she been there all this time?"

MacLean nodded. "Yes, we believe so."

When both husband and wife were silent, MacLean continued. "What did you believe had happened to her, Alice?"

She blinked several times and then replied, her voice quiet. "I thought she ran away."

MacLean looked at Bill. "What about you? Did you think that also?"

Again, the shrug. "She had no reason to run away. I thought she just decided not to come home because she couldn't be bothered. That, or maybe she was taken. We were told that she was seen hitch-hiking. I told her not to, but she never listened to me." He turned to stare at his wife. "No one listens to me."

Alice turned her head to look at Albright, avoiding her husband's eyes.

Albright glanced at MacLean, and he gave her a small nod.

Albright stood. "This tea is cold by now. Let's get a fresh pot organized, Alice. Are you up to helping me?"

Alice pulled herself out of her chair and walked down the hall towards the kitchen, leaving Albright to take the mug from MacLean and gather the tray with tea things.

MacLean heard their voices and the clatter of crockery from the kitchen and he turned back to focus on Bill. "How were things here at home before your daughter disappeared?"

"Things were fine. I didn't see much of her. She always seemed to be out somewhere gallivanting when I was home."

MacLean pulled out a small notebook and pen from his top pocket. "Gallivanting. Was she a party girl?"

Bill Campbell frowned. "I don't know what you mean by party girl. She wasn't a slut."

MacLean twitched at the harsh word. "I didn't mean to imply that. I wondered if she enjoyed going out to clubs or parties with her friends. She was old enough to take a drink, so it would be quite normal for her to enjoy those kinds of things."

Campbell pulled off his cap, scratched his scalp and put his cap back on. "I don't know. She had a job, so that took up some of her time. Other than that, I have no idea what she did when she was out."

MacLean nodded. "It's not easy to be the father of a teenager, especially when they are old enough to go their own way."

"You got that right. She got real mouthy the last few years."

"You argued a lot?"

"She was always at me for taking a drink. I work hard and should be allowed to relax without getting grief from a kid or my wife."

"I can see that."

Campbell stretched out his legs. "At first I just thought she was being a pain in the ass by not coming home. I figured she was with a girlfriend somewhere."

MacLean made a note, *Didn't want to come home?* "Did you and your wife check with her friends?"

Campbell pointed a thumb in the direction of the kitchen. "She did. I wouldn't have a clue who to call."

"You said you heard that Sarah sometimes hitchhiked. Do you have any idea who may have given her a lift, either on the day she disappeared or on other occasions?"

"Nope."

MacLean heard the women coming back down the hall. "Bill, is there anything else you can think of that might be helpful in figuring out what happened to your daughter?"

He shook his head.

Albright set down the tray with a fresh pot of tea and rinsed out mugs.

MacLean stood and glanced at Albright. "While the tea is steeping, you and I will take a look at Sarah's room."

Alice stood hovering uncertainly. Albright touched her arm. "You don't need to come up with us. Why don't you wait here with your husband and we'll be back in a few moments?"

Alice nodded and licked her lips, glancing towards her husband.

MacLean led the way to Sarah's room and stood for a moment to listen. *Even with this huge event, they have nothing to say to each other.*

He shook his head and closed the door softly. "How did it go in the kitchen?"

Albright shook her head. "That's a very unhappy woman. I would say she's been that way long before her daughter disappeared, but that was the final straw. She's just going through the motions now." She stood frowning. "There's something odd, though."

MacLean raised his eyebrows.

"I can't quite put my finger on it, but it seemed like she had been jealous of her daughter."

"Jealous, how?"

"I said that Sarah had been a beautiful girl. I expected her to say thank you or agree or something along that line."

"And?"

"She said that she herself had been beautiful once and if she hadn't gotten pregnant when she was twenty, she might have been a model."

"Interesting."

"She never acknowledged my compliment about Sarah."

"Did you get a sense of whether or not they were close?"

"I asked her that. She said that often they were more like sisters, and all sisters argue at times. I asked her what sort of things they argued about."

"Don't tell me clothes."

She gave a soft laugh. "No. At least not that she told me about." Albright got serious again. "No, she said that Sarah was angry with her because she wouldn't leave her father."

CHAPTER 6

ON THE DRIVE BACK to Big Pond, MacLean mulled over what they had learned. *An unhappy family. An angry young woman.*

In the light of oncoming cars, he glanced at Albright's face, furrowed in thought. "What are you thinking?"

She sighed. "I'm not sure. It seemed like a strange relationship between mother and daughter. Mom seemed to blame Sarah for the way her life had turned out."

MacLean nodded. "If you hadn't been born, my life would have been wonderful."

"Yeah. That kind of thing. But still. Surely if Alice felt strongly, she would have lashed out before this."

"Maybe. Maybe it all came to a head once Sarah was old enough to stand up and argue. They fought. It got out of hand."

"Could be. I've had some pretty heated exchanges with my mother once or twice."

MacLean smiled. "Must be a girl thing."

"Jesus."

"Kidding, Roxanne. Just kidding."

"So, what about the dad? If Sarah was so keen for her mother to leave him, he must have been a real picnic."

MacLean thought of the smell. The boozy wave carried on an undertone of poor hygiene. He tried not to think of the years he had lived with that smell greeting him at home.

"Gordie?"

He shook his head to clear his thoughts. "Dad seemed pretty unconcerned about what had originally happened. Bill told me he just assumed she had decided not to come home. Not so much running away, but just being, as he said, 'a pain in the ass.'"

"Was he unconcerned because he knew what had happened, do you think?"

MacLean thought about it for a moment. "I think he didn't care enough to take that kind of step. I can see him taking a swipe at her in a drunken rage, but to take her and bury her out there? That just feels like it required more effort than he'd bother with."

"Don't forget it's a number of years ago now. He may have been more concerned back then. Afraid of being caught."

He nodded. "Could be."

"Where do we go from here?"

He turned into her driveway. "We've got that list of friends that Alice gave us. We'll connect with them to see what they knew. It's a shame there was no diary and no phone. We've got the number though, so hopefully we can still get a record of her calls. It's a long time ago, so I'm not holding my breath. By tomorrow we'll have the official manner and cause of death, although I don't think there's really any doubt. Even I could see the dent in the back of her skull."

Albright got out of the car. She leaned back in before closing the door. "Thank you."

"For what?"

"For not treating me like I'm something you scraped off the bottom of your shoe."

MacLean chuckled. "We are all juniors at some point. I appreciate the extra set of eyes and ears."

***

MacLean bent down to ruffle his dog's thick fur. "Taz, my darlin', I'm glad to see you."

She poked him in the crotch and then his behind as he walked down the hall to the kitchen. He was used to her enthusiastic nudging. "Yes, yes. All right. Enough of that now."

He gave her a biscuit and picked up the note from his neighbour, which confirmed that she had fed Taz.

"Let's go out for a walk. I need to think."

He clipped her leather leash to her collar and then set off. He smelled the brine in the cool spring air. It was not quite drizzling, but the moisture clung to his hair like a cobweb. It felt cleansing.

He talked aloud to the dog, as he often did. "We have two parents who each seem like they had problems with the daughter. Lots of parents do, of course. Teenagers can be headstrong. I've seen enough domestics to know that by now, but is either one capable of murder? What would be the motivation?" He looked down at the dog and she gazed up at him, wagging her tail. "What would they gain, Taz? Unless somebody just flew off the handle and walloped her. But the dent is on the back of her head. She had to be walking away. I guess that could set someone off all right."

He pictured it. *She and Dad have an argument. She hollers, "Leave me alone. I'm old enough to make my own decisions." She turns to walk away. He shouts at her. "Don't you walk away from me." She keeps going. He picks something up and bang. Down she goes.*

He thought of his own father. Long dead now, but MacLean felt his heart beat faster as he remembered the arguments. *You'll do as I say as long as you're living under my roof.* MacLean left the day he turned seventeen.

"Come on Taz, we better head back. I'm starving."

As they walked back, Taz stopping routinely to sniff something in the brown wet grass along the side of the road, MacLean thought about Alice. "Do you think a woman has it in her to hit her daughter so hard that she dies?"

Taz shook, spraying a thin mist of water against MacLean. He smiled. "No, I agree. It's hard to imagine, isn't it? Happens, though. Usually there's drink involved in those cases, and I don't think Alice is a drinker. She's a funny one, though. If Roxanne's right, the mother blamed Sarah for the life she missed out on."

He walked on, letting the damp air wash him. He felt the tension of the day evaporate and he turned his thoughts to the owner of the house where Sarah's body was found. "What do you think of Vanessa Hunt, Taz? She seems pretty nice, eh? She didn't get all wired about finding a body in her garden like most people I know would have. And I learned something new from her. A bunch of crows is a murder. Poor Sarah Campbell inspired a murder."

CHAPTER 7

MACLEAN WAS UP EARLY the next morning, so he
could take Taz for a walk before heading into the office.
There was a cold rain falling, blowing across the water
from the north in a blustery gale that left him feeling raw. He kept
his hands stuffed into his pocket and let Taz off the leash while they
walked along the quiet roadside. Taz lifted her muzzle to scent the
stories carried on the wind. She made short dashes into the under-
brush, returning every few moments to MacLean's side.

"Sorry girl, we'll have to turn back. No time for a long walk
today. Come on. Let's go home."

He turned, and Taz followed. The wind lifted her long white hair
and streamed it behind her. MacLean pulled out his handkerchief
and wiped at his wet face and blew his nose. "You love this, don't
you, Taz? This is your kind of weather."

They went back in and MacLean rubbed his hands together. *I
should get a wood stove like Vanessa has. Gives off such a nice heat.* He
shook his head while he got Taz her breakfast and put two slices of

whole wheat bread into the toaster for himself. *I have to stop thinking about that woman so much.*

He ate his breakfast, made himself a coffee in his travel mug, gave Taz another loving stroke on the top of her head and then set off for the office.

By the time he arrived, MacLean was ready with a mental list of priorities. Albright was already at her desk when he got there. He hung his jacket on the back of his chair. "I can see I have to get up even earlier to beat you in."

She grinned. "I'm a morning person. Besides, I live closer than you."

"Thanks for that. What have you got?"

She carried over a yellow pad on which she'd been making notes. "I looked up the names we got from Alice yesterday."

"Find anything of interest?"

She shrugged. "I found a Facebook page for the best girlfriend, Mary-Catherine Cameron. She doesn't have much security on it, so I was able to take a look at some of her photos without sending her a friend request."

"OK. I'll take your word for that."

She raised an eyebrow. "Not a big Facebook user?"

He tilted his head and gave a half-smile. "Ah, no."

"Well, she does love taking photos of herself. Me at the pub. Me at the ballgame. Lots of that sort of thing."

"Isn't that normal these days?"

She nodded. "Yes, selfies are definitely common, but this just feels a little over the top."

"What about the other names? Find anything?"

"The ex-boyfriend, James MacNeil, has a Facebook page as well, but I couldn't get much from it. Either it's blocked to outsiders or he just doesn't use it much. Not sure which."

"Hmm. Were you able to get an address for him?"

"Yes. According to his driver's license, it looks like he's moved away from home now and has a place of his own in Port Mulroy."

"Good work. Anything else?"

"That's it."

"That's a good start." He looked at his watch. "I'm going to brief Sarge and by then Allan will be in and we can see if he's ready to pronounce on manner and cause of death."

Albright nodded. "That'll give me time to get a cup of tea. By the way..."

He looked up from his notebook.

"I wouldn't let Sergeant Arsenault hear you calling him Sarge."

MacLean smiled. "For your ears only."

***

After MacLean brought his boss up to date, he took a few moments to step outside for a cigarette. He thought about the meeting he just had and smiled. *You don't like the fact that I'm making progress. Figured I'd be floundering, didn't you, Sarge?* He took a deep drag and stubbed out the cigarette into the metal can filled with sand. He went back inside and as he walked down the hall, he popped out a piece of breath-freshening gum from the packet he always kept in his top pocket.

He dropped the file on his desk and then nodded to Albright. "Ready?"

She followed him down the steps to the basement where the lab was. They pushed through the swinging door and into the brightly lit room. Stainless steel and white tile reflected the fluorescent lights and made it seem even brighter than it was.

MacLean made his way to the small office where John Allan peered at his computer screen as he typed notes. "Morning, John."

Allan leaned back, took the black glasses off and rubbed his eyes. "Morning, Gordie. Detective Albright."

Albright frowned. "Roxanne, please."

He nodded and gave a small smile. "Roxanne."

MacLean leaned against the door frame. "You look beat, John."

"It's just these glasses. I really need to get different ones for the computer." He put them back on and stood up. "You've given me a good excuse to leave the report writing for a few moments."

MacLean stepped out of Allan's way and then he and Albright followed the tall man to the table where Sarah Campbell's remains were laid out. It appeared as if all the bones had been found and the skeleton lay looking complete.

Allan picked up the skull and turned it, so the back was visible to MacLean and Albright. "You can see here..." he circled the indentation on the back of the skull "the occipital bone has been fractured."

Albright leaned in to take a closer look. "Are these gaps part of the injury?"

Allan shook his head. "No. Because of her age, the sphenoid bone and the occipital haven't fused yet. It's one of the markers that told us the victim was most likely between the ages of eighteen and twenty-five. But these lines," he pointed to a pattern of webbing leading out from the depression "they were certainly a result of the trauma."

MacLean wanted to be sure. "So, this is what killed her?"

"Yes. Blunt force trauma."

"Any thoughts on what cracked her skull? Could it have been an accident?"

Allan shook his head. "Very unlikely that it was an accident. Even if she fell backwards and hit her head on concrete, the depression is too great. It would have taken force."

He gripped MacLean by the shoulders. "Someone would have had to grab her like this and slam her against a brick wall or a concrete floor. A simple shove and stumble wouldn't be enough."

He pointed again to the crack. "I would say that something like a length of wood, or something else with a square shape was used to strike her once, extremely hard. You see here? There is a slight impression at the left edge of the depression which wouldn't occur if she had come in to contact with a flat surface like a floor."

Albright suggested. "A curbstone maybe?"

Allan shook his head. "Unlikely. There would have been a more distinct 'v' shape in that case. No. I would say it was a deliberate strike from behind with a square shaped weapon."

"Are you calling it a homicide then?"

Allan set the skull down. "That isn't for me to say. Only the Medical Examiner can pronounce on the cause and manner of death."

MacLean frowned. "He's in Dartmouth. Does that mean all this has to be done again in Dartmouth? Or will he come here?"

Allan led the way back to his office. "We don't often have a case like this, of course, but I've spoken with him and he's told me to ship him off all the records. He shouldn't have to see the physical remains."

"Is it safe to assume that he'll rule it a homicide?"

Allan nodded. "Yes. Homicide, as a result of blunt force trauma."

"Anything else we should know about the remains that might help us?"

"I'm afraid not."

"Then the living people who knew her will have to tell us the rest of her story."

MacLean was ready for a decent coffee. He and Albright went back upstairs, and he lifted his jacket from the back of his chair. "Timmy's?"

Albright opened the narrow locker beside her desk and put on her coat. "Sounds good. I'll drive."

He nodded. *I like her. She's not afraid to take charge.*

Albright parked her Ford Escape in the mall parking lot, and they went in and joined the mid-morning lineup at Tim Horton's. He moved to pull out his wallet, but she held up a hand. "My round."

"I'm having something with the coffee."

She smiled. "Go crazy."

The middle-aged woman behind the counter smiled. "Medium double-double, Gordie?"

"And an oatcake to go with it please, Lynn."

"You'll take a rub of butter on that?"

51

He patted his stomach. "I shouldn't."

She picked up the butter knife. "But you will."

"All right. I will. By the way, this is my new partner, Detective Roxanne Albright."

"If you're Gordie's partner, I suppose we'll be seeing a lot of you, Roxanne. You're new to the station?"

"I'll have a medium steeped tea. No sugar, but yes to milk. And yes, I'm new here."

Lynn poured the tea in a proper mug rather than a paper cup. "Anything to go with the tea?"

"I'll have an old-fashioned plain donut, thank you. Lynn."

MacLean set the drinks and snacks on a tray while Albright paid. He heard Lynn say, "Welcome to the neighbourhood and have fun working with Gordie. He may not always be the most talkative, but underneath he's an old softie."

Albright joined MacLean at the table. "You've got a fan there."

He shrugged. "I just take the time to get to know people and they seem to think that's special."

MacLean pulled out his notebook. "I want to set up some of these interviews. People will now know that the remains we found are Sarah's since the Chief held the news conference. That means we can really get on with it."

"I thought they might wait until the DNA confirmed the identification."

"There really isn't any doubt. The Chief did say that it was a tentative identification pending DNA confirmation, but we can move forward with the investigation now."

Albright made a note in her book. "Where do you want to start?"

"I want to meet with the ex-boyfriend and Sarah's closest friend first. Can you call both of them and set up some time to meet?"

"Do you want them to come in or will we go there?"

"We'll go there. I want to see where she went. What she saw. At least for the first round. Give her old boss a call as well. We'll want to go to her job and see what went on there. Did she have any friends there, that sort of thing."

He took another bite of oatcake before continuing. "While you're doing that, I'll talk to the original investigators to see what they remember. They must have talked to some of these same people and I want to get their impressions."

***

MacLean took the file with the original missing persons report and walked down the hall past the briefing room to where the General Investigations Unit had their workstations and on to his former sergeant's office. He knocked on the door and let himself in at the call from within.

"Detective MacLean. What brings you down to your old stomping grounds?"

MacLean sat down across from his old boss, Sergeant Peddipas. "I want to talk to a couple of the boys about a missing person case, they looked into nine years ago. Sarah Campbell."

"That's a while ago. Still open?"

"We found her remains. It's now a homicide, or it will be when the ME says it is."

Peddipas rubbed his hand across the short steel-grey bristles of his brush cut. "Of course. I heard about this on the news. Damn. I remember her. It's still posted on our website. Pretty schoolgirl, wasn't she?"

"Nineteen. Out of high school and working part time at the Super Save."

Peddipas tapped the name into his computer. "Right. Constables MacDougal and Gould did the initial inquiry. MacDougal is gone now. Moved out west, but Gould is still here."

"Is he in today?"

Peddipas tapped into his computer again to pull up the shift schedule. "You're in luck. He's on shift, but he's out working with

Traffic at the moment. There was a tractor trailer overturned on 125."

"I heard about that. Came off the ferry from Newfoundland, didn't it?"

"Yeah. He should just about be done there by now. Let me find out when he thinks he'll be back."

MacLean stood up and walked to the window to admire the view while Sergeant Peddipas called Constable Gould.

"Right. Give him half an hour. He was already on his way back. I'll have him come down and see you."

"Great. Maybe he'll remember something that will give us a head start."

MacLean returned to his desk, and Albright drew a rolling chair over beside him. "I got a hold of all three."

"How did it go?"

"I don't think anyone was too surprised to hear from us. That ex-boyfriend, James MacNeil, is a real piece of work."

"Oh?"

"He was in a hurry to tell me that everyone thought Sarah was such a nice girl and all, but she could be a real bitch at times. His exact words."

"Interesting. Did he elaborate?"

"I didn't really let him. I arranged to meet with him and left it at that."

MacLean nodded. "Good. It's always better to meet a person face to face to hear what they have to say. What about the others? The girlfriend and the boss?"

She nodded. "Got through to both of them. The boss, Mr. Sandy MacIsaac, sounded harassed, but I don't think it had anything to do with my call. And the girlfriend, Mary-Catherine Cameron, sounded excited to talk to us..."

"OK, let's split them up for this first round. I'll meet with this

Mary-Catherine and you meet with the boss and then we'll see this James fella together."

Albright smiled. "Sounds like a plan."

They arranged the next day's schedule and where to meet, and then MacLean left her to work on seeing about getting cell phone records from the provider, Aliant. MacLean meanwhile sat behind his computer to see what the media had said previously and now about Sarah. He knew reporters were often quite dogged about unearthing tidbits that proved useful. Caught up with reading the news stories, he didn't realize until the man sat down, that a constable had come over.

MacLean removed his computer glasses and stuck out his hand. "Gould, hello. Thank you for coming to see me. I'm Gordie MacLean."

Gould nodded. His shiny dark hair was longer than the way some constables wore their hair, and his sensitive brown eyes were the almond shape that spoke of his Mi'kmaq heritage. "Peter Gould."

He shook MacLean's hand. "I pulled out my notebook from the original inquiry."

"Excellent. What were your impressions?"

Gould flipped open the book and found the page he needed, unfolded it and took a moment to read the page and the next few, each one neatly noted in black ink.

MacLean sat patiently waiting for Gould to review his notes, opening his own book in case there was anything that was useful.

Gould looked up and leaned back in the chair. "The father was obnoxious. He was drunk the first time we talked to him and wasn't inclined to talk to me. He focussed his entire interview on my partner."

MacLean nodded. "That is obnoxious."

Gould shrugged. "It happens. That wasn't the obnoxious part. It was his attitude towards his missing daughter that bugged me. It was like he didn't really believe she was missing, even though she hadn't been seen for two days. She didn't have a history of disappearing, at least according to her mother. The dad didn't seem to know one way or another."

MacLean turned back the pages of his own book. "He told us that Sarah had been seen hitchhiking. Does that ring a bell with you?"

Gould nodded. "We heard that too, but the description of the car was too vague to make much of it. A small or midsize two or four door. Blue or black."

"Very helpful."

Gould continued. "The boyfriend was someone we looked at closely. They had split up a couple of months before Sarah went missing, but no one could really tell us why. She didn't have a new guy, but she dumped him, which seemed to surprise some friends because he was good for giving them all drives to the dances."

MacLean smiled. "He had his uses, then."

"Apparently. I always wondered if he was handy with his fists though, and that's why she gave him the boot. My experience told me that most girls don't get rid of a guy that, as you said, had his uses, without a reason."

"The best friend, Mary-Catherine Cameron, didn't shed any light on it?"

"Nope. Claimed she didn't know."

"Doesn't sound like much of a best friend."

"Sarah sounded like an all-around nice kid with no real reason to take off. She was in the church youth group, she had a job and she had friends. She didn't seem like a wild party-girl kid who was likely to take off for the bright lights of Halifax or Toronto, but we couldn't find any evidence to say she didn't. We had to just leave it as an open missing persons case and move on. Every year Crime Stoppers does a little piece on her, but it's never brought in any new information."

MacLean looked at the notes he took. "The church youth group. Did she have any special friends there that we could talk to? Her mother didn't mention that to us."

Gould flipped through the pages again. "This Mary-Catherine went to the same group, so she might be able to direct you to others. It didn't give us any leads to follow. The priest was concerned and said it was out of character for Sarah to just disappear, but other than that, couldn't tell us anything."

"All right. Thank you for digging that up for me. That was Our Lady of Mercy, I assume?"

Gould nodded and carefully folded the pages of his notebook again.

MacLean smiled. "Were you in the military?"

Gould frowned. "Yes. Five years in the Communications and Electronics Branch. Well, now they've gone back to the old name of Royal Canadian Corps of Signals." Gould smiled. "We all just called it Sigs. Why did you ask?"

"The way you fold your pages to mark them as complete. I've seen other Signalers do that too."

Gould smiled and rose from the chair. "Old habits. You're observant. If there's anything else you think I can do, let me know."

MacLean stood as well. "What did you think happened to her, based on what people told you?"

Gould shrugged. "I didn't think she ran away out west or anything. She didn't take anything with her. If I'm honest, I thought she was dead. I didn't think we'd ever find any sign of her. It's too easy to rent a boat around here."

MacLean nodded. "Good point."

"Still, I'm sorry to have my suspicions confirmed. It would have been nice to have a happy ending. Pretty girl, did well in school. Someone robbed her of her future."

Gould left MacLean to his thoughts.

Why not a boat? Of course, it isn't as easy to make a corpse disappear in the water as people think, but few people know that. They were rushed and panicked. No time for the whole logistical problem of getting a boat. Why bury her at the house? There's so much Crown land around.

Why not there where she'd be less likely to be found? This was unplanned and hasty.

MacLean shook his head. So many questions and no answers. *We'll find the answers, Sarah. Slowly but surely, we'll figure it out.*

MacLean packed up his laptop and went to Albright's desk. "Any luck with the phone records?"

"I haven't even found the right person to talk to yet, and then I'm guessing I'll have to get a court order."

MacLean nodded. "OK, stick with it. I'm heading out and will work from home. I want to prepare my questions for tomorrow. I didn't get much from the previous investigator, but he gave me some food for thought. I just need to pull it all together. I'll see you tomorrow. Let me know if anything comes up."

"Right, Boss."

MacLean grimaced. *Boss? I guess I am, but can't say I like the idea.*

He was glad to climb into his SUV, turn up his favourite station and head out. His phone rang when he was halfway home. Gordie pushed the button on his steering wheel to answer. "Detective MacLean."

"Where the hell are you?"

MacLean took a deep breath before answering. "On the way back to my place, Sergeant."

"I walked down the hall expecting to find you at your desk and your partner informed me you had left already."

So, if you knew where I am, why ask? MacLean said nothing, waiting for his sergeant to get to the point.

"Why are you on your way home when there's an investigation underway?"

"I plan to work on my interviews for tomorrow and I do that better in a quiet place. Was there something you need me for? I can easily turn back if you do."

The voice was grudging. "I want an update. The Chief was down asking me, so naturally I thought I could talk to you."

"And now you are." Before Sergeant Arsenault could complain any further, MacLean continued. "I spoke with the initial investigator. It sounds like both the father and the ex-boyfriend raised some red flags, but nothing they could follow up on without a body or evidence to follow. Tomorrow we'll be doing a series of interviews including the ex. I'll meet with the closest girlfriend. Albright will connect with Sarah's former boss, and then we'll interview the ex together."

"What about phone records? Have you done anything about that?"

"Albright is chasing that. The provider was Aliant and we're hoping they'll cooperate without a warrant, but these days it seems standard. Maybe you could help with that, Sergeant?" MacLean smiled as he suggested it, knowing that Sergeant Arsenault wouldn't want to get down and dirty with the investigation.

"I think it's better that the team executing the warrant get it set up."

"Right, then. I'll wait to hear if Albright manages to get the records without it, and if not, we'll get it sorted."

"Anything else?"

"I'm still waiting to hear that the M.E. has signed off on the determination of homicide, but I know Allan will let me know as soon as he hears."

"All right. In future, don't make me chase you down for an update. I don't need the Chief breathing down my neck. I want to be informed every step of the way. And MacLean, remember that you aren't a lone wolf anymore. You've got a partner. Work with her."

"Right, sure." The phone disengaged, and the music came through the radio again.

Chief breathing down your neck, my ass. I worked with him long enough when I was in General Investigations to know that isn't his style. Just yours.

After MacLean got over his irritation with Sergeant Arsenault chasing him down, he thought about what he had said about having a partner. He felt the sweat prickle under his arms, and he frowned. *Maybe you're right there. I'm used to working alone, but that's not fair to Albright.* He nodded. *OK. In the future, we'll work together. I won't just assign her work like she's just another pair of hands. I can do this. It's been a while, but I can work with a partner. Dammit, Sarge. I hate it when you make a fair point.*

CHAPTER 8

MACLEAN FELT REFRESHED IN the morning. He had time to take Taz for a good walk. The wind had blown in off the water, stinging his face with cold, but Taz had grinned a happy dog smile as it streamed her long hair. She lifted her muzzle to greet each gust as MacLean wiped his eyes and nose with a big white handkerchief.

Back at the house MacLean had to dampen his hair in order to brush the thick white-grey mop back into a semblance of tidiness. He made himself a coffee to take with him in the car and headed off, ready to meet the people who knew Sarah best.

Mary-Catherine Cameron lived in an apartment above the Waterview Café on Main Street in Port Mulroy. The white-sided building with green trim and roof was a pretty three-storey building, once a wealthy family's home. Several decades ago, they had transformed the house into a shop with two apartments above, which were accessed through a door at the side of the building. He rang the buzzer and MacLean heard the door click open. He mounted the steps and as he reached the top landing, the apartment door opened.

Mary-Catherine was twenty-eight years old, the same age that Sarah would have been had she lived. She was petite with her chestnut hair worn in a high ponytail, making her seem a little taller. She held herself erect, exuding confidence.

She held out her hand to MacLean and shook his hand with a firm grip. "Hi. I'm Mary-Catherine Cameron." The name came out in one breath. *Mary-Catherine-Cameron.* As if she was unused to simply saying Mary-Catherine.

MacLean pulled out his identification. "I'm Detective MacLean."

She waved his identification aside without looking at it and pointed to a forest green easy chair. "Please sit. I have the kettle on. Will you have tea?"

"Thank you. That would be nice."

The kitchen ran along one wall of the same room as the living room, so the girl continued to talk as she made the tea. "It was shocking to read in the paper that Sarah's body was found. And so close by. I just can't believe it."

MacLean waited until she brought him his tea and was settled on the matching green sofa before he began. The sofa was under a large window overlooking Main Street, and squinting, he saw in the distance, St. George's Bay. He was at a disadvantage because the sun was in his eyes and he wondered if she had managed the arrangement on purpose. He wanted to see her face clearly and study her body language as she answered questions.

"Miss Cameron, would you mind lowering the blinds?"

She set her mug on the coffee table. "I'm so sorry. Of course." She let the blinds down and it took a moment for MacLean's eyes to adjust to the dim light.

"Thank you. That's better."

She smiled and picked up her cup again. "I just love the sun, so I always try to get as much of it as I can."

He nodded. "I understand completely."

"So how can I help you?"

MacLean had his notebook out. He wrote her name in block letters along with the date and time and then began. "Tell me about Sarah. I just want to get a sense of who she was."

Some people would hesitate with such a wide-open question, not knowing what to pick to talk about. Mary-Catherine took a deep breath, as if she had been waiting for just this question.

"We were friends for years. We were in school together, of course. She had it rough at home, so she spent a lot of time at my place. My parents liked her, and she liked them. We were almost like sisters."

MacLean thought about Sarah's mother, and how she had also said they were like sisters. "Go on."

Mary-Catherine tossed her head, setting the ponytail swinging. "I helped her through things. You know, like when she had a hard time making friends at school, she hung around with me and my friends. I made sure no one made fun of her."

"Would they have, if you hadn't been there to look out for her?"

She shrugged. "She could be awkward. Girls can zoom in on someone with no confidence and give them a hard time."

MacLean made a note. *Awkward? No real friends? Bullied?* "Was there anyone in particular who might have given her a hard time?"

"Not that I can recall. Other than her ex, of course."

"We'll get to him in a moment. Tell me about what you two did together. Did you go to special places, clubs or dances, that sort of thing?"

She pursed her lips. "Just what everyone else did, really. We went to the school dances of course and then they had youth dances at the church hall, and then when we turned seventeen, we started going to the adult dances at the Legion."

"Did you drive? Or did your parents drive you? How did you get to the Legion dances?"

"Sarah and I both got our licenses as soon as we could, but before I could drive and borrow the car off my Dad, someone would drive us. Sometimes James, sometimes I'd be dating someone, and they'd drive. Sometimes someone else would. It all depended."

"Depended on what?"

She frowned. "Depended on what else was going on, I guess. It wasn't always the same people that went."

"All right. Did you ever go to dances without James?"

"Sure, of course."

"Even when Sarah was dating him?"

"Um. Maybe. Probably. She didn't really like him that much, so she was always on the lookout for a better offer."

"That sounds calculating on her part. Is that how she was?"

She frowned. "I didn't mean that. I just think she took up with James without really liking him enough for it to last. She was young."

MacLean smiled. "And what about you? Did you have a boy-friend at that time? Did you double date?"

Again, the head toss. "Oh, no. I knew better than getting stuck with one guy."

"Right. So, what else did you do besides the dances?"

Mary-Catherine paused, deep in thought. "We sometimes we went bowling. And then, we were in the church youth group for a while."

"What was that about?"

She set the empty mug on the coffee table, pulled her legs up under her on the sofa and folded her arms across her chest. "Just discussions, mostly. Passages from the Bible and then sometimes the conversation would move on to how the passage was relevant to today's world or someone's life. That kind of thing."

"You say mostly. What else did the group do?"

She sighed. "Nothing. Well, once in a while we'd take a day trip like to St. Peter's in Ingonish or Saint Ninian's in Antigonish. Once we went to the Mother of Sorrows Pioneer Shrine in Mabou."

"Did Sarah have any special friends in the group?"

Mary-Catherine pouted. "She had me. That was enough. We had a laugh together, and it was free. Just something to do, you know?"

"What about when she got a job? Were you still close then?"

She stretched out languidly on the couch. "Do you want more tea?"

He shook his head. "No, thank you."

"Work. Well, sure we were still friends just the same. Sarah was glad to have the job. She gave her Mom some of her wages, but mostly she spent some on proper clothes and was saving for a car. Sometimes she had to work the evening shift on a Saturday night, so that was a drag and I'd go without her, but mostly we still hung out. I was trying to get a job too."

"Were you jealous that she was earning money, and you weren't?"

She raised one eyebrow. "Seriously? Working in a grocery store? I could have done that if I'd wanted to. No chance. No, I was waiting for the right thing. I was watching for maybe a job in Sydney or Halifax. In an office. I'm really fast on a keyboard."

"Did you end up moving away for a time?"

"No, nothing really appealed to me and then I got a job working here in town on a summer placement thing which ended up growing into a full-time job with the medical clinic. It's a good job, so I just stayed put."

MacLean nodded. "OK, tell me a bit about James and Sarah's relationship as you saw it."

Mary-Catherine sat up, swung her feet on the floor and leaned forward. "He was a problem from the beginning. I warned her, you know. I told her he was no good."

"Why do you say that? What specifically gave you that feeling?"

"He was really possessive. You know, controlling."

"What sort of things did he do?"

"Like he would try to tell her what to wear. Once she started making money and was buying nicer clothes, he'd complain if her skirt was too short or if she wore a crop top. He'd say she looked slutty."

"What did you think of her choices?"

"They looked good on her. She was pretty when she made an effort. I think he liked it when she looked plain because then she'd just be his. No other guy would look at her."

"How did she react when he would try to control her?"

"Most of the time she'd try to keep the peace. At least at first. She'd change if we were being picked up at her place, or she'd wear something else if she knew he didn't like something, even though I told her she looked good in a dress or whatever."

"It sounds like she tried to appease him?"

"Yes. At first."

"What changed?"

"She started to ignore what he wanted. It's like she decided the heck with him."

"When did that start?"

"I think they were together for about six months or more when she started to push back on him. It wasn't just clothes. If we were all at a dance, sometimes a guy would ask her to dance, and we all knew it meant nothing. Lots of guys just go because they like dancing and if the guy was a geek or something and he wanted to dance, Sarah would sometimes say yes."

"And James didn't like that."

"Hell, no. He'd be pissed off for the rest of the night. At first, she'd always say no, and then she just said yes once in a while."

"Why do you think she started to change?"

She shrugged that one shoulder lift again. "I don't know. Just got brave, I guess, and I kept telling her to stand up to him. That probably helped." She put a hand over her mouth. "Oh, my God. Do you think I helped to get her killed because I encouraged her to stand up for herself?"

MacLean shook his head. "No, Mary-Catherine. The only person responsible for this is the one who killed her, and we certainly are a long way away from determining that James did it. This may very well have absolutely nothing to do with him, so don't fret yourself."

She uncovered her mouth and gave him a lopsided grin. "Yes, all right. I understand. I suppose you can't just go around accusing people of things."

MacLean narrowed his eyes. "That's true. Mary-Catherine, is there anything else you can think of that might help to find the person or persons responsible for this?"

She seemed to consider the question, then shook her head. "No, I'm afraid not."

"What did you think when you first learned that she had disappeared?"

She blinked. "Think? I don't know. It was a long time ago."

"Do you recall being surprised? Or did you believe she had simply left town?"

She shook her head. "I didn't think she'd just leave without telling me, so yes, I guess it surprised me."

"Worried?"

"Of course."

"Did you have any speculation, however far-fetched it may seem now, about what may have happened?"

She blinked again, rapidly. "I might have thought after a few days, that she was picked up hitchhiking and that she met someone nasty that way."

"Yes, hitchhiking. I heard did that sometimes. Did that happen often?"

"I wouldn't say often, but once in a while when she missed the bus and couldn't get a ride from anyone she knew, she might."

MacLean nodded. "There's a report that she was seen getting into a dark car on the day she disappeared. Do you know anyone who might have driven something like that?"

"I don't really notice what kind of cars people drive. I know if it's a pickup versus an SUV versus a car, but that's about it. So, no. I don't know who it might have been. I was asked that before." She sounded wounded, as if she believed he was trying to trick her.

"I understand you answered all these questions years ago, but sometimes details come to mind long after an event. Something may occur to you that didn't seem important previously but now, in hindsight, it takes on a new significance."

She nodded, mollified. "That makes sense, I guess."

MacLean pulled out a business card and stood up to hand it to her. "Thank you for your time. If anything like that comes to mind, even some minor detail that might help, please don't hesitate to call me."

She was all smiles again. "I'd certainly like to help. I'll give it lots of thought."

"Very good. I'd appreciate that."

She stood up and followed him to the door. "I hope you find him soon."

He turned. "You seem convinced that it's a him. Any reason why?"

She swallowed. "No. It just seems more likely to me."

He nodded and opened the door. "Thank you again, Mary-Catherine." He resisted the urge to say "Mary-Catherine Cameron."

MacLean made his way down the steep stairs and out into the spring sunshine. It was the sort of day that brought crocuses and daffodils pushing through the ground. As he thought about gardening, he glanced at his watch. He had an hour before meeting Albright.

I'll do a drive by the crime scene and see if it's all cleared up by now. He climbed into his SUV and made a mental note to get a car wash. *I could do it now.* Instead, he drove the few moments to Parish Lane and up the driveway. The dead tree was gone, all the wood tidied away, and the torn earth where Sarah had lain all these years, smoothed over leaving no sign of the trauma.

He parked and knocked on the door.

Vanessa Hunt opened the door, wearing reading glasses perched on the end of her nose. "Oh! How nice. Detective, please come in." She peered around him. "No Taz?"

He smiled. "No, I'm afraid not. Poor Taz has been sadly neglected this last while."

She led the way into the living room where the fire burned low in the wood stove. "You're here on business, then?"

He hesitated, searching for a response. Finally, he shrugged. "Not really. I wanted to see if you had gotten everything put back in order out here, so that's my story and I'm sticking to it."

She removed her glasses and set them beside the book she had been reading. "You're actually here for a cup of tea, then."

"Yes. That's the truth of it."

She went to put the kettle on. "I baked yesterday. Can I interest you in an oatcake?"

"The magic words."

He heard her putting the hard biscuits on a plate. He glanced around the room, enjoying the warmth and serenity.

She came back with the plate of oatcakes and two mugs. "I was thinking about what you said about Taz. You know, I'd love to have her here for the day if you ever think it would be convenient. I realize I'm in the opposite direction of you and your office, but still, the offer is there. I would happily serve as a doggie daycare for her."

"That's very kind of you. I'll keep it in mind. She certainly seemed to take to you, so I know she'd enjoy it."

The kettle whistled, and Vanessa went to make the tea.

He picked up an oatcake and a serviette to catch the crumbs. "I actually haven't got long. I'm in between appointments. I probably should have gone to Tim Horton's instead of disturbing you."

She poured out the tea and nodded to the jug with milk. "I think you don't take sugar, is that right?"

"Good memory."

"I'm very glad you came here instead of Timmy's. I have been dying to contact you and see what progress you all have made. I read in the paper about the identity of the person, of course. I had various news people here trying to make a bigger story than I could provide, but that's all in the past already."

He nodded. "You had your fifteen minutes of fame or whatever that saying is."

She smiled. "Yes, fifteen minutes. That apparently originated from Andy Warhol. Before that the saying was nine days wonder."

He chuckled. "It's a sign of our times. People have a very short attention span these days."

"Fifteen minutes or nine days. I'm glad it's over and I am back to being ordinary me in my quiet little house."

He heard classical music playing quietly from the stereo. "It is pretty tranquil here."

She smiled. "Thank you."

The conversation lapsed, and they listened to the music and sipped their tea. MacLean didn't feel awkward. *I like that she doesn't always chatter.*

He cocked his head. "I rarely listen to this type of music. What is this?"

"This particular piece is called Morning Mood. It's part of a larger suite called Peer Gynt by Edvard Grieg."

MacLean listened to the flute. "It's pretty."

The piece ended and Vanessa poured herself more tea. "Can I top you up?"

"Better not. I'll have to be going in a minute."

"May I ask how the investigation is going?"

"There isn't a lot to tell, really. It's early days. We're just trying to get a sense of who she was and what her life was like."

Vanessa nodded. "Poor girl."

"Does it spook you, knowing that she's been there all this time while you've lived here?"

"Spook me? No. Sadden me? Yes, a little. I feel now that the crows were trying to tell me she was there, but I wasn't listening." She gave a small laugh. "That probably sounds silly to you, but I am a great believer in the harmony of nature and that there are messages to be found all over the place, if only one pays attention."

"I'm not sure about messages, but I love nature too."

She nodded and then broke into a grin. "Speaking of nature, I've started all sorts of seedlings and they are thriving. I'm looking forward to planting lots of colourful things in that new garden bed to make up for the previous darkness."

"I'll have to come by and see it when it's done." He drained his cup and stood. "In the meantime, could I just use your bathroom before I go?"

She stood. "Of course." She pointed him down the hall. "First door on the left."

In the small powder room, the windowsill held pots of geraniums that looked to be a few years old. *She brings them in for the winter. Nice.*

She was standing looking out the living room window when he returned. She turned to walk him to the door. "I hope you won't wait until the garden is in full bloom before returning."

He reached out to shake her hand. "Thank you for the tea. If I'm in the area, I'll drop by." He hesitated. "Unless it's better to call first?"

"Not at all necessary. Come by whenever it suits you."

Her hand was warm in his and he was suddenly aware that it still rested in his. He released her hand. "All right, then. Take care."

She stood in the doorway. "Bye, now."

The door closed softly behind him as MacLean made his way back to the car. He felt rested and somehow rejuvenated.

CHAPTER 9

MACLEAN PARKED OUTSIDE THE older model mini home in Mulroy Estates. He waited in the car and within ten minutes Albright pulled in behind him. He got out of the car and waited until she gathered up her brown leather portfolio, locked her car door, and approached him.

Her forehead wrinkled. "Have you been waiting long?"

"Not at all. I was early. How did it go with the store manager?"

She corrected him. "Franchise Owner. He seemed harassed and genuinely upset about Sarah's death."

"What did he think had happened to her when she disappeared?"

"He thought she had left town on her own. He said that she seemed distracted for a week or so before she left. After she was gone, he thought she must have been planning to leave, and that's why her mind wasn't on her work. The only thing that he couldn't figure out was why she would leave before payday. That was on the Thursday after she disappeared, so she had a few days' wages coming to her. Eventually he gave the money to the mother."

The door opened, and a scruffy-looking young man peered out

at them. "Are you people coming in or what? I've got the dog in the bedroom and she's going nuts, so either I let her out again and she jumps all over you or you come in."

MacLean nodded. "I apologize. We're coming now."

They went inside, and MacLean made to take off his boots.

The man shook his head. "Leave 'em on. The dog tracks mud in and we only clean the floors on weekends."

"If you're sure?"

"Yes. Come in and sit down. I'll let her out, then. She won't jump on you if you're sitting."

MacLean and Albright followed through the kitchen-dining room combination into the living room and sat down, side by side on the worn brown plaid sofa. A blanket was thrown on the floor beside the sofa, and MacLean suspected it was usually on the furniture to keep the worst of the mud and dog hair off the couch.

They heard the bedroom door open and a second later a dark brown mixed breed dog came hurtling in, her tail wagging so hard that her entire back end squirmed back and forth. She gave Albright a cursory sniff before focussing all her attention on MacLean.

MacLean smiled and gently pulled on the dog's ears, which were long and velvety. "Yes, yes. I see you. You can smell Taz on me, can't you?"

The young man came back in and shouted at the dog. "Hilda, off!"

The dog ignored her owner and continued to nudge and push against MacLean.

Albright pulled out her identification and held it up. "I'm Detective Albright and this is Detective MacLean."

The man nodded. "Obviously you know I'm Jamie MacNeil."

Albright looked at MacLean, who nodded to her to continue.

She zipped open her portfolio and took out a pad of paper with prepared interview questions as well as her smaller notebook in which she prepared to record her interview. "Mr. MacNeil..."

He interrupted her. "Jamie."

She nodded. "Jamie, you know why we're here?"

He nodded. "To talk to me about Sarah."

"Yes. You were once her boyfriend."

"Yeah, but we broke up before anything happened to her. I wasn't seeing her anymore when she disappeared."

"Why did you break up, Jamie?"

He shrugged. "I never really knew. One day we were doing just fine and the next she said she didn't think it was working out and I should find someone new."

The dog had settled down and was now lying across MacLean's feet while he continued to caress her head and ears with one hand.

Albright continued. "You must have asked her about that. What did she mean when she said it wasn't working out?"

"I don't know, do I? I asked her. Of course, I did, but she wouldn't say."

"Had you had an argument that triggered the break-up?"

He shrugged. "Nothing, really. All couples argue, but there was nothing major. I have bigger arguments with my girlfriend now and she doesn't split up with me over it. We just make up again. That's how it goes. Normally."

"But it wasn't normal with Sarah?"

"No. Like I said, it just came out of the blue."

"That must have bugged you. Did you follow her? Did you try to get her to come back to you or at least explain things to you?"

Jamie's ears turned pink. "It's a long time ago. I don't really remember."

Albright frowned and tapped her pen against her notebook. "I think you remember, Jamie. It was a pretty big thing at the time for you."

He sighed. "Yes, all right. I did."

"Did what?"

"I parked down the street from her house to see if she was dating anyone else. Sometimes I did the same at her work. I only did it a few times."

"And what did you see?"

He shrugged. "Nothing. She just did the same things she always did before. She went to work. Once she went out after work for a pizza with a couple of girlfriends. Sometimes she went over to Mary-Catherine's place, or the two of them went to that church group she had joined. There was nothing, though. She didn't even go to a dance, while I was watching her, anyway. I didn't get it. Why she didn't want to be with me if she didn't have someone new."

"And did you ever try to talk to her about that? Try to convince her to come back to you?"

"I phoned her a couple of times once I knew she wasn't seeing someone else. She stopped taking my calls after a while." He frowned. "She blocked my number."

"That must have made you angry."

"I was pissed with her, but I just gave up. I got drunk with some buddies and they convinced me I could do better than her, anyway. Why should I waste my energy on her when she wasn't interested?"

As Albright referred to her questions, MacLean spoke. "Jamie, you've given this lots of thought. Back then and especially now after you heard it was Sarah that we found. What did you think? What do you think now in hindsight?"

He frowned. "I don't know. Sure, I've thought about it. Linda and I have talked about it. Linda's my girlfriend now. She knew Sarah too, but not well. They weren't friends or anything."

"What is Linda's last name?"

Jamie frowned. "Frazer."

Gordie made a note and then looked back up. "And what do you and Linda think?"

"She could be mouthy sometimes. That was one of the things Sarah and I sometimes argued about. I'd make a casual comment or suggestion and she'd get all huffy. Like maybe that what she was wearing wasn't right for where we were going or whatever, and she'd just give me lip about it. So maybe she gave lip to the wrong person."

MacLean glanced back to Albright, who had made some tiny check marks on her list of questions. She seemed ready to go on. "Can you think of anyone that she might have given lip to in particular?"

"Her dad. He was always drunk, and she could really set him off when he was like that."

Albright nodded. "Did you ever witness big arguments between them?"

"Every day was an argument in that house. Once when I was there, he asked her for money because he knew she had just been paid. He said that she should contribute more to the household. That's what he said, but of course we all knew that he just wanted beer money. Sarah said that she contributed enough already and that she brought groceries home. That was her contribution. That's what she said."

"How did he react?"

"I thought he was going to hit her and I stepped up and put my arm around her shoulder. If he had touched her, I would have pounded him. He knew that, and he backed off. He sat down in that big recliner of his and turned on the TV Her mom just sat at the dining room table sniffing. She didn't step in to tell him to back off Sarah or anything. She was scared of him too."

A vision of his own father flitted through MacLean's mind. A raised hand. His mother cowering, ready to be struck, standing in front of his sister to ensure the twelve-year-old girl didn't take the punishment for speaking back to their father. At eight-years-old, Gordie himself was wide-eyed in the doorway of the kitchen, too frightened to move. MacLean blinked, and the tableau disappeared. He heard Albright speaking.

"What was Sarah's reaction after that incident?"

"She said that one day he'd go too far."

"What did she mean by that? Was she afraid of him?"

"Funny enough, I don't think she was. Sometimes it seemed like she egged him on." He shrugged. "I don't know what she meant. She didn't want to talk about it. We left right after that to go out. She made her mother stand up to give her a hug and then kind of pushed her back to the kitchen."

"When we were in the car, I asked her if she was afraid that her dad might hurt her mom. She said no, not now. Her dad would probably just fall asleep. That was the end of it."

Albright bit her lip. "Were there ever times that Sarah goaded you in the same way? To the point that you were ready to give her a smack?"

He shook his head. "No, never. She called me a control freak sometimes, and maybe I did tell her what to do sometimes. I was a kid and thought it was a man's job to be a strong leader with your woman, but I never got close to hitting her."

As if in sympathy, the dog stood up and moved over to sit by her owner, the dog's chin resting on Jamie's knee. "I know better now. Linda taught me." He gently stroked the dog's head.

Albright waited to see if he would say anything further, but he seemed lost in thought. "Jamie, do you remember what car you were driving on the day Sarah disappeared?"

He looked up with a grin. "A white Chevy Metro. Grey interior."

Albright raised an eyebrow, and he continued. "With added-on fog lights and…"

She raised a hand, and he stopped. "You have a good memory for the car. What about for what you were doing the day Sarah went missing?"

He shrugged. "Of course, I remember the car. She was my first car and you always remember your first, don't you? What was I doing? God, I don't know exactly. I know I told you people back then. Can't you just look it up?"

MacLean interjected. "We'd like to know if you remember anything new, Jamie. More than what was in the original report."

He frowned. "I hardly remember what I did last week." He sighed. "OK, I think I was working during that day. I was doing some construction labour work that summer. They were doing repairs over at the college and I got hired on. After work, let me think. Oh, yeah. I think I went to the Legion because there was a band playing that I liked. Actually, I kind of thought I'd see Sarah there, but when she didn't show up, I didn't really care. I was dancing and having a good time. I didn't need her." He nodded and looked pleased that he had been able to recall the details.

Albright made some notes and then continued. "Going back to cars for a moment. We heard Sarah was seen talking to someone in a dark-coloured car. Blue or black. Did you know anyone who drove a car like that?"

He shook his head. "Nope. Most of my buddies had pickups or motorbikes." He looked at his watch then. "Are you guys just about done? Linda will be home any minute and you'll have to move your cars, so she can get in."

Albright looked at MacLean. "Anything else you'd like to ask?"

He stood up. "No, I think we're done here." He pulled out a business card. "If anything comes back to you, anything at all, please call us."

Jamie stood and took the card while the dog stretched. "Sure."

Albright led the way to the door. "Thank you for your cooperation, Jamie."

Jamie reached down to hold Hilda by the collar as Albright and MacLean went out.

MacLean pulled his sunglasses out of the inside pocket of his jacket. "Let's get a coffee."

Albright nodded. "Or tea. There's a Robin's down on Mary Street. OK to go there? They have a nice green tea."

"Sure. I'll see you there in a minute."

Albright had driven away, and MacLean backed out on to the street when a black pickup truck pulled into the driveway.

MacLean parked on the shoulder and got back out of his car. "Linda?"

The young woman with platinum bleached spikey hair turned on her way to the front door. "Yes." From inside the house Hilda was barking enthusiastically.

He pulled out his identification. "Detective MacLean."

She nodded. "Oh, right. Jamie said someone was coming today. You're all done, though, right?"

"I understand you knew Sarah as well?"

She shrugged. "I met her a couple of times. I didn't really know her."

"Where did you meet?"

"The church group. I went a couple of times, but it wasn't really my thing."

MacLean cocked his head. "I'm a bit surprised by how many people seemed to go to that youth group."

She laughed. "Yeah. Mostly girls." At that moment the front door opened, and Hilda bounded outside and started jumping against Linda. She put up her arms to fend off the dog. "Yes, OK, OK. Off! Off!"

MacLean smiled at the dog's excitement. He remembered those days. "Thank you for your time. I'll leave you to it."

Linda barely glanced at him, nodded and made a grab for the dog's collar. "Come on, mutt. Inside, inside now."

***

She already had a large green tea and a strudel when MacLean arrived. He got himself a double-double coffee and an old-fashioned plain donut. She was flipping through her notebook and cross-checking with her prepared questions.

"Did you get everything answered that you were looking for?"

She nodded. "I think so."

"So, what did we learn?"

She set down her pen and used her fingers to track her points. "Number one, he wasn't driving the car that she was seen near, unless he borrowed someone else's. Two, he didn't seem to be obsessed about her, although that could be a good act he's putting on now. And three, he himself admits he was a bit of a control freak and doesn't seem to hold it against her that she chafed against his ways."

MacLean nodded. "Good. You picked out the important things. What does your gut tell you about him? Could he do it? Did he do it?"

She bit her lip and then took a sip of tea as she considered the question. "No. I really don't think he did it. Could he do it? Probably. Especially back then when he was a hot-headed kid, but my sense is that he didn't."

"OK. I agree. What do you think about his suggestion that her dad might be responsible?"

She nodded. "I think it's worth looking into further. If he was at her for money and she got mouthy, well, you and I have both seen enough domestics to know that it could get out of control pretty easily."

MacLean frowned. "Would the mom stay with him all these years if she knew he was responsible?"

"But maybe she wasn't home when it happened. I think the news that we found Sarah genuinely upset her."

Albright finished her strudel and wiped her fingers on a paper napkin. "How did your interview with the friend go?"

MacLean drained his coffee cup. "She's interesting."

"Oh? Interesting how? Like she has the solution to climate change?"

MacLean smiled. "Unlikely. No, interesting in that she's a bit of a mystery. She's hiding something, but I can't think what it might be about."

"What makes you think that?"

He narrowed his eyes as he thought about his conversation with the girl. "I can't put my finger on it. Something in her body language made the hairs on my arms rise."

She laughed. "Oh, my. Hate to tell you this, Boss, but most people would say that's just called sexual attraction."

MacLean smiled. "No worries there. She's pretty, but not my type. No, there's something sly about her. I don't know if it's just because she's avoiding responsibility over what happened to Sarah or something else. I think she knows something she isn't telling us."

"Hmm. That is interesting. So, we need to bring the dad in and this Mary-Catherine for more questioning. Is that right?"

"I think the girl would clam right up if we brought her in. I think with her it'll take a bit of coaxing. But yes, for the dad. Let's schedule him for a proper interview at the station. Tell me about the store owner."

Albright shrugged. "Sandy MacIsaac. I'm not sure if there's anything there. According to him, Sarah was a good worker. Always on time. Got along with the other staff."

"But? It sounds like there's a 'but' there."

"He seemed to try too hard, if you know what I mean. I felt he was telling me everything I might want to hear so I'd hurry and leave."

"You told me he seemed harassed. Was it very busy there? Phone ringing, people knocking on the office door?"

She shook her head. "Nothing like that. Maybe harassed isn't the right word. Stressed, maybe."

"Because you were asking him questions?"

"Could be. He was pretty twitchy. Kept tapping his pen on his desk until I looked at it and then he stopped."

"Hmm. Did he say anything about whether Sarah had any friends in particular at work?"

"There was one woman. She still works there, but she's off on holiday for a few days. Visiting someone in Montreal. I've made a note to follow up with her when she gets back. Her name's Lorraine Doyle."

"Did you ask MacIsaac what sort of a car he drove?"

She nodded. "A white Ford cargo van."

"How did he seem when he talked about Sarah? Did he seem very fond?"

"You're wondering whether she was having an affair with him?"

He shrugged. "Stranger things have happened."

"He seemed upset to imagine she'd been dead all this time. He mentioned his wife and daughters. Talked about how his wife is so upset about the thought of a killer in the area. He said that he was glad his daughters are too young to really understand it all."

"Interesting. I wonder what it is he doesn't want the daughters to understand."

"He made it sound like just the fact of a murder, but like I said, there could be more there."

MacLean toyed with his empty cup. "OK, let's put him on the list as well for a follow-up at the office. I'd like to know more about his relationship with her. Did he ever drive her home, did he ever see her outside the store, things like that? I wonder if he had access to another car. A dark one."

He went on. "OK, so that's MacIsaac. Who else is there that we need to consider? I think it's unlikely to be a stranger just passing through. He would have taken the body away from town. The other thing that bothers me is the location of the grave. It's pretty bold to bury a body right on the outskirts of town. Why? Why wouldn't someone go further out rather than there?"

"Are we sure it wasn't the previous homeowner?"

MacLean raised an eyebrow. "An elderly woman? She was in her eighties, wasn't she?"

Albright nodded. "Fair enough. So now what? Head back to the office to see if the phone records are in yet?"

"I want to make one more stop. I asked Linda on the way out about her relationship with Sarah and she said she just met her a couple of times. They were in the same church group. That's also where Mary-Catherine and Sarah went sometimes."

"Wow. Must have been a hopping youth group."

"Let's go and see what the attraction is."

They stood up and Albright gathered up the empty mugs to set them on the dish return tray by the garbage bins. "I'll follow you."

For the second time that day MacLean drove past Parish Lane and Vanessa Hunt's house. He didn't think of the grave. Instead, he had a fleeting image of Vanessa sitting by the wood stove in her big comfortable-looking recliner with her book. He pushed the vision away to think of the interview ahead of him instead of her.

He pulled in and climbed out of the car as he waited for Albright to park and join him. He looked up at Our Lady of Mercy, the old-fashioned large church, its white siding shining in the spring sun. The belfry loomed three storeys above him, and he felt small.

Albright joined him. "Do you go to church?"

He considered the question. "I do the holidays. Christmas, Easter, that sort of thing, but otherwise I'm a great believer in the Church of Mother Nature."

She offered her own position. "I go most Sundays when I'm not working, but mostly for Nana's sake. Are you taking the lead here?"

"Sure." He looked at her before they went inside. "You did a good job there with Jamie. He wasn't what I was expecting. It was good to just watch and listen while you asked the questions."

She flushed. "Thanks."

He pulled open the heavy wooden door and stopped for a moment to let his eyes adjust to the dimness inside.

Passing through the foyer into the church proper, he led the way up towards the front of the church. He stopped and looked at Albright, who shrugged. He turned right and found a door leading to a room beside the altar. Walking through this to another door at the back of the room, he heard a radio playing. He knocked.

"Come in."

MacLean and Albright passed through a tiny outer reception area and into the priest's office. It was a surprisingly large space with a loveseat tucked under a window and a desk with two chairs placed to face the priest. The priest stood and came around to shake hands with MacLean and Albright, who both pulled out their identification.

"I'm Father John Sullivan." He was of average height, with thinning white hair. He wore large square-framed glasses which accentuated his pale grey eyes, and when he smiled at them, he showed off a gap between his two front teeth. "How can I help you, Detectives?" He gestured to the chairs as he went back to his own big leather chair.

MacLean sat down. "We're investigating the death of one of your former parishioners, Sarah Campbell."

The priest steepled his fingers. "Ah, yes. I read about that. Terrible business."

MacLean continued. "Did you know her well, Father?"

Father John laughed. "Me? Not at all. I wasn't here when she went missing."

MacLean's shoulders slumped. "Oh. When did you arrive here?"

"I've been here for almost seven years now. I got here in the summer of 2011."

"I see. Who was here before that?"

"That was Father Peter. The Reverend Peter West, that is."

"Do you know where he went when he left here?"

"He's not far--just up to Antigonish. Father Peter was very keen to go there and they granted his request for transfer in the fall of 2011."

"Why was he keen to go there?"

"I think this was just too small a parish for him. He wanted to be at St. Ninian. I think he enjoys the larger scope for his talents there. He's the Diocesan Spokesperson"

"Public Relations?"

"Oh, it's much more than that. It's very much a community engagement role."

"I understand he ran a youth group when he was here. When you got here, did you take that over?"

"I did indeed."

"It seems like a popular club or group, not sure what you'd call it. I understand Sarah was a regular attendee. Is it still so popular?"

"It folded about a year after Father Peter left."

"Is that so? What happened there?"

Father John stood up. "Let me show you a photo of one of the groups." He led MacLean and Albright back into the room they had passed through to get to the office. There were several framed photos on the wall, taken at different events.

Father John pointed to one. "This is Father Peter."

MacLean looked at the photo of a priest surrounded by six young girls. He glanced at Albright, who said, "Handsome man."

The photo showed a man of about six feet tall, with a face and smile reminiscent of Tom Cruise in the movie Top Gun.

Albright nodded. "I can see what the attraction was."

Father John led the way back to his office. "I understand he was a great favourite and had a way of communicating with young people that I just couldn't match. I think that when Sarah went missing, it took some of the heart out of the group, including Father Peter."

MacLean sat down again. "Why would that be? Did Father Peter think something had happened to Sarah? It appeared some simply thought she had left town for more interesting adventures. He didn't think so?"

Father John leaned back in his chair. "You'd have to ask him. We didn't discuss it. When I say that the heart went out of the group, that was simply my observation and don't forget that was quite some time after she was gone. I only heard her name once or twice and that was in passing, and in fact I think it was at Christmas or Easter when she was included in prayers for the lost or ill."

Father John stood again. "If there's nothing else?"

MacLean stood up, feeling that he had only just sat down. "I'd like to speak with Father Peter. Do you have a number where we could reach him?"

The priest wrote a number on a pad and then tore off the sheet to give to MacLean, wordlessly.

"Thank you." MacLean handed over his card. "If you think of anything else, please do let us know."

Father John put the card in the edge of his desk blotter. "Certainly."

MacLean and Albright stood together in the bright sunlight on the front step for a moment.

Albright raised an eyebrow. "Did it get distinctly chilly in the room at the end, or was that my imagination?"

"Definitely. I don't know what that was about. He seemed quite chatty, and then it seemed as though he suddenly remembered who we were and shut up on principle."

She tilted her head. "Odd, isn't it?"

"Maybe because the Church has gotten so much bad press in the past few years, that they've all been warned off talking to us. I can sympathize."

"But we're not talking about abuse of altar boys."

MacLean shook his head. "We'll set something up and go visit with the handsome Reverend West and see if he'll be a little more forthcoming."

The afternoon was waning, and they agreed to head home and meet at the office first thing in the morning.

On the drive home MacLean called Sergeant Arsenault. He gave his boss the highlights of the day's interviews.

"So you're bringing some of these people in for further questioning, then?"

"We are. Bill Campbell, the dad and this store owner Sandy MacIsaac interest me."

"You're saying the ex-boyfriend isn't worth a further look?"

"I'll go back and check his alibi now that we know the actual date that Sarah went missing, but my sense is no."

"Didn't that girlfriend seem to think the ex was violent?"

"That's what she said, but I'm not convinced. I think she may know more than she's saying, and I'll follow up on that later when I have a better idea of what it may be about, but right now I just feel that chasing the ex is a waste of time."

Even through the tinny sound of the speakerphone and road noises, MacLean heard the irritation in Arsenault's voice. "I want you to follow the facts, MacLean, not a feeling."

MacLean stifled a sigh. "Obviously, I'll follow the facts."

"That domestic file you worked on two weeks ago is still open. When you get in here tomorrow, come see me. Norris closed his open case today so he may be better suited to take this over from you and you can go back to your previous files." With that, Arsenault hung up.

MacLean gritted his teeth. *If he takes me off this case, I'll go above his head.* He drove the rest of the way home, stomach churning. He slammed the car door harder than he intended to and walked in the house, still steaming.

Taz bounded to him and flung herself against him, knocking him against the wall. She leaned her hundred and ten pounds against him, and he bent over to stroke her big head. "Yes, girl, yes, yes. All right. I know I haven't been around much, but here I am now." She nudged her nose against his sleeve and then poked at his legs and crotch, sniffing every spot that Hilda, the dog belonging to James MacNeil, had touched.

MacLean knelt down and Taz laid her head on his shoulder. "You're right. It isn't worth getting all worked up about, is it? You always set me right, Taz. I'll just deal with the sarge when I see what his plan is. Meanwhile, let's you and I get outside and clear our heads and worry about tomorrow, tomorrow."

CHAPTER 10

ALBRIGHT WAS ALREADY AT her desk when MacLean arrived at the office. She nodded towards his desk. "Got you a double-double."

He smiled. "I think I like working with a partner."

She raised her eyebrows. "Hopefully, I'm good for more than a coffee?"

"Prove it to me. What's the news on the phone records?"

She grimaced. "I'm afraid that was a dead end. Depending on the data, they keep it for differing lengths of time. Text data is kept for twenty-four months and call history is now kept for seven years. That's the policy effective 2015, but before that it was five years."

"So, there's nothing."

"No."

"Damn." He took a sip of his coffee. "All right. And we didn't find her laptop. Remind me, was there a computer in the house? A family computer?"

She frowned. "I'm not sure. We didn't search the house, only Sarah's room. I'll call Alice and ask."

"Do that and then while you're calling there, set it up for Bill to come in. Actually, have them both come in. We'll talk to them separately, but I want to understand this family dynamic better. He may have been the one with the temper, but she has eyes and ears. She must have known what was going on there."

Albright nodded. "Right."

"Then go ahead and get MacIsaac in as well. I have to go down the hall." MacLean jerked his head towards Arsenault's office.

Albright nodded. "Good luck."

"Do I need it?"

Albright smiled. "I'm new. I'm not an idiot."

MacLean gave her a tight smile and then walked down to rap on the open door of his sergeant's office. "Good morning."

Arsenault looked up from the computer he had been tapping into. "Have a seat. I just want to finish this email."

MacLean sat. He studied Arsenault's face while his boss finished his correspondence. He wore a scowl, and his lips were clenched in a thin line. *Is that because of me or whatever he's writing about?*

Arsenault clicked what must have been 'send' and then turned his attention to MacLean. "Well?"

MacLean frowned. "Well, what?"

"Do you have an update for me?"

"I just got in. Not much has changed since I spoke with you last evening." MacLean made an effort to keep his voice calm and easy. "The one update is not great news. We can't get any information about her phone calls."

Arsenault folded his arms across his chest. "And why is that?"

"No phone, as you know. No laptop and now no records from the phone company. They don't keep records going back nine years."

"Right. Now that you've told me what you don't have, what about something you do have. Any suspects?"

MacLean shook his head. "Look, Sergeant. As I just mentioned, nothing has changed since we last spoke, so why don't you just get it over with and tell me whatever it is that you want to say. On the phone you acted like you were going to pull me from the case."

Arsenault's face flushed. "I was just thinking out loud. I considered your other cases and wondered if you should be focussed on those and have Norris take over this case, but on further consideration I've decided to switch it around. You'll stay on this case and you'll brief Norris on your open files that need follow-up."

MacLean sat there, waiting for more.

Arsenault raised his eyebrows. "Since you have nothing else to report, you might as well get back to it."

MacLean stood. "Right."

Albright rolled her chair over to his desk when he came back and sat down. "So?"

MacLean shrugged. "So, nothing. I have no idea what just happened. Last night on the phone it sounded like he intended to pull me from the case and now he isn't."

Albright smiled.

MacLean tilted his head. "Do you know something I don't?"

She hunched over his desk, so she was leaning in close. "When I came in this morning, I heard him on the phone. I was the only one here, and it was very quiet. I didn't plan on listening."

"Yeah, yeah. Go on."

"He was really pissed, and he practically shouted something like 'if you aren't going to let me run the department the way I think it should be run, why did you put me here?'"

Suddenly it was clear to MacLean. "The Chief wouldn't let him pull me."

Albright smiled again and kept her voice very low. "Sounds like it. Honestly, I don't get why he'd want to. Do you two have bad blood or something?"

MacLean shook his head. "Not on my part. He just doesn't like the fact that I'm older than he is, and I've earned the respect of others so I can just carry on independently. He likes people who kow-tow to him."

"What? And you won't?"

"That's not my style, especially at this stage in my life."

She straightened up. "Good. I've gotten used to you; I don't want to start again with a new partner.."

"Not to worry. He's more bark than bite."

She sat back and cocked her head. "Seriously, though. You know he can't discriminate against you for your age or anything else. You'd be well within your rights to file a grievance if he tried."

MacLean huffed, something between a snort and a laugh. "No. Call me old-fashioned, but I won't go down that route. Besides, maybe that's the warning the Chief gave. Just the threat is probably enough. We'll get through this."

Albright shook her head. "Take it from someone who has had a lot of snide comments and other harassment thrown her way. You can't always just take it."

He nodded. "I can imagine what you've had to put up with. This is probably pretty mild in comparison, so I'm going to focus on the work and get on with the job. Let's get back to the case and prove Sarge wrong with his worries. The old man and the girl. Between us we'll get this done."

She flipped open her notebook. "I got a hold of the Campbells and they'll be in later this afternoon after Bill finishes work."

MacLean nodded. "And hopefully before he stops off at the Legion."

"Next on my list is to schedule MacIsaac."

"Good. I'm going to track down the buddies that MacNeil said he was with and get his alibi confirmed. I also want to go back to the original reports to see if we can find which witness said they saw Sarah and that car."

As Albright rolled away from the desk, she stopped. "Oh, and I asked Alice about a home computer. They do have one, but it doesn't sound like Sarah ever used it. It really is just Alice who uses it. She seemed very reluctant to let us have it."

"It can't be the same one from nine years ago. I wonder if she has a backup of her old computer somewhere. I'd still like to take a look. When she gets here, we'll pursue that."

***

After lunch, Sandy MacIsaac reported to the front desk, and Albright went to get him. When MacLean joined them in the interview room, MacIsaac was dipping a tea bag up and down in a cup of grey-looking water since it already had milk in it. When it was a darker shade of grey, MacIsaac squeezed the bag and laid it on the paper towel that Albright had provided.

MacLean took the lead. "Thank you for coming in, Mr. MacIsaac. I'm Detective MacLean and of course you already know my partner, Detective Albright."

MacIsaac nodded, took a sip of the tea and winced. He set the cup back down. "I don't know why I'm here. I told you everything I already know."

MacLean continued. "Just a few more questions. How long did Sarah work for you?"

The store owner frowned. "About two years, I guess."

"Would you say that you got to know her fairly well in that time?"

He shrugged. "As well as I know any of my employees."

"She didn't have a car. Did you ever give her a lift home or somewhere else?"

He folded his arms across his chest. "Sure. Once in a while. If she missed the bus or her boyfriend couldn't pick her up. I'd do the same for anyone."

"Did you?"

"Did I what?"

"Did you do the same for other employees? Drive them home?"

MacIsaac's ears pinked. "Most of them have their own cars or they live close enough to walk."

92

"So that would be no."

"I may have. I'm sure I have over the years, but nothing springs to mind at the moment."

"Sarah often worked the evening shift, is that right?"

"Yes. She started when she was still in school and just kept on even when she finished school. She liked that shift."

"You gave her quite a bit of responsibility for such a young woman. Sometimes she'd even lock up the store, am I right?"

"Yes. She was a reliable girl."

"Did you ever come to do the lock-up yourself when she was there?"

"Yes, of course. Often."

"In that case, there would just be the two of you. Is that right?"

"Yes, but if I was there, she'd usually just go on. It didn't take two of us to lock up."

"But sometimes she'd stay? The door locked? Maybe the two of you in the office or storeroom?"

Now his face flushed as well. "What are you getting at? I'm a happily married man."

"Happily married men sometimes find a pretty young girl like Sarah hard to resist. Was that what happened? Was she hard to resist? Perhaps you read it wrong and she got upset when you made a pass at her?"

He stood up. "No. Absolutely not. Nothing like that ever happened. She was just an employee. I liked her and trusted her because she was always cheerful with the customers and reliable. That's it."

"Sit down, please, Mr. MacIsaac."

He took a deep breath and sat down again.

"Let's move on. The day she disappeared. The seventeenth of August 2009. It was a Friday night. She had worked the day shift, which was not her usual shift. Why did she switch shifts?"

MacIsaac frowned. "I don't recall. It wasn't unusual for staff to work other shifts. Maybe it wasn't even her choice. It could have been that someone was on summer vacation and she was covering their shift. I don't remember."

"OK. Were you working that day?"

"Yes."

"Do you recall seeing her leave at the end of her shift?"

"I only remember because I was asked about it after she went missing. There was nothing special that happened."

"Tell me what you remember."

The flush in his face had faded, and he closed his eyes briefly as if conjuring up the picture of that afternoon. "She was wearing a new dress. I remember that. All the employees wear a yellow smock over their street clothes, so I hadn't noticed it until she was leaving. She left her smock in her locker and when she left, I was at the front of the store cutting up and flattening boxes. She stood outside the store for a moment and made a phone call on her cell phone, so I noticed the dress and how summery she looked in it. It had big flowers, and she wore some kind of red shoes that matched some of the flower pattern. The girls wear sneakers when they're working because they're on their feet all the time and we found them later in her locker. She had a big bag over her shoulder where I think she sometimes carried her laptop."

"You have a good eye for detail, Mr. MacIsaac. What else did you notice? Did someone come to pick her up after her call?"

"Not that I saw. She turned to walk along the front of the store and when she turned, she saw me through the window and waved. I waved back. That was it. She turned down Water Street in the direction of the library, but I wasn't watching to see where she went or if anyone picked her up. I wasn't watching her, you know? I was just working." He emphasized the point that he wasn't watching her and then pursed his lips.

"All right. Going back to other days when she left before you. You may know that she broke up with her boyfriend some time before she disappeared?"

"Yes, I knew. I hear the girls talking on their lunch hour sometimes. We're a friendly group and people chat about their weekends or kids or whatever, so yes I knew."

"Do you know if she was seeing someone else?"

"That, I don't know. I never heard her mention anyone, so if she was, she didn't talk about it. I heard her talk about going to dances with her girlfriends, but I didn't hear of any new beau."

MacLean's lips twitched at the old-fashioned word. "And do you recall ever seeing someone pick her up after she split up with her boyfriend?"

"Nothing stands out in my memory. If it happened, it was so inconsequential that I don't remember it."

MacLean looked at Albright. "Is there anything else you'd like to add, Detective?"

She shook her head. "Not at this time."

MacLean leaned on the table. "Just one last thing. Can you please remind me where you were on the evening of August seventeenth, 2009?"

"As I've said previously, I was at home with my wife and daughters. It was a nice summer evening, and we had a barbecue."

"Did someone else lock up for you that evening?"

MacIsaac's Adam's apple bobbed as he swallowed. "No, I went back for a few minutes to lock up. The girls had cashed out already and had everything ready to hand over to me. I put the takings in the safe, turned off the lights, set the alarm and locked up. The whole thing didn't take more than half an hour and then I rejoined my wife, and we had some wine together, sitting out on the deck."

MacLean stood up. "We appreciate your time. We'll let you know if we have any further questions." When MacIsaac stood up, MacLean reached across the table to shake his hand. MacIsaac's hand was clammy with sweat and after Albright led him out of the room, MacLean wiped his hand on his pant leg.

When Albright rejoined MacLean, he pulled his jacket off the back of his chair. "Ready for a tea?"

She nodded and retrieved her jacket and then followed him out to his car.

Once seated with their drinks at Tim Horton's, he raised his eyebrows. "Well, what did you think?"

I still think he's OK. I know he had time when he went to close the store, but he'd have to be quick unless he was prepared to have his wife grill him on where he'd been."

MacLean took a sip of coffee. "Maybe. We only have his say-so that he went back to sit on the deck with his wife. Maybe she went to bed early or watched TV. We'd have to confirm that. Do you think there was anything more between him and Sarah?"

"Not really. I'm just not feeling it. What do you think?"

"The jury's still out. I think he had daily contact with a pretty, young girl and it would be an easy thing for him to cross the line. Maybe he was driving her home and instead of dropping her at home, he took her somewhere else and she protested. Things got heated, and he smacked her with something handy. He didn't want to take the chance that she'd run around town saying what he'd done. It would ruin him."

Albright pulled out her notebook. "I'll call the wife. See what she recalls."

MacLean nodded. "Right. Do it right away before he gets to her. Of course, if there was something he wanted to hide, he'd probably keep quiet now. The last thing he'd want is for the wife to start thinking about that night. Anyway, let's just see what you can find out, but he's still on my list right now."

They went back to the office and while Albright reached out to Mrs. MacIsaac, MacLean updated the whiteboard. He worked on the timeline of Sarah's last day. *She was at work until four o'clock, if we believe MacIsaac. She made a phone call and then walked off down Water Street. Where were you going, Sarah?*

MacLean opened the file with the original missing person's report. The notes showed that the witness who saw Sarah talking to someone through the passenger window of the dark car said it was late afternoon. The car was parked on Union Street down from the library. *That tallies with what MacIsaac had said. He saw her turn down Water towards the library, which sits on the corner of Water and Union. She went past the library and turned down Union.*

MacLean muttered out loud. "Damn it. Why didn't you watch for another moment? Did she get into the car or not?"

The witness had been driving along Union and noticed Sarah in passing. The woman knew her to see her as one of the checkout girls where she shopped but didn't have enough interest to look closely at Sarah or the car.

MacLean was still staring at the board when Albright joined him. He turned to her. "Did you reach the wife?"

"I did. She tells the same basic story as he did. He left for a short while but came back pretty quickly."

"Do you think he called her when he left here?"

"I don't think so. She had to think back and then there was a lot of detail about the dinner they ate because the daughters didn't like fish done on the barbecue and yada, yada."

"OK. We'll cross him off for now unless something new comes up." He left the board and went back to his desk.

Albright pulled her chair over to his desk and sat down. "We've got the parents coming in at four o'clock. What's the plan there?"

"Let's take them one at a time. Put Alice in Interview Room One and Bill in Two. I want to see if we can rattle him a bit, so we'll leave him to stew while we talk to Alice. For her, I want to go over the family dynamic. How did Sarah get on with both of them? Then I want to know what she saw or heard on the day Sarah went missing. Did she talk to her daughter after Sarah left work? After we go through some of those details, we'll go in and talk to him. He won't know what Alice has said, so I may exaggerate a bit to see what his reaction is. Feel free to jump in with either of them if you want to."

"Do we want to mention what Jamie said?"

"Definitely." He continued on, tapping on one of the pages in the file "Can you give the original witness a call to see if she can add anything to the original report about that car? Does she think that Sarah got in? Maybe in hindsight she remembers Sarah opening the car door or something."

"Sure. I'll call her, but it's nine years ago. Hard to imagine she'll remember anything new after all this time."

MacLean shrugged. "Can't hurt to try."

Albright went back to her desk while MacLean spent the time updating his notes on the system to make them available to Sergeant Arsenault if he wanted to read them.

Shortly after four o'clock Albright went down to bring the Campbells in. MacLean heard Bill complain about being separated from his wife. He heard Albright offer him a cup of tea or coffee and the abrupt 'no' in response.

MacLean took the file with notes and crime scene photos along with a pad of paper into the interview room where Albright sat with Alice Campbell. He nodded to Albright to begin recording and then sat across from Alice. "Thank you for coming in, Alice. This must be a difficult time for you, and I appreciate your help."

She frowned. "I don't know which is harder, not knowing what happened or knowing. At least before I always hoped she would call me or come home. Now there's no hope."

"That's true. Now all we can do is get justice for Sarah. That's where you come in."

She folded her arms across her chest. "I really don't know how I can help."

"You probably know more than you even realize. That's why we want to spend some time talking it through."

"I think it would be better if Bill and I were together. Sometimes he remembers more than I do."

"No, I think you can speak more openly without him in the room."

Her eyes widened, and she licked her lips.

"Alice, let's go back to that time. To the days and weeks before Sarah disappeared. What was it like at home?"

"What do you mean?"

"Were there a lot of arguments? We heard Sarah didn't really get along with her dad."

She breathed deeply through her nose as if to stay calm. "She didn't always get along with him. That's true. She was getting very independent, but she was working, and I guess that happens. She was an adult. At her age I was the same."

"What did they argue about?"

She shrugged. "Just about everything. Bill felt Sarah should pay more since she was working full time, but Sarah was trying to put some money by for a place of her own. She brought groceries home from the store quite often and, although Bill didn't know it, she sometimes gave me money."

"Did Bill ever get so angry with Sarah that it became physical?" As MacLean asked, a vision of his father's balled fist swinging for his mother flashed through his mind. He gritted his teeth and focussed on Alice.

"Not really."

"Can you elaborate? What does 'not really' mean?"

She swallowed. "A couple of weeks before she went missing, they really got into it. Bill complained about what Sarah was wearing. She told him he had no right to tell her what to wear or not. It was about the top she was wearing, which was flimsy and you could see her bra. Her Dad went nuts and told her she couldn't go out in a negligee."

"But she defied him?"

"Yes. It was clear she was going to go out. He had been drinking, and he made to grab her arm, but she pulled away and he ended up ripping the sleeve of this thing. She was furious. She started screaming at him and he slapped her across the face."

"What did she do, Alice?"

"She was shocked. I think she wanted to hit him back, but she thought better of it and she turned and ran up the stairs crying."

"And Bill? What was his reaction?"

Alice's voice was very low. "I think he felt like he did a good thing. He got his way. She had to go change."

"He wasn't disturbed by his own behaviour?"

She shook her head. "I don't think so."

"Thank you for your honesty, Alice. Let's move on to the day she went missing. Sarah worked the day shift that day. Did she call you in the afternoon to let you know what her schedule was for after work? It was a Friday, and she may have had plans?"

Alice swallowed, and this time bit her lip. "No. I didn't talk to her."

"Was that usual? Would she normally call you?"

"Sometimes, but not always."

MacLean frowned. *There's something here.* "So, you're saying she didn't call you? We've asked the phone company for her call history from that day, Alice. Is there anything we should know?" MacLean saw Albright give him a quick glance before turning her attention back to Alice.

"I wasn't home. We didn't have call display or anything, so if she called the house I wouldn't know."

"I see. Where were you that afternoon, Alice?"

She looked down at her hands, which now rested on the table. "I was with a friend."

MacLean slid the pad of paper and his pen over to Alice. "Can you please write your friend's name and number down for us?"

Alice stared at the pad without picking up the pen. "My friend doesn't live here anymore, so no, I can't."

MacLean looked at Albright. She leaned over and touched Alice's hand. "Alice, is this friend someone that no one else knows about?"

Alice blinked without responding, head down.

Albright tried again. "Alice. Please tell us about your friend. We do need to know. It may have some bearing on Sarah's case."

Alice looked up at Albright. "It doesn't. I swear it doesn't."

"How can you know that?"

Alice took a deep breath. "Because we were together that afternoon and into the evening. We went out for supper and then he dropped me off at the corner of my street at about 9:30."

Albright continued softly. "We need his name, Alice. We'll need to talk to him."

As if resigned, now that she had admitted as much as she had, Alice wrote down a name and email address on the pad.

MacLean slid it around, so he and Albright could read it. *Jan Visser.*

He took over again from Albright. "So, this Jan..." he pronounced it as if it were the start of the name Janet.

Alice corrected him sharply. "It's pronounced *Yun.*"

He held up his hand. "Sorry. Jan. He was someone you had an affair with? Is that correct?"

She sighed. "Yes. Briefly. He is an engineer, who was here from the Netherlands for a few months. I didn't mean for it to happen, but I met him at the YMCA and we became friends. He was so different from Bill."

"Does Bill know?"

"Oh my God, no." The colour fled, leaving her face pasty white. "Do you have to tell him?"

"I can't make any promises, Alice. Perhaps you might want to tell him first."

"No. I don't want to tell him at all. It's long in the past. Jan went home a couple of months after Sarah disappeared."

"Did Sarah know about him?"

"No. I'm sure she didn't. She asked me where I was, once or twice, but didn't really seem interested in the answer."

"What would have happened if either your husband or Sarah had found out?"

Alice shrugged. "Bill would have gone ballistic, but Sarah? I think she would have cheered. She was often after me to leave, but I had no job, no money." She gave a wan smile. "I think though, that Jan and I could have made a go of it. He liked Canada. They offered him a job at the quarry in Quality Control. That's what he was there for. He analyzed the rock before they loaded it on to the ship for his company. Then it all went wrong, when Sarah went missing. It came between us because I was so distracted. Even Jan seemed upset. He didn't know her, but he knew enough of her from me to care about what happened to her. In the end he just went home, but once in a while we still email each other. He's married now and living happily ever after. And me? I'm just here. Once again, Sarah came between me and happiness." Her voice was bitter, and MacLean felt the hairs on the back of his neck rise.

CHAPTER 11

THEY LEFT ALICE WITH a cup of coffee and went down the hall to talk to Bill Campbell. Before they went into the room, they stood and spoke quietly in the hall. MacLean shook his head. "I wasn't expecting that."

"Are you going to tell the husband?"

"Not if I don't have to. I'll skirt around it and see what his reactions are. If I think he already knows, I'll ask."

Albright nodded. "What did you think about that last comment, about Sarah coming between her and happiness?"

"Strange."

She nodded. "Not very motherly."

"When was the first time that Sarah got in the way?"

"I think she meant that if she hadn't gotten pregnant with Sarah, she would have had a different life."

"Hmm. Right. Strange, but she wouldn't be the first mother who was jealous of a pretty daughter."

He put his hand on the door handle. "Shall we do this?"

She nodded and followed him into the room.

Bill pushed away from the table and stood up. His face grew red, as if ready to blow a fuse. "It's about bloody time. You have no right to keep me sitting here all this time waiting around. I have things I need to do. I'll be calling my lawyer. You can bet on that."

MacLean waited until Bill ran out of steam. "Please sit down again, Bill. I apologize for keeping you waiting so long."

All three sat down, and Albright started the tape to record the session.

MacLean made a show of opening the file and studying the notes. "Bill, we've just had a chat with your wife."

"Oh yeah? And what did she have to say that kept you interested for so long?" Bill Campbell frowned and tapped his thick forefinger on the table.

"Quite a few things. She's a very observant woman, and we had a great talk. We were discussing the weeks leading up to your daughter's disappearance. I'd like to go over the same time frame with you. See what you remember. See if you saw things in the same way."

Campbell's eyebrows pulled into a deep crease. "What things? What did she say?"

"Let's just focus on you. This is your chance to tell your side of the story."

Campbell's nose and cheeks flushed the deep broken-vessel-red of a long-time drinker. "What story?"

"How was your relationship with Sarah in the days and weeks leading up to that August day when she went missing?"

"Fine. I mean, we had the odd argument, but all parents and teenagers do. Do you have kids?"

MacLean ignored the question. "What did you argue about?"

Campbell shrugged. "Lots of things. What time she came home, what she wore. Things like that. I was just doing what any caring father would do."

"What about money? Did you argue about that? Did you expect Sarah to pay more for the privilege of living in your home?"

"I wouldn't put it like that. Of course, I expected her to contribute. Why not?"

"We heard that you once almost came to blows when she stood up to you and said she wouldn't give you any money."

Campbell's eyes narrowed. "That MacNeil kid. He's lying. He's the one who had a temper. Not me."

"You must recall a certain incident to think that James MacNeil told us anything."

Campbell studied his hands and picked at the cuticle of his thumb. "Once I shouted at her when he was there. It was no big deal."

"Were there other times that she defied you and you became furious?"

"She was always defying me by the end. It wasn't right. She was living under my roof and she should have paid attention to me."

MacLean nodded. "I can see how you'd be annoyed with that attitude."

"Right. She had an attitude problem."

"What about the night she disappeared? Did she come home after work? Did she give you some back-talk that annoyed you?"

Campbell shook his head. "I told you already I didn't see her that night. There was a darts tournament at the Legion, and I was there until closing."

"Are you good at darts? Are you on the team?"

Bill Campbell licked his lips. "No, I'm not on the team, but I support the team. I was there to cheer them on."

"I see. Who can we talk to that will verify that you were there the entire evening?"

He shrugged. "I don't know. It was a long time ago. Who remembers one night in the Legion from nine years ago?"

MacLean nodded. "You weren't sitting with a good pal that might remember?"

Campbell shook his head. "No. I'm friends with everyone, so I just talk to this one and that one. No one in particular."

"All right. So you weren't home that evening. Did Sarah call you?"

"No. Why would she?"

"What about your wife? Did you talk to her during the evening?"

"No. She knows not to bug me when I'm having a night out with the boys."

"I see. So as far as you know, your wife was at home and waiting for your return. What time did you get home?"

"Probably a little after midnight. It closes at midnight."

"And what time did you arrive there?"

"I got off work at four, so probably got there about four-twenty."

"You didn't go home first?"

"No. They serve burgers at the Legion. They have a barbecue out back in the summer and I had that for supper."

"Did you drive home?"

"No. I can walk. I left my car there and went back in the morning for it."

MacLean smiled. "Good. Did you see your wife when you got home?"

"She was in bed, I guess. I sometimes sleep in the spare room, so I don't disturb her with my snoring. She didn't wake up, so if she says I wasn't there, she's wrong."

MacLean looked at Albright, who shrugged. "All right, Bill. I think that's all for now."

"You dragged me all the way in here and kept me waiting all this time for that?"

MacLean stood up. "I appreciate your cooperation."

Campbell got up and followed MacLean out into the hallway. "Where's my wife?"

MacLean nodded to Albright. "Detective Albright will find her and bring her down to the lobby. You can come with me and I'll take you down."

After the Campbells left, MacLean updated the whiteboard, noting the alibi of each under their names.

Albright sat in one of the chairs facing the board. "What do you think?"

"We'll have to get a hold of that Dutch guy and talk to him. Send him an email and ask him for his number." MacLean stood back and scratched his neck while he studied the board. "The house is within walking distance. Campbell could easily have decided to go home for some reason. To get changed out of his work clothes, to get something to eat, to get more money. Maybe that's it. Maybe he decided to see if his daughter was home and touch her up for some money."

Albright continued the story. "He gets there. He's already half-cut. Maybe he's searching her room when she comes home, and they get into it. She turns him down as usual, only this time he isn't taking no for an answer. He picks up something heavy and squarish and when she turns to walk out on him, he swings it. A chair? The laptop?"

MacLean nods. "Could be. He's got it in him." He sighed. "We have absolutely no evidence, though. And everything we know suggests she didn't go home. She's wearing what she wore when she left work. Her phone and computer weren't found. He doesn't seem like the kind of guy who would think through all these details."

MacLean tapped the board with the marker. "What about the mom? She seemed to harbour a lot of jealousy and anger towards Sarah. What if Sarah found out about the affair? Threatened to tell her father?"

She shook her head. "I can't see it. Why would Sarah tell her father? By all accounts, she'd be pleased for her mother to leave her dad."

"What if Sarah met this Jan Visser guy somehow, and she fancied him for herself? He's foreign, he's got some money from this good job, she imagines he could be her ticket out of Port Mulroy. Mom wouldn't like that."

She nodded. "She wouldn't have liked that. It would account for her reaction there, when she said that Sarah came between her and happiness."

"When you get this guy's number, let's call him together. We'll ask him about meeting Sarah. See what he has to say." He shook his head. "I hate to let the dad go, but the pieces aren't fitting there. I don't think there was anything there with Sandy MacIsaac either. What about you?"

"No. He would have had to be the calmest guy in the world to sit and have dinner with the family if he killed her between the end of Sarah's shift and him going home, and he would have had to be fast since he got home somewhere around 5. He wouldn't have had time to kill her and bury her in the short time he was away to lock up."

MacLean wrote *No Time. No motive* under MacIsaac's name on the board. Under Bill Campbell's name he wrote *Money? Rage?* And under Alice's name he wrote *Jealousy?*

He set down the pen. "OK, you see if you can get a hold of this guy in Holland and I'll track down this priest that used to run the youth group. I just want to close that loop. See if he knows someone else we should check into. I'm also going to call Mary-Catherine Cameron in. There's something she knows. I'm sure of it, but we'll talk to the priest first and see if something comes from that conversation we can use when we bring the girl in."

By the end of the day, they had interviews set up for the following day. First thing in the morning they would speak with Mr. Jan Visser in the Netherlands, who had responded very quickly to Albright's request for a phone call, and in the afternoon the priest, the Reverend Peter West who had said he had several appointments so couldn't come all the way out to see them. MacLean told him they'd be happy to come see him. They scheduled the afternoon for a trip to Antigonish.

On the drive home, MacLean reran the interviews in his mind. *Dad. Drunk and wanting money. He had the opportunity. He could easily have wandered home without anyone noticing, but then what? How did he get her body out to bury it? Could he have driven home early on, like right after work, and then gone over to the Legion after it was all over?* MacLean shook his head. *He wouldn't have done it sober. He would have had to be drunk, but if he was drunk, he's not likely to have the wherewithal to take the body and bury it at that house. Would he?*

MacLean knew he was biased against the father. He was reluctant to take him out of the picture, but it was hard to make it all add up.

What about Mom? She seemed controlled by Dad, but maybe not as much as we first thought. She had the nerve to have an affair. What if she really believed somehow Sarah was coming between her and her fella? I wonder what kind of car he drove? MacLean made a mental note to ask him when they spoke in the morning.

At least I think we can eliminate MacIsaac. That's one off the list, at least.

Taz was in a frenzy when MacLean got home. Her back ended up with her tail waving its feathery plume in a wild swoosh, and front end down. Taz wanted to play.

"All right, my girl. Let's go out for a drive. How's that?" MacLean opened the hatch-back and the dog sailed in.

MacLean settled in the driver's seat and made a phone call. "Hi, Vanessa? It's Gordie MacLean. I'm just out for a drive with Taz and thought we might drop by."

He smiled into the rear-view mirror as he set off. "I know you'd like to see that nice lady again, Taz. I'm doing this for you."

The moment MacLean parked the car, Vanessa Hunt came out of the house wearing a light jacket. He opened the hatch and let Taz out, who bounded over to receive the hugs and petting Vanessa lavished on the dog.

MacLean watched the enthusiasm between both Taz and Vanessa. "You don't mind us dropping by?"

Vanessa cocked her head. "Please, Gordie. Does it look like I mind? I'm delighted. Do you want to go for a walk before we go inside?"

"That would be great."

"To the water or back towards the woods?"

MacLean pointed towards the woods. "That seems like a quieter way."

They walked along Parish Lane away from the shore towards a forested area at the end of the road. "Is that Crown land down there?"

She nodded. "Yes. It's nice to have that so close to the house, and with it being government owned, I don't think they will ever develop it."

They chatted about the weather, the spring flowers and other inconsequential things. She didn't ask about the investigation and he didn't mention it. She seemed to sense that he needed to take a break from it.

They didn't stay out for long. It was getting dark by the time they walked to the woods and turned back to return the same way.

When they got back to her place, MacLean stopped at the car. She turned to look at him. "Won't you come in for a cup of tea or a glass of something?"

"No, thank you. This has been just what I needed, but I have another early start tomorrow and need to head back."

She looked disappointed and then smiled. "I'm glad you dropped by. You're welcome anytime."

Taz jumped back into the car and then MacLean stood for a moment before climbing back in himself. "It's very restful here. I like that."

"Good. I'm glad."

"I'll see you again. I don't know when, but I'll call."

"I look forward to it."

She waved them off and stood outside, watching until he turned on to Route 19. She was still standing there when he glanced in the rear-view mirror just before turning.

MacLean spoke to the dog and saw one ear lift at the sound of his voice. "Did you enjoy that, Taz? Will we go back again sometime?"

CHAPTER 12

MACLEAN WAS AT THE office early the next morning. He felt rested and revived after a short, brisk walk with Taz, and bacon and eggs at home. Albright found him at his desk, making notes on his lined pad.

She peered over his shoulder as she stood behind him and read the heading: "Questions for Jan Visser." Fetching her chair from her desk, she rolled it over to his. "What do you have?"

"Apart from the obvious ones concerning his relationship with Alice, and whether he knew Sarah?"

She nodded.

"I want to know what car he was driving. I also want to know if Alice talked about Sarah and Bill."

"You want to know if he thinks Bill could have done it?"

"Or Alice."

"You're assuming he wasn't involved?"

"Don't know that yet, but I think we'll get a sense of it as we talk to him. But let's assume for the moment that yes, he's in the clear. He may have a good perspective on what was going on in that house."

Officers were moving into the briefing room. MacLean looked at his watch. "Let's get the briefing over and then we'll be ready to call this guy. We'll do it in the small boardroom so we can be on the speaker with him."

MacLean spent fifteen minutes bringing Sergeant Arsenault and the other detectives up to speed on where the investigation stood.

Arsenault stood with his arms folded the entire time, leaning against the door frame. "It sounds like you aren't much further than when you last briefed us."

MacLean took a breath. In through the nose and out through the mouth. "Slow and steady, Sergeant. The discovery that the mom was having an affair is significant in my view, and Albright and I will be talking to that man shortly to ascertain where he fits in to the picture. We also now believe we can rule out the store manager, so I think we are actually making some progress."

MacLean saw a couple of his colleagues nodding. They understood these things took time, and one answer may lead to additional questions previously not asked. It was an iterative process.

Arsenault's voice was thick with sarcasm. "Don't let us keep you from it, then."

MacLean put his whiteboard marker down and the detectives started to stand up, but at that moment Detective Norris called out. "I've got some capacity. If you need a hand, just let me know."

MacLean pushed back the thought that Arsenault had set this up. He'd take the offer as genuine. "That's great. Thanks, Rob. We may just take you up on that. I'll let you know."

After the briefing MacLean and Albright got ready in the boardroom with their cups, notes, and files arrayed around them and the speakerphone between them. Albright dialed the number and on the second ring, a heavily accented voice answered: "Jan Visser."

MacLean took the lead. "Mr. Visser, this is Detective Gordie MacLean and Detective Roxanne Albright, calling from the Cape

Breton Regional Police Service. Good morning. Actually, I suppose it's good afternoon for you."

"Yes. It is afternoon here. How can I help you, Detectives?"

MacLean had wondered if the man's English would be easy to follow over the phone, but he was relieved to hear that Visser spoke impeccable English. "We're calling about the death of Sarah Campbell."

"Yes, I heard about that." There was a light chuckle. "I have the Cape Breton Post in my favourites, so keep up with the news there."

"I see. Did the name ring a bell with you?"

"Yes, of course. I'm sure you know about Alice and me or else you wouldn't be contacting me. I knew immediately when I read the story of the discovery of her remains. It's very, very sad. I think Alice always hoped she would turn up somewhere happy and healthy."

"Thank you for your honesty, Mr. Visser."

"Please call me Jan."

"All right, Jan. We'd like to go over some details with you since you were around at the time of Sarah's disappearance. Can you tell me what you remember about the day she went missing? And also, your memories of the time leading up to the actual day."

Jan Visser spoke clearly, confirming what Alice had said. They were together. No, he never met the girl, and knew nothing other than what Alice had said. His sense was that she was a typical teen-ager, displaying some rebellious moments, but she was working and contributed by giving her mother some money and bringing home groceries. Jan Visser didn't know much about Sarah, but from what he recalled, she had sounded like a normal girl on the cusp of becoming an adult. Alice spoke fondly of her, although she some-times wished that Sarah wouldn't push her father so much.

MacLean closed the conversation by asking about the car.

"I had a leased car. It was much bigger than what I'm used to. It was a white Ford Escape. I loved it. Here in the Netherlands, we drive smaller cars and I admit I enjoyed the power of the larger car." His voice held a wistful note.

Albright's mouth turned down and MacLean shrugged. *Don't be disappointed.*

"Thank you for your assistance, Jan. We won't keep you any longer."

"No problem at all. Detective?"

"Yes?"

Visser hesitated. "How is Alice doing with all this?"

"I think she's coping. Once she got over the shock of the discovery, I think she's getting used to it."

"Thank you. I always wished her well. I would have liked…well, that's all water under the bridge now."

"Jan, it sounds like you enjoyed her company. May I ask why it didn't work out?"

Again, the wistful tone was obvious despite the distance. "When Sarah went missing, Alice pulled away. It seemed to me that she felt she was being punished for her transgression."

"I see. I'm sorry it didn't work out. Goodbye, Jan. Thank you again."

"If you have any further questions, please don't hesitate to call me or send me an email."

After hanging up, they sat on and MacLean looked at the notes he had made. "Well, it looks like we can eliminate Alice. I believed him. What about you?"

She nodded. "Yes. He sounded legit. There's no reason for him to lie."

They went back to the briefing room and added the timeline of Alice's movements and then went back to MacLean's desk. He noted, *No Opportunity,* below her name.

He circled the note about Visser's vehicle. "Contact the rental company he mentioned and see if you can get confirmation on the car, just to close that loop. We've got Mary-Catherine Cameron in shortly. I want to see if we can winkle some more information out of her about Sarah's movements on that last day. Best friends know every step of what their pals are doing, don't they?"

"Unless the pal in question is trying to hide something from her best friend."

"That in itself would be interesting."

MacLean listened to his messages and raised his eyebrows. "While you're chasing down the car, I'll go see Allan. He tells me they've found some trace that might be interesting."

He made his way down to the lab. "What have you got?"

John Allan pulled out two photographs of extreme close-ups of several hairs. "We got some hairs from her dress."

"Not hers?"

The Forensics Identification technician pulled his mouth in a sneer. "Really, Gordie? Would I call you about that?"

MacLean held up his hands. "Sorry. Tell me then." His heart began to race. "DNA?"

"Not the kind you're hoping for, I'm afraid, but we did send the hairs to Halifax and they're running a mitochondrial DNA analysis."

MacLean frowned. "Refresh my memory. What does that mean again?"

"The hairs didn't contain a nucleus, which is what we want for a solid identification. We can do an identification of sorts based on the mitochondrial DNA, which is inherited from the mother. If you get a suspect, we can compare the two and while it won't be definitive because if the suspect has siblings from the same mother, or indeed the mother, there could be an argument that the hairs came from them. It narrows the field, though."

"OK. I get it. What it also tells me, though, is that she was pretty close to this other person for these hairs to adhere to her dress."

"That makes sense."

"All right, well this is interesting. Can you tell if the hairs are male or female?"

"No, I'm afraid not. I believe there are experiments with new procedures going on, but right now that's beyond the ability of the labs we have access to. I can tell you that the hair showed no sign of being dyed."

"All right, well, it'll still be useful as corroboration when we have a suspect. And no dye may mean it came from a male, but even that isn't certain."

"No."

"OK, well, it's better than nothing. No scrapings under the nails or anything else useful?"

"No, too much time has passed for that. There was no sign of defensive marks."

"She didn't see it coming."

"No, but we retrieved a few slivers of wood, which confirms our thinking that the weapon was a piece of wood."

MacLean sighed. "All right. Confirmation is something I suppose, although I'm sure the wood is long gone into someone's fire by now."

MacLean thanked John Allan, and he returned to his desk to think about the piece of wood. *Does this mean it was a murder of opportunity? Surely if you were intending to kill someone, you'd take something more convenient and practical than a piece of wood. If it was convenience, does that mean it took place at a building site?*

***

MacLean made his way back to Albright's desk and mentioned his thinking about the building site. "Do you think we could find out what places were under construction in Port Mulroy in August of 2009?"

She thought for a moment. "I'm not sure how useful that would even be. Think about all the home renovation jobs going on at any point in time. Maybe someone was doing up their basement or something."

"We might get a list of building permits issued for that period."

She raised an eyebrow. "Does everyone doing a weekend job with a 2-4 and a bunch of guys, apply for a building permit?"

"Not likely" he acknowledged. The 2-4 she referred to was not a piece of wood but rather a case of 24 beers, the common payment for a small job that a group of friends could manage during a weekend.

He went back to his desk to mull over the problem as they waited for Mary-Catherine Cameron to arrive.

CHAPTER 13

DETECTIVE ALBRIGHT OFFERED MARY-CATH-
ERINE a cup of tea as they settled into the interview
room. At Mary-Catherine's nod, Albright went off to get
the standard cup of dark tea in a paper cup that was all that was on
offer in the lunchroom.

Today the young woman wore her hair down, the hair cascad-
ing below her shoulders, and as she lowered her head, the chestnut
waves formed a curtain, obscuring part of her face. Mary-Catherine
wrapped her fingers around the tepid cup and stared down into the
liquid but didn't immediately drink any tea while MacLean and
Albright arranged notebooks and pens in front of them on the table.
In this larger interview room, the session was automatically recorded
by the small camera fixed to the corner where the ceiling met the
wall. MacLean waited until Mary-Catherine looked up at him.

She frowned. "Why did I have to come in here? I answered all
your questions already."

MacLean tilted his head. "There are always more questions,

Mary-Catherine. Right up until the person who murdered Sarah is put into jail."

Albright nodded. "And maybe even after that."

Mary-Catherine shrugged, a one-shouldered, defiant twitch. "So, go ahead then. Ask away."

MacLean leaned in, resting his folded arms on the table. "Mary-Catherine, I think you know more than you've shared with us so far. Why don't you tell us what you've been holding back?"

The girl moved her hand away from her cup and pressed back into the chair, arms folded across her chest. "I don't know what you mean."

MacLean slowly shook his head. "Don't you want to find the culprit who did this to your best friend? She *was* your best friend, wasn't she?"

Mary-Catherine flushed. "Yes. 'Course she was. I do want to punish the person who did this, but there's just nothing more I can tell you."

MacLean smiled and leaned back in his chair. "OK. Maybe you just don't realize that you know something important. Why don't you just tell me a bit more about Sarah as a person? What did you like about her? Why were you friends?"

Mary-Catherine's shoulders dropped, and she unfolded her arms. She picked up the cup as she considered the question and took a sip of tea. She put the cup back down and slid it away. "We were friends because we didn't judge each other. Like, sometimes I might go out with a guy she didn't like, but she never gave me a hard time. You know?"

Albright looked up from her notebook. "She was there for you."

Mary-Catherine nodded. "Yes. She was always there for me. And I tried to be there for her, but it was different."

MacLean nodded. "How was it different?"

Mary-Catherine blinked rapidly. "Her family was a pain and even when I knew they upset her, she didn't talk about it too much."

Albright's voice was soothing. "You didn't know how to help her."

"No. I didn't know what to do. I'd ask if everything was OK, and she'd say yes, even though I could see she'd been crying. I didn't want to make it worse, so sometimes I'd just move on, right?"

MacLean leaned forward, but kept his arms resting on his chair. "Do you think there was violence in the house, Mary-Catherine?"

The girl's eyes flickered off to the side. "I don't know."

"Even if she didn't actually tell you, you must have speculated. I'm just asking for your opinion."

She nodded. "I think her father hit her mom. Sometimes Sarah would be really pissed off, and she'd just say something like 'I don't understand why some women let a man push them around.'"

"And you concluded she was talking about her mother?"

"Yes."

"Did you ever see any unexplained bruises on Sarah? Do you think she ever tried to get in the middle of things?"

"I never saw any bruising, but sometimes she'd wear long sleeves even when it was warm out, so who knows?"

MacLean nodded. "See now? You're doing well and are really helping me to get a picture of Sarah. Now, can you tell me a bit more about what the two of you did together? I know you said you went to dances. Tell me more about a typical evening together."

Mary-Catherine sighed. "Sometimes we'd just hang out at my place and watch a movie or play cribbage." Mary-Catherine smiled as she remembered. "She was such a fiend for cribbage. You could wake her up in the night and ask her for a game, and she'd be happy. Fifteen-two, Fifteen-four. She could add faster than anyone I knew."

"Sounds like she was clever."

"Oh yes. She could have been anything she wanted."

"But she didn't plan to go to university?"

The smile slid away from Mary-Catherine's face. "No."

MacLean frowned. "Why not?"

The one-shouldered shrug. "No money?"

"She could have applied for student grants or loans."

"She had other plans, I guess."

MacLean felt Albright shift in the chair beside him. He kept his voice easy. "What sort of plans?"

Mary-Catherine put her hand in front of her mouth, touching her lips before speaking. "I don't know exactly. Just not more school. That's all I know."

"I see. OK, go on. So, sometimes you just hung out at home and sometimes you went to dances. What else?"

Mary-Catherine frowned. "Just ordinary stuff that people do. Nothing amazing or weird. We didn't go rock climbing or skydiving or anything, you know?"

MacLean leaned forward with his arms on the table again. "Did you double date?"

She shook her head. "I didn't really like James, and he didn't like me or anyone really, so they didn't double date."

"But what about after she and James broke up?"

"No, we never double dated."

"But she did date other people after James, right?"

"Sure, she was popular. She went out sometimes."

"Can you remember anyone in particular?"

Mary-Catherine licked her lips, and she looked down at the cold cup of tea. "I don't remember anyone in particular."

Albright glanced at MacLean, and MacLean nodded. The girl had shut down again. Albright stood and picked up the cold tea. "Do you want a fresh cup?"

Mary-Catherine shook her head. "No. I just want to get this done. I have things to do."

Albright sat back down.

MacLean leaned back and studied Mary-Catherine, waiting for her to return his gaze. When she did, he suddenly sat forward, startling her, her eyes widening. "Mary-Catherine, I think you're holding out on me. Who was she dating?"

Her lips pursed. "I don't know."

"I think you do. Is it someone you liked? Were you angry at her for going out with someone that you wanted? Is that it? Were you jealous?"

Mary-Catherine bit her lip. She spoke slowly, the anger in her voice barely controlled. "She never went out with anyone that I wanted. We had different tastes in men."

"You're lying about something, Mary-Catherine. The only reason I can think that you would lie is because somehow you feel responsible about what happened."

Her voice went up half an octave. "I'm not responsible. I did nothing. She was my friend."

"So, what is it? I will find out, Mary-Catherine. I won't rest until I do."

Tears welled in Mary-Catherine's eyes. She seemed to deflate, as the defiance left her. She stared down at the table. "I knew she was seeing someone, but she didn't tell me who." She looked up at MacLean, eyes fully gazing into his. "Honestly, she wouldn't tell me."

MacLean nodded. "And she usually did, right?"

Mary-Catherine nodded. "If I'd only asked her more. If I'd demanded she tell me, then maybe none of this would have happened."

"Do you think he was married? Is that why she wouldn't tell you?"

She blinked rapidly. "I don't know. Maybe."

"There had to be a reason she wouldn't say, right?"

She sighed deeply and took a moment to respond. "Could be. Yes, usually we told each other everything." A shadow crossed her face. A memory recalled. Mary-Catherine rolled her shoulders. Her mouth tightened and she straightened up in her chair.

"Looking back, do you have any ideas or suspicions about who it might have been?"

She shook her head. "No. Look, I really need to go. Are we finished here?"

MacLean looked at Albright to see if she had any further

questions, but she shook her head. "All right. Thank you for your help. If you think of anything else, make sure you let us know. It doesn't matter how small, or if you don't know something for certain, but just have a feeling, I'd appreciate a call."

Mary-Catherine was on her feet. "Yeah, OK."

When Albright came back after escorting Mary-Catherine out, MacLean stood. "Let's get some lunch. I'll buy. I'm feeling like we had a breakthrough there, but this isn't the last we're seeing of that girl. She is still holding out and I want to know what it is."

Albright glanced through her notebook as they walked to MacLean's car. "You did good, Boss. I would have cut her loose much earlier." She put the book away into her breast pocket. "What makes you think there's more to tell?"

"She lied. Her voice, the way she kept looking off to the side or at the table. She's definitely lying about something. I just don't know what it is, but I could see that she had gotten a grip on herself again after she told us about Sarah seeing someone. We weren't going to get anything else today, so we'll give her a break and now that we have this lead, we'll see if anyone else knows anything."

"Like her mother?"

Maclean parked the car as close to the Tim Horton's in the mall as he could. As they walked, he answered her question. "I don't think the mother will have a clue. She was too wrapped up in her own issues. Between her drunken husband, and her affair, I'm guessing she hardly even knew where Sarah was on any given day, let alone know who her mysterious boyfriend was."

They ordered lunch. A toasted bagel with cream cheese for her and a grilled cheese sandwich for him. When they settled at their favourite table in the corner with lunch in front of them, Albright suddenly stopped eating. "What if it was the same man her mom was seeing? That would explain the secrecy."

MacLean raised his eyebrows and smiled. "You have a devious mind. Where did that come from?"

"Dunno. I'm just trying to imagine why a girl would keep the information about a new man away from her best friend. Even if he were married, like, let's say, her boss at the store, I don't think it would be enough to keep her quiet. Girls share secrets."

MacLean thought about it as he chewed. He finished his sandwich and brushed the crumbs from the front of his shirt and then sat back, stretching out his legs as he drank his coffee. He shook his head. "It's possible, of course. Anything's possible, but personally I can't see it. Sarah wanted to protect her mother. If she knew about her mother's affair, I can't see her hurting her mom by dating him. If she didn't know, how would she even come to meet the man? I know we only spoke with the fellow over the phone, but he didn't strike me as a real scoundrel. He sounded like he was sorry that it didn't work out with Alice."

Albright nodded. "Yeah. He sounded genuine, but who knows? Maybe Sarah found out something about the guy and wanted to expose him, so dated him, just to show him up to her mother?"

"And then what? He has a solid alibi for her murder. He was with the mother."

Her face fell. "Right. OK. It was just a thought."

MacLean grinned. "Keep the thoughts coming, partner. I'm not Sergeant Arsenault, who only wants to hear the final result. I'm good with theories. We'll go back to the shop, figure out our next steps, and then I need to head home and clear my head with a good long walk with Taz. There's something Mary-Catherine said today that's niggling at me, but I just can't grab it."

CHAPTER 14

B Y THE TIME GORDIE had driven home and loaded Taz
in the car, he was ready for an easy walk, so he drove the
fifteen minutes to Pondville Beach to walk along the long
stretch of sandy beach. Taz loped off to sniff and roll in the seaweed
while he strolled, deep in thought.

*Dammit. I wish I remembered what it was that girl said that bothers
me. She's still hiding something, but I can't put my finger on it.* He mentally
shook his head. *It'll come. Meanwhile, we've got other people to question
again. I want to see what that Jamie fellow knows about a new boyfriend.
He was trailing around after her. Some people would call it stalking.*

He turned his gaze from the water to see Taz lying on the damp
sand eating something. "Taz. Come on. Leave it now, let's go." The
dog thumped her tail on the ground and kept crunching. Gordie
quickened his pace and tried to wheedle the piece of lobster shell
away from the dog. "Come on. Drop it."

Taz ran off with her prize and crunched some more. Gordie
shook his head and gave up. "Don't blame me when you have a stom-
ach-ache." He walked on, suddenly reminded of walks on the beach

with his mother when he was a boy. He'd delighted in picking up all sorts of things including half rotten pieces of rope, shells, stones, pieces of broken lobster trap and interesting twists of driftwood. It was a treasure trove for a boy and his best friend, his sister Jean. Those were the best days, when it was just the three of them. On the rare occasion when his father came, it was a whole different experience. His father might be angry because he'd been dragged along on the family outing when he'd rather be at the Legion. Or maybe he'd been out somewhere drinking already, and then it was even worse because he'd go from happy and playful to angry and mean in a minute without warning. Gordie and Jeanie learned to read the moods like a farmer read the sky.

Gordie shivered as the wind off the water swirled around his neck. "Come on, Taz. Let's go home."

The big dog came sprinting after him as MacLean turned and headed back along the beach. The wind was fresh and made his eyes water. He stopped. *Punished. That's the word Mary-Catherine used.* He asked her if she wanted the culprit caught and she said she wanted the culprit punished. That was what was bothering him. *Does that mean anything? Why not echo my word 'caught'?*

Gordie was more convinced than ever that she knew something important. *We'll give her a couple of days while we talk to some of the others. Then maybe I'll have something more that I can confront her with. Something that will break down those last defences.* He mulled it over as he and Taz got back in the car. *Punished. Does that mean she already knows the culprit? Is it her after all? Is she feeling guilty?*

***

The next day was Saturday, and Gordie called his mother. "Hi, Mum. How are you?"

His mother chatted away about the card club and the seniors' lunch club for a while. He let her chat while he washed the breakfast dishes, the cordless phone clamped between his shoulder and ear.

When his mother wound down, he dried his hands and sat at

the table. "I'm thinking of running down for a visit. What do you think? Will your busy schedule have room for me?" He smiled at her enthusiastic response. "Do you think Jeanie's around? Maybe I could take my two favourite ladies out for lunch."

He nodded. "OK. You phone her and I'm going to give a friend of mine a call to see if she'll take Taz for the day. I've been leaving her on her own a lot this week, and I hate the idea of another long day for her. I'll see you around noon."

He hung up the phone and sat for a moment, caressing his dog's ears as she rested her head on his knees. "What do you think, Taz? Should I call her? Would you like to go there for a visit? You know I'd love to take you with me, but I can't take you out for lunch with us, and you'd end up sitting in the car all day. That's no fun."

He took a deep breath and called Vanessa. "Hi, Vanessa. It's Detective Gordie MacLean. Well, since it's just a social call, I guess I should just say it's Gordie MacLean." He rolled his eyes at Taz and felt himself flush.

Her voice was soothing, and he felt himself relaxing a little. "Vanessa, I have a favour to ask and please feel free to say no. I'm going to Halifax for the day, but I can't take Taz with me." Before he even asked, she offered to take her. "Are you sure? I know it's an imposition, but she's been on her own so much that…" He listened to her protests. "Well, thank you. Will it be convenient if I head over shortly?"

He hung up the phone and felt his heart racing. "Well, Taz, I think you have a real fan there. I'm afraid you won't want to come home." Taz tilted her head and pressed against the hand that scratched behind her ear. Gordie sat smiling at Taz for several moments before he jumped up to get cleaned up.

When Gordie pulled into Vanessa's driveway, he felt his heart race again. *Oh, for God's sake. Settle down.*

She came out to greet him. "Good morning. I'm so glad you called me to take her rather than leave her in the house all day. She's welcome here any time."

Taz leaped out of the back when Gordie opened the door and she trotted over to Vanessa. Gordie slammed the hatch down and joined Taz. "Thank you for this. As thanks…"

Vanessa held up her hand. "No, thanks necessary."

Gordie continued. "As thanks, I hope you'll let me take you out for supper tomorrow evening."

Vanessa smiled. "I'd love that. Do you have time for a cup of tea or coffee before you go?"

Gordie glanced at his watch. "No, I better get going. I said I'd pick up my mother at noon."

"Oh, you're meeting your mother. How lovely."

"And my sister. We don't get together very often, but I was thinking about them yesterday and just decided to make the trek down. My mother is eighty-two and time goes by so fast, you know?"

She nodded. "I do know, and you're so right. Enjoy these times while you can."

"I should be back by about six or six-thirty to pick her up again."

"Shall I feed her something?"

"Oh, no. I'll feed her when I get home. She's easygoing about supper time. She's used to me and my unpredictable schedule by now."

He handed over the leather leash he had taken out of the car. "You might feel more comfortable walking her on the leash if you decide to go for a walk. She's usually pretty good, but sometimes she does have a mind of her own."

Vanessa took the leash. "Exactly as it should be. Everyone should have a bit of unpredictability in them."

Gordie walked them to the house to make sure Taz didn't try to turn back for the car and once Vanessa and the dog were inside, he went back to the car, thinking about her words.

***

They went to a restaurant right on the waterfront with a view of the harbour.

Gordie's mother had protested. "It's so expensive. You can get the same food for half the price if you go up a few streets."

Gordie patted her hand. "The view is worth it. No arguments. It's not like we do this every day."

Jean raised an eyebrow. "You seem remarkably cheerful. What's going on?"

He shrugged. "Nothing. You two were on my mind, so I decided to come for a visit. Does there have to be a reason?"

Jean cracked a smile. "Of course not, but there usually is."

"Today there isn't." He flipped open the menu and pointed out some options to his mother. He knew she didn't have a big appetite these days, so didn't bother with the steaks. They settled on what they'd have: a pound of mussels between him and his mother to start while Jean had a bowl of seafood chowder, and a Caesar salad for his mother after that and a burger for him. Jean ordered pasta.

His mother closed the menu. "Well, give us all the gossip. What's been happening in your life?"

He settled back comfortably in the chair. "Have you read in the paper about the bones that were found up in Port Mulroy?"

Jean set the glass of water back down that she had just picked up. "Are you working on that case?"

"It's my case."

His mother clasped her hands together as if she would clap, but decided against it at the last second. "Oh, Gordie! Your first big case, isn't it?"

He nodded. "It is, Mum."

"I'm so proud of you."

Jean's eyes sparkled. "Well, tell us all about it."

"I can't tell you all the details, of course. A lot of its confidential, but I know that some of the basics have already made it into the paper." He told them about the discovery of the bones and some high-level activities since then, including the identification of Sarah.

Jean's eyes narrowed. "This Vanessa woman. Is she involved, do you think?"

"No, no. She didn't even move to Nova Scotia until after Sarah was murdered. We're sure of that. She's simply an innocent bystander."

"Your voice just seemed to, I don't know, quicken, when you talked about her, so I thought she might be a suspect, but you couldn't say so."

"Not at all. In fact, she's looking after Taz today."

He saw the look exchanged between his mother and sister. "What's that look for?"

Jean smiled. "Nothing. I just never knew you to leave Taz with someone before. Usually she just stays home, and you get someone in to look after her if need be."

Gordie felt sweat prickle under his arms and hoped he wasn't blushing. "I told you. Taz was with me when I first went out there and Vanessa and Taz seem to really like each other, so I just thought I'd take the woman up on her offer to mind her. That's all."

Gordie was glad that the starters arrived at that moment, and they tucked into their lunches. As they ate, Gordie caught up on what his sister had been up to since they had last seen each other. He spoke to his mother on the phone every week so knew much of it, but it was nice to hear the details of Jean's work and travels directly from her.

Over coffee and cheesecake, the conversation turned back to his case. Under pressing from his mother for more details, Gordie talked a little about Sarah and her family.

"The father really gets to me. I have to work to keep my cool around him."

His mother frowned. "That's not like you. You're usually pretty easygoing around people. What is it about this man?"

Gordie took a deep breath. "I suppose he reminds me too much of..."

Jean finished the sentence "of Dad?"

Gordie shrugged. "Yeah. I guess so."

Jean nodded. "A drunk, then."

His mother flushed. "Oh, Jeanie. Don't call him that. Your Dad had problems, but he tried to make a good life for us."

Jean closed her eyes for a second. "Mum. *You* tried to make a good life for us. *He* never did. He was a nightmare."

Gordie nodded. "Mum, you know Jeanie's right. He was brutal. So now, when I meet someone like that, I feel the blood pressure go up."

His mother turned to look out the window at the harbour. "He wasn't always like that."

Gordie made an effort to unclench his jaw. "It's all we ever knew of him."

She nodded and sighed. "Did this man do something to his daughter, do you think?"

Gordie picked up his fork to finish his dessert. "I'm not really sure, but I'm keeping my eye on him." He put a morsel of cherry cheesecake on his fork and turned it towards his mother. "Will you have a bite, Mum?"

***

Gordie was too tired to socialize by the time he got back to pick up Taz, so he simply picked up the dog, thanked Vanessa, and arranged to pick her up at five o'clock the next day. On Sunday, when he got back to her house again, he felt better. A sound sleep and puttering around for the day including a walk left him refreshed.

She welcomed him inside and again he was immediately struck by the warm and cozy feel of the house.

She invited him to sit down. "Do we have time for a drink or cup of tea?"

He smiled. "We're in no rush, but I'm not much of a drinker. I made a reservation at the Shoreside for six, so we have time for a quick cup of tea, or by all means have a drink yourself. I'm driving so you can relax."

She nodded. "I'll put the kettle on."

He sat down on the sofa, looking across where a book lay open on the wing chair by the fire. Every detail of the room spoke of comfort.

She came back carrying a tray with a pot and cups. He stood to take it from her, placed it on the coffee table, and then sat back down.

She lifted the pot and swirled it to help the tea steep. "How did your visit go yesterday?"

"It was good, although there were some old memories that got stirred up that aren't the most pleasant."

She raised her eyebrows as she handed him his cup. "Oh?"

He shook his head. "Nothing major. Just the inevitable stuff that comes when family gets together. Nothing that would cause arguments between us three, though. I get on well with my mother and sister, so overall it was a nice afternoon."

She smiled. "I'm glad. Taz and I had a lovely afternoon as well. We went for a long walk and she was as good as gold walking on the leash. I really should get a dog. It forces a person outside, and that's so good for mind and body."

"I agree. I'm sure I'd just sit in front of the TV if I didn't have Taz."

They spoke about dogs for a bit and then Vanessa stood. "We'd better get going if we want to make our reservation."

Gordie looked at his watch. "Good Lord. I had no idea it was that time already."

Gordie hadn't had an evening like this for a very long time. It slipped away in easy conversation. Any women he'd dated in the last few years always made him feel stressed, as though he were performing in some way. He'd had fun with a few, but nothing stuck. With Vanessa, he felt different, although he couldn't think why when he lay in bed later that night reviewing the evening. He fell asleep still wondering.

***

Gordie turned the radio up on the way to work early Monday morning. The usually calm voice of the news announcer was more frantic than normal as he read the story of the overnight hit and run. A young woman was in hospital fighting for her life. Gordie almost drove off the road when he heard that Mary-Catherine Cameron, aged 29, had been struck as she walked on a rural road in an isolated spot outside Port Mulroy. The victim was in a coma with life-threatening injuries.

Gordie's eyes widened, and he burst out loud. "Oh, my God. It's Mary-Catherine. Someone tried to kill her."

CHAPTER 15

I KNEW IT. I DAMN well knew she was hiding something. And now we may never know what it was.

Gordie cranked down the radio and pushed the button on his steering wheel for the phone.

"Arsenault."

"Sergeant, it's MacLean. Did you hear the news about the hit and run?"

"Just heard it. The name rang a bell. Who is she?"

"She's one of the witnesses in my case. Damn. I can't believe it."

"I'm assigning Norris to the case."

Gordie gripped the steering wheel. He took a deep breath and before he could say anything, his sergeant's voice came through again. "Did you hear me? Are you still there?"

"I'm here. Sergeant, this is connected to my case. I know it."

"And I know that I'm still in charge of assignments. Come see me when you get in."

The phone disengaged, and Gordie's radio came on again. He tried to concentrate on the sweet sound of the Rankin family singing

Fare Thee Well Love as he took deep breaths. *Damn him. What the hell's the matter with him? It's like he would rather do everything in his power to make me fail instead of helping to solve this.* And in a flash of insight, Gordie realized that's exactly what was happening. *Sarge wants me to fail so he'll have an excuse to get rid of me. News for you, Sarge. It's not happening.*

By the time Gordie arrived at the office, he was determined to keep his temper. He dropped his jacket over his chair and walked down the hall to Arsenault's office. The door was closed, so he knocked and went in when he heard Arsenault's abrupt "Come."

Detective Norris sat in one chair across from Arsenault. Gordie took the other and shifted the angle slightly to face Norris instead of Arsenault.

Norris nodded. "How are you now?" He ran the words together, so it sounded more like "howaryanow?"

Gordie ignored his sergeant and grinned at Norris. "Norris, you sound more like a Newfoundlander than a Newfoundlander."

Norris laughed. "The wife's got family visiting for a couple of weeks and when you get all of them going a mile a minute, you might as well be sitting in St. John's. It's hard *not* to fall into it right along with them."

From the corner of his eye, Gordie saw Arsenault fold his arms, a sure sign he was annoyed.

Arsenault cleared his throat. "If you ladies are finished gossiping, can we get on with it?"

The grin slipped from Norris' face. "Sorry, Sergeant."

Gordie turned his head to look at his boss but didn't say anything.

Arsenault shifted to unfold his arms and tidied a stack of files on his desk. Then he looked up and glared at Gordie. "I've assigned Norris to take the lead on the new case."

Gordie nodded once. "So, you said."

Norris pulled a notebook and pen out of his pocket, clearly expecting Gordie to give him some details.

Gordie sat on without speaking.

Arsenault frowned. "I expect you to cooperate."

Gordie unclenched his jaw. "I imagine you do."

A flush rose up Arsenault's throat and turned his face a deep purple. "Are you saying you won't?"

Gordie raised his eyebrows. "I didn't say that."

Arsenault's voice rose in volume. "Detective MacLean, there's no discussion here. This is my decision. You may feel this case belongs to you, but I have no evidence other than your...*intuition* to suggest it should be." The way he said intuition was clearly meant as an insult.

Gordie stood.

The muscles squeezed into Sergeant Arsenault's shirt sleeves rippled. Gordie gave a hint of a smile. *He'd love to punch me right now.*

"Where the hell are you going?"

"I heard you say there was no discussion. I understood that meant that this meeting is over."

Arsenault stood, perhaps feeling at a disadvantage to argue with a man looming over him.

"I expect you to fully brief Detective Norris."

Gordie frowned. "What is there to brief if the case isn't connected to mine?"

Norris rose as well. "We can leave you to your work, Sergeant. I'll get some basic information about the victim from Detective MacLean and I'm sure we'll figure out the information-sharing process as we move forward."

When MacLean and Norris were back at MacLean's desk, Norris rolled a chair over to sit with him. "Look, I didn't ask for this."

MacLean nodded. "I know. I'm not against you working the case, but it's connected, and he damn well knows it. He's only doing this to rile me."

Norris sighed. "I don't know why he gives you so much aggravation, but look, I'm not taking over. Work for you, work with you, it's all the same. We want the same thing and that's getting it solved."

Gordie nodded. He stood again and waved over to Albright. "Come on. We've got a new team member. This deserves a decent cup of coffee." MacLean led the way to his car to drive over to the coffee shop. Norris went to get into the front seat but before he did, Gordie pointed to Albright. "My partner rides shotgun. Sorry, buddy."

Norris clambered into the back silently.

At the coffee shop, Gordie bought the drinks while Norris and Albright talked about the victim.

Norris pulled out his notebook. "What can you tell me about her, MacLean? Did she live a high-risk lifestyle or have any known enemies? Or is this just an accident in fact?"

MacLean shook his head. "It's not a bloody accident, and no, her lifestyle is not high-risk generally speaking."

Albright interjected. "Not that we know of, anyway."

MacLean nodded. "Not that we know of. I didn't see anything that would lead me to believe that she was into drugs or that she went out with a lot of different guys." He turned to Albright. "You agree?"

She nodded. "I agree."

Norris tapped his pen on the table. "Well, someone wanted her dead."

MacLean slammed his hand on the table and the few other patrons all looked over, startled expressions on their faces. "It's because of Sarah. That's what I keep saying. Mary-Catherine knew something. We were working on her, but it's been a slow process."

Norris leaned back and took a drink. "What kind of thing did she know? You must be guessing something."

MacLean nodded. "I think she knew who killed Sarah."

"Why wouldn't she say so then?"

MacLean rubbed his hand across his forehead. "I don't know. And maybe she didn't know it for a fact, but she had an idea and maybe she confronted the person."

"That's a lot of maybes."

Albright flipped open her book. "We got more out of her in the last interview than the first time. We were making progress."

Norris turned to her. "Like what? What new information did you get out of her?"

Before Albright could answer, MacLean interrupted. "That doesn't have any bearing on your case. It was information pertinent to Sarah only. Since Sarge is adamant that you focus on the Cameron case, I think we better not muddy the waters by going over what she said about Sarah."

Norris frowned. "He also expects you to fully brief me."

MacLean drained his cup. "We're briefing you on anything relevant to the Cameron case. Let's talk about next steps. I suggest Norris, that you and I go through Cameron's apartment and Albright, I want you to set up the next round of interviews with Jamie and Sarah's family."

Albright made a note. "Do you need them to come in?"

"I doubt Jamie would come all this way. No, let's go there again."

When they were back in the office, Norris and MacLean made arrangements to each drive out to Mary-Catherine's apartment. Neither suggested they drive together.

The landlord let them in. When they were inside, Norris took a quick tour of the small unit and then leaned against the bedroom door frame while MacLean opened drawers and flipped through the papers on a desk.

Norris watched for a moment and then sighed. "Do you want to tell me what you're looking for?"

MacLean looked up. "I'll know when I see it. That's how it works, isn't it?"

Norris held up his hands as if to ward off the anger radiating from MacLean. "Look, Gordie, I just want to help. I'm not interested in taking over your investigation, but it would be great if we could be on the same page here."

MacLean straightened up. "You may not be interested in taking over, but that bastard is going to push you into it whether you want to or not."

"I won't let him. If I can show him evidence that this wasn't an accident, I'll tell Arsenault myself that it makes little sense to run parallel investigations. I'll let him know that you're the lead on this. Just give me something I can use."

MacLean's anger faded. He usually got on with Norris and couldn't keep up directing the anger he felt towards his sergeant at Norris. "All right. I'm convinced Mary-Catherine knows or at least speculates who killed Sarah. I believe the killer is convinced of the same thing. They've been watching her or talking to her or just got worried for no reason at all and that's what triggered this attack." He sighed. "The truth is, I feel responsible. I should have stuck with it, but I let her go and now this happened."

"You couldn't know anything would happen. Right. OK, so we're looking for something that would show she met with someone that's outside her usual circle, then."

MacLean nodded. "If we could get her phone records, we might find something faster, but in the meantime I was hoping to find some handwritten note or a diary entry or something along that line."

"Do we know who her phone carrier is?"

"I don't but I'm sure it wouldn't take Albright long to find out."

"Let's get her on it, then."

Gordie nodded and called his partner. "We're going through the apartment. Nothing helpful so far, but if you can get the phone records, we might find something there."

Gordie listened as Albright agreed to follow up. She gave short, cool answers. He stood and walked as far away from Norris as the small apartment allowed. "Listen, there is no way I'm treating you as my personal lackey. You have experience with the phone companies, which makes you the person for the job. I'm here with Norris, but tomorrow you and I are going back to talk to James again, right?"

He heard her voice thaw as she said she'd confirm the

appointment with James. Gordie nodded, even though he knew she didn't see him. "Great. Let me know when you've talked to him. I'll probably meet you there if it's in the morning."

Norris finished going through all the kitchen drawers and cabinets. "Nothing here. I'm going over to the hospital to see what the news is there. You coming?"

Gordie took one final look around the bedroom, lifting the mattress from the box spring to ensure there was nothing hidden there. "Yeah. I'll let the landlord know we're done here, and I'll meet you there."

On his way out of the apartment, Gordie passed a shelf of photo albums. Half a dozen self-adhesive albums with fading pictures placed under yellowing plastic were shelved in-between old schoolbooks. On a whim, he scooped them up and set them on the arm of the sofa to take with him. He also picked a piece of mail out of the wastepaper basket tucked under the shelving. It was a notice from the credit union informing her of the upcoming annual general meeting. She banks at the credit union. He sent a text to Albright to ask her to get a warrant for Mary-Catherine's bank records as well.

**

Gordie walked down the hall of the hospital. The smell of disinfectant combined with a general miasma of sick and decay always made his stomach roil. He turned the corner to the critical care wing and found Norris in conversation with the doctor. Nearby, a sixty-something woman cried while a man with a shocked, pale face rubbed her back.

Norris left the doctor to greet Gordie. "She just died."

"Damn." He nodded towards the couple. "They the parents?"

Norris nodded.

"Did you get a chance to talk to them?"

"No. The doctor was just giving them the news when I arrived."

Gordie sighed. "I should have pushed her. I knew there was something. Dammit, I should have pushed her."

Norris stuck his hands into his jacket pocket. "We don't know for sure yet if it's connected."

Gordie frowned. "Right. Well, you carry on trying to figure out another reason why she was killed like this and I'll go on with my investigation before we have a third victim on our hands."

"Jesus, MacLean. Don't take everything so personally. We'll continue to work on this together and see where it leads."

Gordie watched as the couple approached where he and Norris stood. They clung to each other, stumbling their way out. Gordie stepped forward. "Mr. and Mrs. Cameron?"

The husband nodded. "Yes."

Gordie pulled out his card, ignoring the frown on Norris' face. "I'm Detective Gordie MacLean. I'm so sorry for your loss. I spoke to your daughter a couple of times recently. She was a lovely girl. She told me how much she loved her job and she seemed content and cheerful."

Mr. Cameron took Gordie's card automatically and put it in his shirt pocket.

Gordie touched Mrs. Cameron on the arm. "Let me drive you folks home. You shouldn't be driving right now."

She didn't seem to hear him or understand what he said, but Mr. Cameron nodded. "Thank you."

Gordie turned and led them back down the long hallway and outside. Mrs. Cameron shaded her eyes from the sun, seeming shocked to see the bright sunny day.

Gordie held the back door open. "Here we are."

Both of them slid into the back seat, Mr. Cameron mumbling a thank you again.

As Gordie climbed into the front, he saw Norris standing in the parking lot watching him. *Tough luck, buddy. You had your chance.*

Mr. Cameron gave Gordie directions and then fell back into silence. When they got to the house, Gordie jumped out and opened the door for them and then followed them up the walkway to the two-storey modern home. Mrs. Cameron pulled keys out of her bag but handed them over to her husband to open the door, as even that act seemed beyond her.

Neither of the Camerons seemed to notice that Gordie followed them into the house. They sat down together on the sofa and for the first time Mary-Catherine's mother spoke. "We have to call Danny." She started to cry again. "Oh God, how do we tell him she's gone?"

Gordie sat on the loveseat across from the couple. "Is Danny Mary-Catherine's brother?"

Mr. Cameron nodded. "He's away working in Alberta. When she was hit, he said he'd arrange for some time off, but it would take a couple of days. He's in Fort McMurray."

Gordie nodded. "I'm sure he's already working on getting here. Is Danny her only sibling?"

Mr. Cameron nodded. "Just the two of them. They're quite close. She went to visit him last year."

Mrs. Cameron looked up, her eyes red and puffy. "I was afraid she'd decide to move there too, but she laughed at me and said she was happy here." She took a tissue from a box on the coffee table and blew her nose. "I should have encouraged her. She'd still be alive today."

Mr. Cameron patted his wife's knee. "You can't say that. You know the Lord works in mysterious ways and if it was her time, it was her time no matter where she was."

She nodded but said nothing to agree with him.

Gordie stood. "Can I put the kettle on to make tea for you both?"

Mrs. Cameron shook her head and stood up. "I can do it."

Gordie let her go and then turned to Mr. Cameron. "Can you think of any reason your daughter would have been out there on that isolated road?"

Mr. Cameron shook his head. "Usually, she took the highway. She wasn't a fan of the smaller roads because they slowed her down."

Gordie nodded. "Was there any place that she might have been going up there? A card play, someone's house, a dance?"

Her father shrugged helplessly. "Not that I know of."

"Did Mary-Catherine have any close friends? We're going to find who did this to her and you can help with that."

Mary-Catherine's father blinked. Tears welled, but he seemed to refuse to let them fall. "First Sarah and now Mary-Catherine. It's unbelievable. Friends? Well, she sometimes goes out with a woman she works with. Janet? Janice? I can't think at the moment."

Mrs. Cameron came back in carrying a tray with a pot and three mugs. The act of making the tea seemed to have steadied her a little bit, although the tray shook as she carried it. Gordie took the tray and set it down on the coffee table. She nodded her thanks. "Janice. That's the name of her friend."

Gordie nodded. "And she works at the medical center on Highland, right?"

They nodded in unison.

Gordie pulled out his notebook and wrote the information down and then slipped it back into his shirt pocket. "I'm going to leave you now. You have calls to make, but you have my card. If you can imagine any reason someone might want to hurt Mary-Catherine, or if you think of anything that's happened in the past few weeks that seemed to upset Mary-Catherine or seemed strange to you, please call me."

Mr. Cameron wrinkled his forehead. "Wasn't this an accident?"

"Quite possibly, but we need to explore every possibility."

Gordie walked back to his car and called Norris. "I've delivered the parents home and left them. Where are you?"

He listened to Norris give him directions to the scene where Mary-Catherine was hit. "I'll be there in fifteen minutes."

Gordie swung past Robin's Donuts and picked up two coffees. Even using his GPS, Gordie struggled to find the spot. It was a little-used road that cut from a subdivision out through the woods to Highway 105. Once it was a busy road heading north, but when the highway was built, which ran almost parallel to this road, it became redundant with only a few locals still using it.

Gordie pulled up behind Norris' car. He held out the coffee to Norris as a peace offering.

Norris took the cup but still grumbled. "What did you find out after poaching my witnesses?"

Gordie shrugged. "Not a lot. Mary-Catherine had a friend called Janice that she worked with. Hopefully she can tell us something, but as far as the parents go, they can't imagine that someone would do this on purpose, and they have no idea why she was on this road. She preferred the highway."

Norris walked along the shoulder and then pointed to the ground. "I'd guess she pulled over and then stood here for a bit."

Gordie crouched down. They were lucky there hadn't been any spring rain since the accident. He saw footprints in the soft gravel. There were small prints with a distinctive imprint of a cross and Doc Martens stamp. Gordie looked up. "You took photos?"

"I did, and the Mounties took a pile as well. There was a piece of chewing gum just here as well that the Mounties took away for evidence. We'll check it for DNA but it seems most likely it's Mary-Catherine's."

Gordie shook his head. "I don't see anyone else's prints. It looks like the girl stood here, walked up and down a bit, maybe on her phone, maybe just watching the road. She probably saw the car coming, spit out her gum and stepped out to wave it down. If she had been standing right next to her car, he wouldn't have been able to hit her like he did."

"He or she."

Gordie nodded. "He or she. You'd have to have pretty steely nerves to simply accelerate and hit a young woman with a car."

Norris shrugged. "I've met women who are capable."

"I guess so."

"Someone hated her."

Gordie frowned. "I don't know if hate is right. Mary-Catherine was confident she wasn't in danger. She came out here expecting to talk to this person. She wasn't afraid of them."

Norris walked back to his car and leaned against the passenger side, drinking his coffee and looking at the thick forest. "Why here? It's the middle of nowhere."

Gordie put his coffee on the ground and lit a cigarette. "It's a perfect place not to be seen."

Norris nodded. "The other person probably suggested it."

"Meaning they know the area. No one that isn't from around here would know this old road existed."

Norris drained his coffee. "So, what next? There was nothing worth looking at in her apartment and her parents know nothing."

Gordie pulled out his notebook. "She was friendly with someone she worked with. Janice something."

Norris looked at his watch. "All right. First thing tomorrow, I'll go to the clinic and meet with the friend. Do you need to come along?"

Gordie heard the tone. "No, you go ahead. I'm heading into the office tomorrow morning and see what Albright's been able to dig out. With any luck, she's been able to get the phone records."

Gordie got back in his car and did a U-turn. He drove back into the subdivision and when he came to the junction with the main road, he paused. Turn right to drive past Vanessa's house. Turn left to go home. He hesitated and then turned.

CHAPTER 16

GORDIE WAS GLAD THAT he had gone straight home the previous evening. He spent a quiet night with Taz snoring at his feet as he wrote out the points he understood so far. His mind was busy while he drove the familiar Route 4 towards Sydney. Usually the hour and forty-five-minute drive seemed endless, but today he hardly noticed. He considered the interviews he wanted to have. He also looked forward to sitting down with Roxanne Albright to see what she had discovered, and more importantly he wanted to bounce some ideas off her to test his thinking.

He picked up a coffee, tea and some oatcakes from Tim Hortons before going to the office.

Detective Albright took the tea from him and nodded her thanks. "Do you want to sit down now?"

"Is there anything big you need to tell me? If not, I better go down the hall first." Gordie nodded towards Sergeant Arsenault's office.

Albright took the lid off the paper cup. "No, nothing I'd want to share there yet. You go ahead and get that over with and then we'll talk."

"Let's meet in the briefing room. I want to use the whiteboard."

"Got it."

Gordie pulled out his notebook and skimmed over his notes as he walked down the hall. His boss's office was open, and Arsenault looked up when Gordie stepped into the open doorway.

"Detective MacLean. Come in."

"Good morning, Sergeant."

"I understand you and Detective Norris were in Port Mulroy yesterday."

"We were. Perhaps you've heard from Detective Norris already?"

Arsenault simply stared at Gordie, waiting for him to continue.

"As you've no doubt heard, at least on the news, is that Mary-Catherine Cameron died yesterday of her injuries. She never regained consciousness, so we were unable to question her about the accident."

"But you were able to whisk away the parents for an interview that didn't include Detective Norris."

Gordie took a deep breath, feeling his coffee churn in his stomach. "The parents were distraught, as you can imagine. I didn't see Detective Norris volunteer to drive them home, so I did. It was more a simple act of kindness than about getting an interview done."

Arsenault tilted back in his chair. "Setting aside Norris' case, do you have *any* update for me on the Sarah Campbell case?"

"I'll be interviewing some of the key witnesses again, given this new situation. There is also a former colleague of Sarah's that I have yet to interview for the first time. She's been away, but I understand she's back now. Detective Albright called her and is arranging a meeting."

"Right. So that would be no. No progress."

Gordie felt the sweat prickle in his armpits. "I'm convinced that Mary-Catherine's death is significant in the Campbell case. I believe she had her suspicions about who killed Sarah, and that's what got her killed."

"Based on what?"

"Based on the fact that she's dead." Gordie knew his voice was too loud and took another deep breath to calm himself. "Norris and I looked at the scene where she was run down. It's clear that she got out of the car on the side of the road and stood there for some time. We can see her boot marks in the soft shoulder where she walked up and down a couple of times. The Mounties collected a piece of gum from the scene and we'll wait to get the DNA back to confirm it was hers, but if it was, it makes it look like she'd been there long enough to get rid of a piece of gum she'd been chewing for a while. In other words, she was waiting for something or someone. The car's been taken in to check it over for mechanical problems and the report will be ready later today, but according to the parents, there was nothing wrong with the car as far as they knew. Mary-Catherine kept it in good shape with regular tune-ups. Assuming there was nothing wrong with the car, there was no mechanical reason for her to pull over. The most obvious reason for her to be there is because she was meeting someone."

Arsenault and Gordie locked eyes. "But why? Why would the girl meet with someone who might be a killer?"

Gordie took a deep breath. "Blackmail."

"Where's that coming from?"

"It's a theory. Because you're right. Why else would anyone meet with someone they suspected of murder? It's not logical. Unless there's a good reason to take the risk."

"Lots of assumptions and no evidence."

"Not yet."

Gordie saw that Arsenault wanted to tell him to leave it alone since he had assigned the case to Detective Norris, but the logic was too overwhelming to continue to insist the cases were not connected. His jaw was clenched, and face flushed, but eventually Arsenault nodded. "I expect you to continue to work closely with Detective Norris."

"Naturally."

Arsenault pulled a file towards him and flipped it open. Gordie closed his notebook and left the office.

He stopped at his desk long enough to check that there were no messages on his desk phone. People rarely called him there as his business card had his cell phone number, but occasionally someone was routed through. He joined Roxanne Albright in the briefing room. She had updated the whiteboard to add Mary-Catherine's date of death.

She raised her eyebrows. "Well?"

Gordie shrugged. "Even the Sarge has silently agreed that Mary-Catherine's death is likely connected to Sarah's murder."

Albright sat down on the edge of the table. "That's a breakthrough."

"It is. I have a theory. I think she was blackmailing the killer. Sarge didn't come out and agree, but he didn't argue with the notion."

She nodded. "Makes sense. Did you find anything at the apartment?"

"Nothing aside from that notice from her credit union." Gordie took a seat in front of the whiteboard. "Bring me up to speed on how your day went. Any luck with the phone records?"

"Luckily, she's on a plan with Aliant, so they have her calls. Once they understood she was dead and we're investigating as a possible homicide, they waived the warrant. I'll have it this afternoon. They'll give me the records going back three months to start with. I figured we'd start with that since I'm not sure there's much point in going back much before Sarah's remains were found."

Gordie nodded. "Good work, Roxanne. I better give Norris a call and bring him up to date. He was going to Mary-Catherine's work today. With any luck, she mentioned going out to meet someone on the night she died and that'll give us something to start with when the phone records come in."

Gordie dialed Norris' number and resisted the temptation to sit back and prop his feet on his desk. That would be the moment Arsenault was sure to step out of his office. Instead, he made some notes as he listened to the phone ring. When Norris answered, Gordie heard the wind blowing, and he had to speak loudly to make himself understood. "Where the hell are you?"

"Back on Old Albert Road. I'm doing a house-to-house along with the Mountie constable from traffic who first answered the call. It's blowing a gale out here."

"When you get back in your car, call me back."

"Right. Give me five minutes."

When Norris called back, Gordie heard the breathless sound of his colleague's voice.

Gordie laughed. "Glad I decided to come into the office today."

"Yeah. Lucky you. What have you got?"

Gordie brought him up to speed. "Have you been to her workplace already?"

"No. They were having some kind of staff meeting this morning complete with a counsellor to help them deal with the news of Mary-Catherine's passing."

"Well, that's good. Maybe after they've talked amongst themselves, they'll have something they can give you. Names to match up or cross off the phone records would be helpful."

Norris grunted in agreement.

"Are you getting anything from the house-to-house?"

"I don't know if it's worth anything, but one guy took that way home and passed Mary-Catherine while she was waiting. He slowed down to see if she needed help, but she just smiled and waved him on, so he didn't even stop to talk. He drove on and he remembers a car passing him coming from the opposite direction, but it could have been anyone, even one of the neighbours. He thinks a guy down the road has a similar car. He didn't get a good look at it, no plate number or anything. Even the description could be just about anything."

"What's the description?"

"A small or midsize two or four-door. Blue or black."

Gordie frowned. *Is that a coincidence?*

Norris' voice was irritated. "You still there?"

"Yeah, I'm here. Norris, that's the same description we had of the car that Sarah Campbell was last seen getting into."

Now it was Norris' turn for silence. Then he snorted. "MacLean, you can't be thinking that the very same car is still driving around out there ten years later. Come on. Give yourself a shake."

Gordie sighed. "Yeah, you're right. Just a coincidence."

"And the fact that it's as vague as saying that the killer was a white male somewhere between five-five and five-ten."

Gordie heard Norris laugh again. "I'll call you when I'm done at Mary-Catherine's work."

CHAPTER 17

GORDIE HELD UP AN oatcake and waved it at Roxanne, who sat at their favourite corner table. She shook her head. He turned back to the girl serving. A new girl. Young. Gordie didn't know her. "Just the one."

The girl grunted. It may have been 'right' or it may have been a cough. She put the coffee, tea and oatcake on a plate with a pat of butter on the side on the tray and slid it across to Gordie.

"Thank you."

She looked up and frowned suspiciously. Perhaps reading that Gordie was sincere, she nodded. "You're welcome. Have a nice day."

He took the tray over to the table. "I miss my usual girl. Do young people not understand the art of customer service anymore?"

Roxanne smiled. "You're showing your age when you say things like that."

"But it's true. How hard is it to be pleasant?"

Roxanne shrugged. "Maybe she's just having a bad day. Maybe someone was rude to her, and she's cautious now."

Gordie nodded. "You have a point. Trust. It's an interesting thing. Why do we trust some people and not others?"

Roxanne wrinkled her forehead. "Where are you going with this?"

Gordie took a sip of coffee. "Mary-Catherine must have trusted the person she planned to meet on that deserted stretch of road. I mean, it's like internet dating. You hear all the time that you should meet in a public place where there are plenty of people around. Wouldn't you think that something like this, something dodgy, would need a place less secluded?"

"But since it was illegal, at least if we're right about the blackmail, then probably neither one would want to be seen."

"So, you figure she was more afraid of being seen, than she was afraid of them."

"Yes, I guess so."

"But then again, we're back to the trust question. She must have had some trust that despite her putting this pressure on the person, she was reasonably safe."

"How could she possibly think that, if she believed the person was a murderer?"

He sighed. True. Then we're down to the simple fact that she was foolish."

"I think that's more probable."

Gordie wiped his buttery fingers on a paper napkin. "I'm keeping my options open, even still. She was foolish, yes. But she also had some degree of trust. Let's say she knew something about the circumstances and knew that whatever triggered the person to kill Sarah, wasn't going to cause the person to kill her as well."

"Maybe she had some kind of insurance. You know, someplace she wrote it all down or photos or something."

"We haven't found anything like that and her place hadn't been searched, or at least it didn't appear to have been. She didn't realize that once a person kills, it gets easier to do it again."

"You and I know that, but if she knew the person, really knew them, she may have believed something else."

"She must have. After all, she went to meet them on that lonely stretch of road."

"Right. I think she knew this person more than just their name. I think she actually knew them, had some kind of relationship, even in passing."

He drained his coffee and stood. "Let's go back and review the list again. See if there's someone that stands out a little more than others."

They spent the afternoon setting up follow-up interviews. First they'd go see Lorraine Doyle, the store employee who had been away during the first round of interviews. After they finished with her, they planned to drive to Antigonish to see the priest who had run the youth group.

Gordie was keen to go see Bill Campbell again. He argued his point with his partner. "Campbell doesn't have a watertight alibi and he tells us he was at the Legion, but not with anyone in particular. There was a darts tournament going on. I say he could easily have slipped out."

Albright leaned back in her chair and propped her feet up on the boardroom table. "I agree, but when? And did he have a serious enough reason? It's a big deal, murdering your daughter. He just doesn't seem motivated enough to me."

MacLean paced in front of the whiteboard. "Men like him don't need a lot of motivation. They have a few drinks and get handy with their fists. No reason other than the attitude his daughter had, and he didn't like."

Albright frowned. "Still. It means he went home after having a few drinks and got into an argument. What did he do with her body until he had a chance to bury her?"

"In the car. We only have his word that he left the car at the Legion. Maybe he drove home for some reason. To get changed out of his work clothes. To get a proper cooked dinner instead of the burgers that were on offer at the Legion. Who knows? But he drives home. Does the deed after getting some lip from his daughter, puts her in the car and hustles back to the Legion to establish an alibi. Late that night he drives out and somehow chooses to bury her at that house and comes back to leave the car in the Legion parking lot. In the morning he goes back and makes a bit of a deal of talking to people, so they know he's there to pick up his car."

Albright swung her feet down and stood up to come closer to the board. She studied Bill Campbell's face from his driving licence enlargement. "It's possible. We've talked to him a couple of times already. I'm not sure we're going to get more out of him until we have something new with which to confront him."

"His wife's affair?"

She cocked her head at Gordie. "Really? Are you ready to drop her in it by telling him?"

MacLean slumped into a chair. "No. You're right. Let's leave him for now. What I'd like is to find someone from the Legion who saw him leave. Can you work on that? Get their membership list and just start calling people."

She picked up her portfolio. "On it."

Gordie went back to his desk and pulled out the box of photo albums. He flipped them open and skimmed through them. The first was when Mary-Catherine was a young teenager. *Must have gotten a camera for a gift.* He turned the pages quickly and the photos of her in various family settings went past. An older teenager wearing a baseball uniform whom Gordie assumed was the brother, proudly held a trophy. Mary-Catherine in shorts, kneeling on the ground with her arms around a dog. The parents sitting on a sofa beside a Christmas tree. The next album was much the same. Mary-Catherine smiling shyly with braces on her teeth. By the end of the album, more photos with friends instead of just family were laid on the sticky paper in angles with small drawings and symbols scribed between them.

Gordie went through that album and the next rapidly. Nothing to be learned here. Photos chronicled Mary-Catherine growing into a young woman. These photos had larger time gaps between them. The braces were suddenly gone, and a large school photo centered on a page displayed the straightened, gleaming grin. Finally, he saw a photo with Sarah. They had become good friends, and like all best girlfriends, became inseparable. It was probably the last year of high school. They were cheerleaders together and stood amongst other girls in short skirts and holding pompoms. Another group shot with a line of them resting a foot each on a red canoe, the five kids with arms around each other. Sarah at the end, the arm of Mary-Catherine's brother slung over her shoulder.

Gordie frowned. *When did he move out west?* He turned the pages more slowly now. He studied each photo, looking for a message from Sarah or Mary-Catherine. *What happened, girls?* By the time he reached the last album, only half the pages were filled with photos and he was no further ahead. The last album held very few family photos. Most were group shots of days out, as if she only remembered the camera on those special days. *Or maybe by then you had a digital camera and didn't bother to print the pictures for albums?*

Gordie walked over to Albright's desk. Roxanne had a list printed out and had put a check mark beside several of the names. She looked up. "I got the membership list from back then. Amazing they still had it. I have a feeling not much has changed since then. Some have died, but a lot of members are still around."

He nodded. "Great work. Did we get Mary-Catherine's computer? I just realized there wasn't one in the apartment."

She shook her head. "Maybe Detective Norris got it?"

"I'll ask. What about her phone?"

"I haven't seen it. I've sent over the paperwork to get her records, but that's from Aliant. The phone itself I haven't seen, but she probably had it at the hospital if it was in her purse."

"OK. I'll check with Norris. Before I do, you're handier than I am with this whole social media business. Can we pull up Mary-Catherine's Facebook page?"

Albright pushed aside the list she was working from and turned her computer monitor so that both of them could look at it. Gordie pulled over a chair and sat down.

She tapped on the keyboard and then searched. "Here we go. She's got security on it so we can't see much. See here? There are a few photos that she's got as public, so we can see that, but they're pretty old. Yup this album is from 2015. Looks like she went on a trip to Mexico, so she's got a few photos from that. We can get a warrant easily enough I'd say and have Facebook provide us access."

"OK. I'll talk to Detective Norris first just to see if he's already on this. I don't actually think we'll get much, but I want to see what else might be on her computer in the way of photos or emails."

"Definitely. If she's like anyone else her age, she's probably got tons of old files and emails saved."

Gordie went back to his desk and called Detective Norris. "Norris. Can you talk for a minute?" He listened as Norris walked for a moment, his footsteps audible on a bare floor. When Norris told him to go ahead, he asked about the computer and phone.

"So, you don't have either one. You asked the parents? All right, all right. I know it's standard. I'm just asking. Are you still at her work? Great. While you're there, can you see if there are any old photos on that computer? I'm interested in any group shots from back before Sarah went missing in August 2009. OK, thanks."

He hung up and opened the last of Mary-Catherine's photo albums again. He flipped through the pages, feeling that there was something here that he couldn't put his finger on, but again nothing stood out. He closed it and put it back in the box with the others under his desk. A faint damp, mouldering smell lifted from the box to his nose, and he pushed the box with his foot further under his desk and out of the way.

***

Albright came to his house where the plan was for her to leave the car. MacLean had vacuumed all the tumbleweeds of Taz's hair up the night before, but by morning there were more balls already gathering in corners and on the blanket on the sofa. He considered taking the blanket away but didn't bother.

The dog followed him around the house in his last-minute efforts to straighten up. "I know, I know. She isn't coming for a visit, but I don't want her to think we live like complete slobs." It had occurred to Gordie as he pushed the old grey Sears vacuum around that Albright was the first of his colleagues ever to come to his house.

When she drove up, he was tempted to immediately go out to meet her in the driveway and get straight in his car but thought it would be rude. *What's the protocol for having a partner come to the house?*

He opened the door and Taz squeezed around him to bump her nose against Roxanne's crotch. "Sorry. It's best just to let her poke at you a couple of times, and then it's done. The more you try to get away from her, the more persistent she gets."

Roxanne stood still, and the dog soon turned to go back to the kitchen. Gordie followed Taz and Albright followed him. He waved her to a kitchen chair. "Do you want a cup of tea before we go?"

"Do we have time?"

Gordie walked over and clicked on the kettle. "Plenty."

Albright glanced around the kitchen, which was bright with spring sun. "This is nice. Cozy."

Gordie flushed, pleased. "Thanks. We like it, don't we, Taz?" He stroked the big white head that leaned against him as he stood waiting for the kettle to boil.

When he had a pot made and the cups out, he sat down and opened his notebook. "I want to get as much as we can from this Lorraine Doyle. They chummed around. Surely to God she'll know something useful. So far it seems like most people hardly knew Sarah. I feel like we're caught in a giant spider web. The strands are clinging to me and I know there's someone out there watching and hoping we give up the struggle."

She smiled. "That's almost poetic."

He snorted. "Hardly. It's frustrating."

"I know you want to meet with Jamie again You really think he can give us something new?"

"I hope that Mary-Catherine's death will make him think twice if he's holding anything back."

"You're sure it's not him?"

"Reasonably sure. His alibi is good, and he just doesn't seem like he had the requisite rage any more by the time she went missing." They drank in silence, and then he drained his cup and stood.

She stood as well and carried her own cup to the sink. She bent down then and clasped Taz's face between her hands. "It was a pleasure to meet you. I've heard lots about you, and I hope we can be friends."

The dog swept her tail slowly from side to side.

Gordie topped up the dog's water dish and then dug a treat out of the bag on the counter. "Here you go, girl."

Taz took the treat and turned to go to the sofa.

Roxanne smiled. "She knows she can't come with you."

"Oh yes. She's clever. She's a good sounding board. We go for long walks and I can see things more clearly as I talk to her. Does that sound strange?"

She slid into the passenger side of the car. "I don't think so. We all need ways to decompress."

They drove without speaking for a while. He glanced at her. "What do you do to decompress?"

"I like to read. I like the classics like Dickens and Jane Austen the best."

"Vanessa likes to read too." The words were out before he thought about them.

"Vanessa?"

He felt himself grow hot. "The woman who owns the house where Sarah's body was buried."

"Yes, that's who I thought you meant. Vanessa."

He considered saying something to downplay his friendship and then decided he'd only dig himself in deeper. Instead, he spoke about the coming interview. They got past the awkward moment and by the time they pulled into Lorraine Doyle's driveway, their minds were fully on the coming meeting and what he hoped to discover.

CHAPTER 18

LORRAINE DOYLE WAS OLDER than Gordie expected. She probably wasn't really that old, but her clothing made her seem more middle-aged than necessary. Her dress was a grey and white baggy cotton shift that hung loosely from her shoulders over her round stomach and fell to below her knees. Her shoulder-length brown hair was streaked with grey.

They sat at the kitchen table with cups of tea. Gordie took a homemade shortbread cookie from the plate sitting on the table. "Lorraine, you know we are here to talk about Sarah and what you might remember of her last days or weeks."

She nodded and fiddled with a simple gold cross that hung around her neck.

"It's been a couple of weeks now since Sarah's body was found. Have you given thought to those days before she died?"

"Yes, but I'm not sure what I can really tell you that you don't already know."

Albright sat with her pen poised over her notebook, ready to take notes. Lorraine glanced at her, blinking rapidly.

Gordie's voice was gentle. "Often we know more than we think. Don't worry about giving us important information. Just tell us about your friendship with her. She was a bit younger than you, is that right?"

Again, the nod. "By almost ten years, but it didn't seem to matter to her. Sarah was nice, and she was very mature for her age. She wasn't like a lot of nineteen-year-olds." Lorraine stopped, lost in thought.

Gordie nudged her. "How so?"

"She was thinking about her future. It wasn't all about just going to movies or dances with her. She wanted to make something of her life."

"She was ambitious?"

Lorraine bit her bottom lip. "Not ambitious, really. I mean, she didn't want to be store manager or anything. She just wanted more than what her mother had. She worried about her mother a lot, and she was determined that she would have a better life. A happier life, I guess."

"Was there anything in particular that stands out in your memory, when you say that she worried about her mother?" Gordie tried not to sound too excited. *The father. Sarah was worried about the father.*

As if Lorraine read his mind, she said, "She told me that she wished her mother would leave her father. She was prepared to get a place for the two of them, her and her mum, if only she could convince her mother to leave."

"Was she close to convincing her, do you think?"

Lorraine shrugged. "If so, she didn't tell me."

"Was she especially worried in the last weeks before she disappeared?"

Lorraine frowned. "There was something all right, but I don't think it was about her mother. I don't know exactly why I think that, but I do. I've gone over it and over it, but I just don't know."

"What have you gone over?"

"The last shift we had together."

Gordie glanced at Roxanne. He felt a chill go down his spine. "Go on. What happened that day?"

"She'd been up and down for a few days. First, she seemed thrilled and then a few days later she seemed down. I asked her if she was OK, but she wasn't really in a talkative mood. Then on the last day she seemed better again."

"What did you make of all that?"

Lorraine flushed. "At the time I thought maybe it was..."

Gordie nodded encouragingly.

"...maybe it was the time of the month."

"But in hindsight you don't believe that anymore?"

"No. The last day was different. It was like she had made up her mind about something and after she was gone, I thought she had decided to leave."

"Why would she leave, though? Especially if she was worried about her mother? Did you think that something was wrong?"

"I thought I had gotten it wrong. I was sad, but I believed she was saying goodbye to me on that last day without actually saying it."

Gordie frowned. "I don't understand. Did she say something odd?"

Lorraine slid the cross along the chain and put her thumb behind it to show it to MacLean and Albright. "She gave me this."

Gordie sat back. "She gave you a gift. Was it your birthday or some other event that prompted her to give you a gift?"

She shook her head. "No. That's the thing. There was no reason. I tried to turn it down. I knew how much she loved it."

Gordie sat forward again. "You mean this was hers? She wore it and then took it off to give you?"

Lorraine nodded, her eyes welling with tears.

"Tell us about that moment. How did it come about?"

"I can hardly even say. I had admired it before. It looked so pretty on her, and she was very fond of it. Her parents gave it to her one year when she was in high school."

Gordie looked at Albright. "I recognize it now. Sarah is wearing it in the school photo we have on file."

Lorraine nodded. "She always wore it. She was religious. Not obsessive or anything, but she always went to church. Sometimes we met and went to Mass together and she was a member of the youth group."

"Yes, we've heard that."

Again, Lorraine was quiet. Gordie touched her arm. "It's hard for you to remember this. You might think you should have known something was wrong, but you couldn't have known. Tell us exactly what happened."

Lorraine drained her tea and set the cup down. "We were almost at the end of the shift. She seemed in good spirits. As I said, it seemed in hindsight like she'd made some kind of decision. It was quiet in the store, so I came over to her lane and bagged for her since I didn't have any customers. We often did that. It's better than standing there doing nothing."

Gordie nodded. "Go on. You're doing great."

Lorraine sighed. "Her customer left and there were customers in the store shopping, but no one standing in line, so for a moment we just stood there. The sun made the cross sparkle, and I said something about it. Like 'I just love that cross. It's so pretty.' I'd said things like that before and she'd just smile or say thank you or whatever. This time she put her hands up to undo the catch. She rested the necklace in her hand for a moment and looked at it, and then stretched out her hand to give it to me. All without a word."

Gordie frowned. "It must have surprised you?"

"Surprised? That's not the word. I was shocked and then I felt so badly because I thought she must have believed that I mentioned it so often because I wanted it." Her eyes filled with tears. "Honestly, I didn't. Even after all these years, I think of how she may have imagined I was asking for it and I feel awful."

Albright leaned over and rubbed Lorraine's back. "I don't think she believed that at all. It sounds like Sarah was a very generous-natured girl and knew that you would treasure it."

Lorraine gave Albright a small smile. She pulled a tissue from her sleeve and blew her nose. She nodded and then continued. "I protested, of course. I said I wouldn't for the world take it, but she leaned over and took my hand and then dropped the necklace into my hand."

Gordie waited for more, and when Lorraine seemed to have run out of words, he nudged her. "Did she say anything at all? Like why she was giving it to you?"

"No. Maybe she would have but then someone came to my lane. I slipped the necklace into my pocket, planning to give it back to her later. I was working the express lane, and I went back to my register. It got sort of busy after that and before I knew it the day was over. She was relieved before me and by the time I went back to the staff room where we have our lockers, she was just about to leave. I tried again to give it back to her, but she shook her head and she said something like 'it's better with you.' Then she just turned and hurried out while I was still changing my shoes. When I came outside, I didn't see her anywhere."

"Did you have any idea what she meant?"

"No, I didn't. I put it on, though because I was terrified that I'd lose it before I could give it back. You know, I fully intended to make her take it back when I saw her again on Monday, but then I never saw her again and after that...well, that's when I thought she meant to leave, and it was a going-away gift. It's never come off since."

Gordie sat quietly when Lorraine finished, deep in thought.

Albright cocked her head. "Lorraine, did you see her talking to anyone else either on that day or in the day or two previously?"

Lorraine shrugged. "Nothing that stands out. She talked to Mr.

MacIsaac a few times, but that's normal. I didn't see her talking to anyone else other than customers, and that was just the usual chit-chat. We know most of our customers, but we mostly talk about the weather or whatever."

Albright pushed a little further. "Would you have been able to hear if any one of those customers were talking about something other than the weather or routine topics?"

Lorraine frowned. "I would if they spoke in a normal voice. Obviously if they were leaning in to speak quietly, I might not."

"And you didn't notice anyone leaning in for a quiet conversation?"

"No, nothing. I mean, it gets busy so it could have happened, and I didn't notice, but she didn't seem upset or anything like that."

Gordie took over. "What about on her phone? Did you notice any sort of agitated calls she may have had?"

Again, Lorraine shook her head. "We didn't take lunch at the same time, so she may have had that kind of call when I wasn't around, but at the end of the day usually we were getting changed and leaving at the same time and there was nothing. Like I said before, there were a couple of days when she was really friendly and full of chat and then a couple when she was quiet, but that's it. We all have moods like that. Lots of times I don't feel like talking to people because I've got lots on my mind, so I really didn't think anything about it at the time."

Gordie looked at Albright. "Anything else from you?"

She shook her head. "No. Not right now."

Gordie stood up. "Lorraine, you've been very helpful. I know it's hard for you to think about all of this so many years later, but you've done very well, and we appreciate it. You were a good friend to Sarah."

Lorraine stood to lead them out of her house. She opened the door, her eyes luminous with unshed tears. "I could have been a better friend."

Gordie and Albright left without saying anything further.

They got back in his car and Gordie headed for the submarine sandwich shop. He threw a quick glance at his partner. "I didn't see that business with the cross coming. Why would Sarah give away something so personal?"

CHAPTER 19

THEY ATE LUNCH AND then set off to Antigonish to talk to Father Peter. As they drove, they continued their lunch discussion.

He shook his head. "Have you ever given something you love away, on a whim?"

"No, never. My nana sometimes gives me things that are special to her, but usually she saves them for birthdays or Christmas."

"I thought maybe it was a girl thing."

"We aren't all the same, you know."

Gordie gave a wry smile. "Fair enough. When we were at lunch, it seemed like you had something on your mind. What was it?"

When she didn't answer, he turned to give her a quick look. "Come on, Roxanne. What are you thinking?"

Albright sighed. "I've heard that people contemplating suicide sometimes give their things away."

He let that idea sink in. "She wouldn't have a crushed skull and wouldn't have gotten buried like that for a suicide."

She shrugged. "I know. It doesn't add up. But what if she had a really good friend that somehow, she convinces to help her. She doesn't have the courage to take pills or whatever."

Gordie let the scenario play out. "She's a good Catholic, so can't do it herself. She knows though that even having someone else kill her, it's wrong, so she gives away her cross. She feels guilty."

Albright nodded. "She doesn't want to see it coming so they agree, her and her accomplice, to do it while her back is turned."

"Good God. But why? I just can't wrap my head around it. She was a smart, pretty girl with her life ahead of her."

Albright's voice was somber. "It happens. I know a family and the boy did it. He wasn't being bullied that anyone could determine. It looked like he had everything going for him, but without warning one day." She stopped to take a deep breath. "The family will never be the same. There was no note, nothing."

"They're sure it was suicide?"

She nodded. "Yes."

"I'm sorry. Sometimes there's just no explaining things. You just hope that there's some grand scheme that isn't obvious to us mere mortals."

"Do you believe that? Are you religious?"

He was quiet for a moment. "I think there are things beyond our understanding and believe there is a God, although I'm not a great churchgoer anymore. What about you?"

"Yes, I go to church but mostly because my nana wants to go. I suppose I don't spend enough time thinking about it although I was raised as a Catholic and so I continue on as one and all that it means."

They drove in silence until a big garishly painted sign proclaimed that this was the exit to take in order to eat at a popular steak house. Gordie read it aloud and then grinned. "Do you ever go there?"

"I don't come out this way too often, but I have eaten there. Name a person from these parts that hasn't."

Gordie shook his head. "I bet they lost business though when the new highway went through. It's great having the divided highway, but I miss going through all the little places."

She nodded. "I know what you mean. I remember as a kid I had some family who lived out this way and when I was visiting them, my cousins and I would go out on our bicycles and later my aunt would know every place we'd been because it had already been reported to her."

"A little like being in Big Pond then."

She laughed. "That's true. One thing about this new highway, a person could go from Cape Breton to Truro and no one would see you to report to the family."

***

They met Father Peter West in an office with tall windows that looked out over parking spaces, a green lawn and the old brick of the university campus buildings. When they entered, the priest had his back to the room and stood gazing out on the view. Albright made a quizzical face at Gordie, but they stood silently waiting until the priest turned to them. His chestnut-brown hair was glossy and thick, still giving him the Tom Cruise look, but had threads of grey through it now. He was dressed in a neat, but not expensive-looking charcoal sport jacket, white shirt with a green tie that brought out the colour of his hazel eyes, and grey flannel slacks. In Gordie's eyes, he didn't look like a priest.

Father Peter approached them to shake hands. "My apologies." He smiled. "It's so easy to get lost in thought looking out at these grand old buildings. I'm Father Peter West, the Diocesan Spokesperson and rector here at St. Ninian Please sit down."

"I'm Detective MacLean and this is Detective Albright. Thank you for meeting with us."

They all sat down, a large desk separating them. Father Peter leaned back in his swivel chair. "I believe you are investigating the death of Sarah Campbell."

Gordie nodded. "We are. We've been told that you knew the girl quite well and I'm hoping you can give us some insight into who she was, and more importantly anything you might know that could lead us to finding who did this."

The priest nodded. "She was one of several young people in a youth group I ran. I knew her to be a kind and thoughtful girl. Perhaps more thoughtful than many others of her age." He frowned and then continued. "At times, she seemed quite troubled. I encouraged her to talk to me and occasionally she did. She didn't have a happy home life. You may have already discovered that?"

"What did she tell you about her home life, Father?"

"Her father drank a lot, and as with so many cases of that nature, he could be troublesome when he had too much to drink."

Gordie swallowed, feeling the old anger beating in his chest. "What do you mean by troublesome? Don't be shy, Father. The more you can tell us, the more it will help. Obviously, I'm not looking for you to break the confessional oath, but anything else would be useful."

"He shouted a lot, he demanded money from Sarah, and I know that on more than one occasion he struck Sarah's mother in anger."

Albright shifted in her chair and wrote a few words in her notebook.

Gordie nodded, keeping quiet.

Father Peter rubbed his forehead. "Sarah wanted her mother to leave her father, but of course I didn't encourage that line of thinking."

Gordie felt the muscles in his neck and shoulder tense. "Of course."

Father Peter frowned. "I suggested I would be happy to meet with Mr. Campbell or indeed the whole family, in an effort to counsel them through the difficulties."

"Did they take you up on that offer?"

"No. I suspect Sarah didn't even broach it at home."

"And you didn't try to meet with the family despite Sarah's reluctance?"

He shook his head. "No. I felt Sarah might see that as a betrayal of her confidence."

"All right. What else can you tell us? What about her friends in the youth group? Who did she hang around with?"

Father Peter chewed on his bottom lip. "It was so many years ago now. I do remember her best friend though. Mary-Catherine. They were as thick as thieves, but aside from her, no one else really stands out in my mind. Sarah got along with everyone, and there were some lovely energetic discussions with the group, but no other single person jumps out at me."

MacLean repeated. "Mary-Catherine Cameron was her closest friend."

"Yes, that's it. Mary-Catherine."

"You know that she recently died?"

Father Peter nodded. "Yes, I remember reading that in the paper. An accident, wasn't it?"

"A hit and run."

He shook his head. "That's terrible. I didn't know her as well as Sarah, but I recall she was a fun-loving girl."

"I would have thought you knew them both about the same, since they were best pals."

"Sarah was more introspective, and I suppose that was more conducive to deeper conversation. Mary-Catherine liked to joke around, and she didn't always come to the meetings, so although the girls stuck together when she did come, Sarah was sometimes on her own."

Albright made a note.

Gordie waited to see if Father Peter had anything else to add. When the silence lengthened, he prompted the priest. "What about any boys?"

"We had a couple of boys, but I don't recall Sarah really connecting with them."

"And were they particularly interested in her? Maybe one of them tried something and was rejected?"

He hesitated. "I don't think so. They were all friendly to each other, but I don't think it was like that. Of course, I don't know what happened when they left the group. Perhaps they were friendlier than I understood."

"Can you please write down their names for me and if you know where they are now, please put that down as well."

The priest tore a piece of paper from the pad on his desk and wrote for a moment. He slid the paper across, and Albright picked it up and folded it into her notebook. Father Peter nodded to the paper. "I think Donny is in Sydney now, but I'm pretty sure Gerard stayed local, working with his father on the farm."

"That's great, thank you for that. Father, did you ever see these kids outside of the church setting? As you say, maybe they were different away from there?"

"We went on a few road trips to religious places of interest. No overnight things naturally, just within an easy drive and we'd have a picnic or stop in a tea room, so yes, I saw them out where things were more casual and, let's face it, more fun, but still I didn't see anything that would suggest one of the boys had an unhealthy interest in Sarah."

"All right. Father, this next question will be difficult, but I want you to give it some serious thought."

Father Peter leaned his elbows on the desk and steepled his fingers. "Go ahead."

"Do you think it possible that Sarah was depressed?"

Father Peter frowned. "What makes you ask that?"

Gordie leaned in and rested his own elbows on the desk. "Is it possible that she considered suicide?"

The rector laid his hands flat on the desk as if to brace himself. "No. I don't think that's at all possible. She was a very spiritual person and that would have gone against everything she believed."

Gordie nodded. "I understand. Suicide wasn't an option, but going back to the first question, was she depressed at all in those days or weeks before she disappeared? You seemed to have known her quite well. Would you have noticed something like that?"

He licked his lips. "I believe I would have noticed, and no, I don't believe she was depressed. Not in the clinical way you're suggesting. She had her ups and downs as most people do, and with her troubled home life, I would say she felt things deeply, but not to the point you are considering. If anything, she tended towards anger rather than depression. I'm not a psychologist by any means, but I think she was a pretty stable person considering what she experienced at home."

MacLean hesitated and then continued. "Father, on the day Sarah disappeared, she gave her gold cross to a friend. Does that surprise you?"

The priest's fingers curled into clenched fists. His face blanched but his voice was calm and measured. "Yes, that surprises me very much. In fact, I am shocked to hear it."

"You know the cross I'm talking about?"

"Yes, she always wore it. As far as I know, she was very fond of it."

"Can you think of any reason why she might give it away?"

"No. Absolutely not. I can see now why you asked me about suicide."

"And does it change your answer on the possibility?"

Father Peter's pursed his lips and shook his head. "No, it doesn't. I can't explain her behaviour, but I continue to be certain she was not a person that would commit suicide."

Gordie leaned back and sighed. "All right, thank you. What did you think happened to her when Sarah disappeared, Father?"

"At first, I was concerned, especially when there were rumours that she had been hitchhiking. But then, we talked about it in the group. Her friends seemed convinced that Sarah had gone to Toronto, and after a bit, I suppose I thought they were right."

Gordie nodded and looked at Albright.

She skimmed through her notes and then looked up. "Father, what kind of car did you drive back in 2009?"

He hesitated for an instant and then chuckled. "I had a red 1999 Mazda Protégé. I bought it second-hand and by then it was forever breaking down, so I often drove the church van, or in good weather I rode my bicycle."

"When you went on road trips with the club you drove this van?"

"Yes, it was an eight-passenger white Ford."

Albright made a note. "And just for our records, where did you live when you were Parish Priest in Port Mulroy?"

"I had a room in a house about a kilometer away from the church. We were looked after by a widow; Mrs. Scott. There was another priest there too, Father Duncan Landry, who looked after the parish in Creignish."

Gordie felt his heart beat a little faster. "Was this house on Parish Lane, Father?"

Father Peter's brow wrinkled in puzzlement. "No, it was on Mary Street."

"Ah, right. Is Father Duncan still living there?"

Father Peter smiled. "No, he's in Edmonton now. He has family there and was anxious to be closer to them. Mrs. Scott died a few years ago."

Albright closed her notebook and Gordie stood up. "I think that's everything for now. If you think of anything else that might help us find who did this, please let us know." Gordie handed Father Peter his card. They all shook hands, and then Gordie and Albright left.

When they were back in the car and out on the highway back to Cape Breton, Gordie threw a glance over at his partner. "Well Roxanne, what did you think of him?"

She shifted to face him. "I think he's very handsome."

"Too handsome for a rector."

She laughed. "What's he supposed to do about that? Get a brush cut, maybe?"

"That'd be a start."

She chuckled again. "Seriously, I thought he was sincere. He wasn't over the top sad about Sarah, because that would be odd after all these years, but he did seem authentic about feeling unhappy. What did you think?"

"I agree with you. At least he gave us some more friends to chase down so it wasn't a wasted trip."

Albright reached over and turned up the radio and they drove in companionable quiet, listening to the radio for the rest of the trip home to Gordie's house.

He offered her a cup of tea before she headed home, but she declined and Gordie didn't argue. He was keen to get Taz and go out.

He needed to think. There was something about today's interviews that niggled at him.

CHAPTER 20

AT THE MORNING BRIEFING, Gordie brought the team up to date on the new information about Sarah giving her cross to her work-friend, Lorraine. "It seems to have been a spur-of-the-moment decision after Lorraine admired the cross."

Sergeant Arsenault stood, as usual, leaning against the door frame of the meeting room with his arms folded. Gordie wasn't sure if his boss was more irritated that there was new information or that they hadn't made more progress. "Detective MacLean, what do you infer from this spontaneous gift giving thing? Is it even relevant?"

"I believe it is. There was a reason she gave that cross away. It had been precious to her for a couple of years, so why now? We need to figure out that reason. That means going back to some previous people for further interviews. I think her mother may know something. Maybe she doesn't even realize she knows it."

One of the other detectives asked about the boys from the youth group. "What about these boys? Do they know anything?"

Gordie lifted his hands in a gesture of 'I don't know.' "We'll be getting a hold of them today, I hope, and we'll find out."

After Gordie finished his briefing, Norris stood and ran through the status on the hit and run. Gordie kept himself from smiling when he saw the same grim look on Arsenault's face when Norris had to admit that they were no further ahead than they had been two days ago.

Arsenault shook his head. "Well, get to it, then. You aren't making progress standing here." He turned and left the room, followed by the other detectives.

Gordie assigned Albright to track down the two boys. "Bring them in here, or we'll go to them. Either way works for me. By the way, did you get anything back on the phone records for Mary-Catherine? I know Norris is keen and I don't want him to take over. Whatever we can keep a hold of, let's do it."

She nodded. "I'll follow up. I sent over the warrant electronically and they told me that was good enough, so I'll run it down."

"Right. Norris and I are going to Mary-Catherine's bank to meet with the manager." He crooked a half smile. "Norris was prepared to go out on his own but has graciously allowed me to tag along."

He turned away, but Albright called him back. "What about the other girls?"

He nodded. "Yes, good point. We should talk to the other girls from that group. Give Father Peter a shout and see if he can give you their names. I knew there was something I missed but couldn't come up with it. Good catch, Roxanne, and call Alice again to see if she's thought of any other friends we should chase down. Someone knows something about what Sarah was doing."

Gordie walked down the hall to meet Detective Norris at the door leading out to the parking lot. "Do you want me to drive?"

Norris held up his keys. "I'm good."

Norris drove straight along Number 4 east to the bank. During the ten-minute drive Norris reminded Gordie that it was his case and Gordie was just along for the ride.

Gordie held up his hands in surrender. "I have complete faith in you. I appreciate that you let me come along."

They were shown into the bank manager's office. Norris stepped forward and showed his badge and handed over the warrant. "Thank you for meeting with us, Mr. Morrison. I'm Detective Norris and this is my colleague, Detective MacLean."

The short, thin man with wire-framed glasses shook hands with each of them, his hand damp. He waved them into the chairs in front of his desk while he retreated to his swivel chair behind it.

The chair squeaked as the bank manager sat down, and he flushed. "I have Ms. Cameron's account printed out here as requested. I went back a year, which is all I can easily do. Did you want to go back further than that?"

Norris took the proffered pages. "Probably not. Let's just take a quick look in case we have questions for you."

As Norris scanned down the first page, his brows pulled together and he glanced at Gordie before handing him the page.

Gordie nodded. He saw what caught the attention of the other detective. A week prior to her accident, Mary-Catherine had made a deposit of 5,000 dollars. It was an extraordinary amount and a flip through the other pages showed that there was nothing else like it over the course of the year. The routine electronic deposit of her pay cheque was essentially the only money going in. In late April there had been a deposit from the Government of Canada, indicating a tax refund. Otherwise, all the entries were for withdrawals and bill payments. She lived month to month, never going into overdraft, but never having more than a small amount left at the end of the month.

Norris slid the top page towards Mr. Morrison. "Are you able to tell me anything at all about this deposit? Was it a cheque? If so, we'll want to see a scan of it."

Morrison tapped into his computer and then shook his head. "Cash, I'm afraid."

"Damn."

Norris folded the pages and put them into his inside pocket. "I think that's everything, unless Detective MacLean has anything."

Gordie stood as well. "I don't suppose there's any point in looking at CCTV of her making the deposit?"

Norris snorted. "Anyone who was careful enough to give her cash is sure as heck not about to be caught on camera doing it."

"I'm sure you're right. Well, it gives us something, anyway. Thank you, Mr. Morrison. You've been very helpful." Gordie stepped away, not wanting to clasp the clammy hand again.

Morrison bobbed his head. "It isn't often we're asked to help the police with inquiries. We're glad to do it, of course. I'm sorry I had to ask you to get the warrant, but those are the rules."

Gordie noticed that Norris stepped out of reach of a handshake and he said goodbye.

Back in the car, Gordie spoke first. "This is the link between the cases. Even Arsenault will have to acknowledge it. Mary-Catherine Cameron blackmailed someone and was killed over it."

Norris held up his hand. "We can't know that for certain. Maybe she won at bingo or chase the ace and just didn't tell anyone. Keeping it quiet to surprise her folks with a fancy gift maybe. We can't assume."

Gordie sighed. "OK. We can't assume, but we can speculate. Can you give me that much?"

Norris grinned. "Fair enough. And the reality is, if she had won on anything around here, the world would have known about it whether she told anyone or not."

They went together to Sergeant Arsenault's office. Their boss waved them in to sit down, his face expectant. "You must have something. What's happened?"

Norris pulled the pages from his pocket. "We believe this links the cases. This is Mary-Catherine Cameron's bank records. It shows a deposit from an unknown source a week before she was hit by the car."

Arsenault looked at the entry and then leaned back. "Blackmail, then."

"We think so."

Arsenault continued to address Norris. "Where do you want to go from here?"

Norris nodded towards Gordie. "We talked it over and we both agree that I continue on looking at the Cameron case, but it gets rolled into Detective MacLean's case. He's the lead and we'll coordinate closely with anything either of us find."

Arsenault frowned. "Or it gets rolled into one and you take the lead. You have the experience."

Gordie and Norris had talked about this possibility, and as hard as it was, Gordie remained quiet and let Norris continue.

"With all due respect, Sergeant, it makes more sense for MacLean to continue as lead. He's already well into the details and has rapport with some of the witnesses."

Arsenault sighed. "All right, fine. Carry on, then."

They left and walked back down the hall to the meeting room with the case whiteboard. Gordie waved to the board. "Update the board and I'll get Albright in to bring her up to speed."

When the two of them returned, Norris had erased some of the entries to move them over, making room for Mary-Catherine's details to be listed side by side with Sarah's.

Albright sat down in the front row and Gordie told her about the payment to Mary-Catherine and how the two cases were now considered as one.

She nodded. "Okay. Well, that's interesting. That makes the phone records even more urgent. I called them and they said they'd have it to me by end of day."

Gordie nodded. "Good. We'll want to see who she's spoken to in the time between Sarah's body being identified and the payment."

Norris nodded. "In the meantime, I'm going to circle back to the parents to see if Mary-Catherine had mentioned this payment to them, and anything else. Maybe she talked about meeting up with an old friend or something. There are also a couple of her friends that I didn't talk to yet. Maybe one of them knows something."

Gordie gave him a light punch in the arm as Norris walked past on his way back to his own desk. "Thanks for today."

Norris shrugged. "It's only right. You're doing a good job, so you might as well keep doing it."

When Norris and Albright left him alone, Gordie stood examining the board. He picked up the marker and began a list to the left of Sarah's name.

Go back to basics, old man. What inspires a person to murder, assuming it's not a random act of a madman?

He wrote down bulleted words: Jealousy/Sexual, Revenge/Retaliation, Money, Fear.

Beside each bullet he assigned a name or a question-mark. For Jealousy, he put Mary-Catherine, Donny, Gerard.

Beside Revenge, he put a question mark. Anything he had heard so far didn't offer any ideas on people that Sarah may have wronged. By all accounts she was pretty kind, even if she was a little mouthy, as Jamie put it. He frowned when he thought of Jamie. *Is it possible Sarah wanted him back? That might make the new girlfriend angry. When did they get together?*

Beside Money, he wrote Bill Cameron. *He wanted money and she wouldn't give it to him.*

Beside Fear, he wrote Alice Cameron. *Sarah might have found out about the affair and threatened to expose it.*

He sat down in front of the board and flipped open his notebook to copy out the list. He wanted to add points to each one to add a weighting system in order to prioritize the ideas. *Which is most likely?*

He was still sitting there when Albright came back and sat down next to him. She stretched out her legs. "Father Peter is unavailable as he and the Bishop have gone to Halifax for two days."

"Hmph. That's a nuisance. Who did you hear that from?"

"The parish secretary who answered his phone."

Gordie grunted again.

"Then I called Jamie MacNeil."

"Oh?"

"Remember, we met his girlfriend, Linda? She was in that group, right?"

Gordie smiled. "I may get used to having a partner."

"Two heads are better than one."

"So I've been told, but before this I didn't believe it."

She smiled. "Jamie gave me Linda's number, and I called her. We had a chat, but she had little to say about it since she only went to this group maybe three times. Linda remembers both Donny and Gerard but doesn't think either of them liked Sarah in that way. She said they were into different things like playing chess and Donny played the fiddle with his sister at some of the dances. Linda had the idea that Donny might have known Sarah slightly because of the dances."

"That doesn't sound hopeful."

"Not really, no. Unless Donny knew Sarah more than he let on. Those dances full of hot sweaty young people and hormones, who knows what thoughts may have gone through his head while he was up on stage watching the action on the dance floor."

"Were you able to reach either Donny or Gerard?"

"I Googled Donny since he's a musician, I figured he might still be playing and voilà!"

Gordie raised his eyebrows.

"Donny and Matine, brother and sister musicians have a website where you can see what events they will be performing at on any given weekend. There's no phone number though, and there are so many listings in the phone book for *D. Boudreau* that it would be a long job to find the right one. I sent a note through the *Contact Us* form on their website. Hopefully, I'll hear back soon. The sister probably has a married name now. I couldn't find her in the phone book at all, and besides, so many people only have a cell phone these days, which isn't listed, so it's tough."

"What about the other one, Gerard?"

"Linda was pretty certain Gerard works on his family farm. She sees him around town sometimes."

"Where's this farm?"

"Out near Horton Lake."

"I think tomorrow you and I will take a drive out there. Do you know exactly where?"

"I'm sure I can find it. Linda gave me directions."

"Well done. Did she say anything about the other girls in the group?"

"When she was there, there was only one other girl. She was someone that had gone to school with Sarah and Mary-Catherine, which was another reason that Linda didn't stay with the group. She felt like an outsider because she had gone to a different school. The girl's name was Donna Wright. Linda isn't sure what happened to her, so I'll do some more digging there. I'm thinking the old high school the three girls went to might have something."

"Good plan."

She turned her attention to the board. "What are you doing here?"

Gordie stood up and walked back to the board. "I'm just regrouping. Going back to see the big picture."

Albright nodded. "Jealousy. Why put Mary-Catherine down?"

"Just remembering how she talked about Sarah. It seemed that there was something there. Of course, now we can speculate that she knew who the murderer was, and that's what she was hiding, but still. I felt like there was something more and the word that came to me was jealous. She seemed envious of Sarah for some reason, and it wasn't because of the job. I don't think." He shrugged.

"We don't know enough about Donny and Gerard, so let's leave jealousy. Money. You still think Sarah's father could have done this for twenty dollars or whatever?"

Gordie nodded. "I think that man's capable, especially when he's been drinking. We know he's got a temper, and he'd gotten physical with her before this. And according to Father Peter, Bill Campbell hits his wife. Dad's got no real alibi for the day Sarah went missing. He claims he was at a barbecue where a darts tournament was going on but could easily have left for some time; driven home, encountered Sarah, getting into a fight with her when she turns him down for money. She tells him to take a hike, he loses it and smack. Maybe he doesn't mean to hit her so hard, but he bashes her in the head. Then, of course he panics and puts her body in the trunk of the car so his wife doesn't find out and goes back to the Legion. Bill chats with a bunch of people, so he's seen and then disappears again when it's dark to go bury the body. He gets back before closing and leaves his car there where people will notice it in the emptying parking lot." Gordie folded his arms across his chest with a nod as if to say, 'case closed.'

Albright nodded. "You're not wrong. It could have happened, but where does Mary-Catherine Cameron fit into it?"

"Maybe the two girls spoke to each other before Sarah's father got home. They're on the phone when Dad walks in. Sarah says, 'my Dad's home. I'll call you back later.'"

"So why does Mary-Catherine wait until Sarah's body is found to blackmail the dad? Why not before this? Or why didn't she say something to the police in the initial investigation when Sarah was reported missing?"

Gordie chewed on his bottom lip. "Good questions. Don't know."

Albright turned her attention back to the board. "You've got Alice up there for fear. You really imagine that Sarah's mother could have killed her daughter for fear of having her affair discovered?"

Gordie lifted a shoulder. "It's weak, I know. But fear of exposure can be a good motive. She may really have been afraid of what her husband would do if he found out. Afraid that he'd beat her and more afraid he'd go after the boyfriend, Jan."

"It's possible, but I still don't see her being so afraid or angry as to kill her, and then how did she get the body buried? You aren't going to suggest the boyfriend helped her?"

"Maybe."

Albright shook her head. "I'm not feeling it."

Gordie set down the marker on the ledge of the board and sat down again. "Okay, Roxanne, your turn. What have I missed?"

She walked to the board and picked up the marker. "Jamie. I think he fits the jealousy angle more than Mary-Catherine. He's on a slow burn over the couple of months since they split up. The boy sees her at the odd dance in those slinky clothes and wants her back for himself. He waits for her that afternoon near her work and somehow convinces her to take a drive with him in his white Chevy Metro."

Gordie grinned and interjected. "with grey interior."

"With grey interior. They go to some quiet place, he knows, and they get out for a walk. He makes a pass at her and she turns him down cold. It's too much for him. Why should these other guys get to dance with her and spend time with her and not him? What's wrong with him? She tells him exactly why not him until he's had enough. He sees red and picks up a piece of wood and that's it."

Gordie nodded. "Okay. Put Jamie's name there beside jealousy."

She wrote it down and came back to sit down. "Where do we go from here?"

"Chip away. We'll meet with the two boys, track down any other friends we can, and meanwhile see if we can get more information about the money that Mary-Catherine received. We'll just keep tightening the net, little by little."

CHAPTER 21

ALBRIGHT PICKED UP GORDIE the next morning for the drive out to see Gerard Smith.

Gordie looked out the window at the passing scenery. "Things look different when you're a passenger."

"Are you enjoying the experience?"

"No. Can't say that I am."

"Why did you agree I could drive?"

"It seemed important to you. It's part of my new collaborative persona."

She laughed. "You may get used to it."

He snorted. "Don't count on it."

She pulled into the yard of a modern, well-kept farm. A sign at the gate proclaimed the name *Ashbourne-Rose Farm*. Sheep dotted the rolling hills around the immediate farmyard. They got out of the car and a Great Pyrenees dog trotted out of the barn and stood barking at them.

Albright grinned. "That should make you feel at home."

"It does."

A young man strode out of the barn and gave a sharp command to the dog, who stopped barking and lay down.

He was tall and wore no jacket; his bare muscular forearms tanned despite the early spring weather. "I'm Gerard Smith." He stuck out his hand and shook Gordie's hand and then Albright's.

They introduced themselves, and then Gordie asked if they could talk for a few moments.

"Come into the barn. It's lambing season and I've got a mother in labour. I don't like to leave her for long."

They followed him into the barn, the dog getting up to accompany them. Gordie had to admire the dog. "I've got a Great Pyr at home, but she's smaller than this fella."

Gerard looked fondly at the dog. "He's great with the sheep. Not a herder, of course, but he stays out in the fields at night with them and I know they'll be safe."

Gordie nodded. "It's what they're bred for, of course." They followed him to the end of the barn where an older man was kneeling in the straw beside a sheep. "Everything all right, Dad?"

"Fine. Not long now, though." He looked up and nodded at the two detectives.

Gerard simply said, "This is my Dad." He led them beyond the stall and stood with his arms folded. "So, what can I do for you? I think" here he nodded at Albright "you said it was to do with Sarah Campbell?"

Albright pulled out her notebook while Gordie arranged the questions in his mind. "You were in this youth group that Father Peter ran, so you knew Sarah, is that correct?"

Gerard nodded. "I didn't know her well, but yes, we both went to that group."

"Did you know her from anywhere else?"

"Not really. I'd seen her at Mass of course but didn't know her to talk to her."

"What sort of relationship did you have once you met her at the group?"

Gerard frowned. "Relationship?"

"Yes. In other words, did you become friends? Did you see her outside of the group?"

"I would say no to both those questions. I liked her all right at the group, but I wouldn't say we became friends. She was usually with that other girl, Mary-Catherine, so they stuck together. I liked that she got properly into the discussions, which Mary-Catherine didn't really do. She was more interested in giggling or making faces, that one." He blushed then, as he suddenly seemed to remember that Mary-Catherine had recently died.

"Did they tease you, Gerard? Girls can do that sometimes."

He shook his head. "No. That's not what I mean." He closed his eyes for a moment. "I remember one time we were talking about being authentic and there was a passage from the bible. Maybe Corinthians. I remember a line that went: *For when I am weak, then I am strong.* Sarah really got hepped up about it. It sounded like she used to be bullied and so there was a whole discussion about how to deal with it based on this notion about weakness being a strength. I liked to listen to her when she was enthusiastic like that. It made me think, you know? But Mary-Catherine wasn't like that. She'd be all quiet, like she was thinking about something else altogether. I think Father Peter did it on purpose."

"Did what on purpose?"

"Get Sarah riled up. He'd kind of smile when she'd get on a tear about something. I suppose that was the point of the whole thing, wasn't it? To get us all thinking about things and how the Bible and God fit into our daily lives."

Gordie nodded. "What about the other boy that was in the group. Donny Boudreau. How did he and Sarah get along?"

Gerard shrugged. "The same as me, I'd say. He and I were buddies, and we'd sometimes meet early before the group all got there to have a game of chess. We both just liked the peace and quiet of it all. Donny's one of seven kids and it was always a madhouse at his place so he came just for the break. I went because it got me away from the endless chores, I guess. Neither of us were into sports, so we weren't on any teams. I went to 4-H for a while when I was younger, but that was all about projects and it seemed to me like it was just an extension of the farm work." He grinned. "Now I love it all and my wife has a hard time dragging me away from here."

"You're married? Congratulations."

"I'm married and we have a little one on the way. You may have noticed the little red house when you turned in, up on the hill behind the barn?"

Gordie nodded.

"That's where we live. One day my folks will move in there and we'll move into the big house and take over the whole farm."

Gordie smiled. "Sounds like you found your calling."

Gerard nodded. "But I haven't forgotten the lessons from Father Peter. He made me think about things in a way I hadn't before and here, surrounded by nature, it's all more obvious to me."

"There were a couple other girls in the group. Linda and Donna. What can you tell me about them?"

"I knew Linda a little from school, but I didn't know Donna at all. Linda didn't really stick around for long. Not her thing, I guess, and the other girls didn't go out of their way to make her feel welcome. Donna obviously knew Sarah and Mary-Catherine from their school, but they didn't seem to be great pals or anything. They'd sit together and yack, but you could tell that Donna wasn't really part of their gang. In the beginning it seemed like they were all friends, but after a while Donna got sort of cool towards Sarah so I don't know if they had an argument or something. I didn't care enough to find out. After a while Donna stopped coming."

"Was that before Sarah disappeared or after?"

"Before. After she disappeared, it seemed like the energy went out of the whole club and then Father Peter left. After that, it was only a few months later that it folded. By then I had started at college and I was glad because I was going to quit, anyway. No time, you know?"

"One last question, Gerard. When Sarah went missing, did you think she had simply left and gone to Toronto or wherever?"

Gerard shook his head. "No. I never thought that. From the way she talked, she was pretty close to her mom. She had a good job that she seemed to like, and I never thought she just threw that all away to run off."

"What did you think happened?"

"I thought something bad. She was a pretty, friendly girl, and when I heard she'd been hitchhiking, I thought she'd met the wrong person. We don't get much of that sort of thing here in Cape Breton, but it isn't unheard of. It might have been a tourist, or a truck driver come off the ferry from Newfoundland on his way to Ontario or something. That's what I thought."

Gordie nodded. "Yes, I can see that."

Gerard's father called out. "Gerard. Come on. It's time."

Gordie put out his hand and shook Gerard's hand. "Thank you for your time. You've been very helpful."

Albright shook his hand as well before the young man hastened to the stall where the sheep had begun to bleat, and the two detectives went back to the car.

Once they were back on the road heading towards Port Mulroy, Gordie tapped out a rhythm on his knees. He wasn't used to being in a car where his hands weren't fully occupied with driving. "Well, what did you think of all that, Roxanne?"

She licked her lips. "It's given me some real food for thought."

"How so?"

"Have we spent enough time considering the stranger angle?"

"You think it's viable?"

"I think it's a possibility we haven't explored."

"Hmph."

"You obviously don't think so."

"No, and here's why." He ticked his comments off on his fingers. "One, how would he, let's say he instead of she, how would he know a quiet place to take her to rape her or simply murder her if that was his thing? Two, would she really get in with a total stranger? Yes, we've heard of her hitchhiking, but it's one thing to get in with someone you've seen around, and a completely different thing to get in with a complete stranger. Three, how would a stranger know where to bury her? There's so much open land around here, or better yet, he could have taken her along until he got to New Brunswick where the Trans-Canada highway goes through so much empty forested land. And last, but definitely not least, how do we explain the payment to Mary-Catherine?"

He put his hands back on his knees, with a feeling of satisfaction.

She nodded as they pulled into Robin's Donuts. "Okay. You've convinced me."

He opened the door to climb out and tossed back a comment over his shoulder. "I'll buy. You deserve it after that lecture. Let's sit down and figure out where we go from here."

CHAPTER 22

H E NURSED HIS LARGE coffee while she read out her notes in a quiet voice at their table in the far corner.

She looked up when she finished. "Did we waste a whole morning here?"

"No, not at all. For one thing, it's clear to me he wasn't involved. If we take him at face value, no motive and just doesn't seem the type. I keep going back to the question of who might have the rage, or passion at least, to do such a thing."

"So, we take him off our list. That's what we achieved here."

"Yes, there's that, and I also got a better sense of Sarah. Any information that builds a better picture of her is helpful."

Albright cocked her head. "And what did you learn today?"

"I learned she was spiritual. I know we heard the same thing from Father Peter, but this confirms it. She wasn't just at the group to meet people or get out of the house. She got involved in the discussions. It makes me wonder even more why she would give her cross away."

Albright slid her cup back and forth, deep in thought.

"Go ahead. Something's occurred to you. Spit it out."

"It's probably way off base."

Gordie sighed. "Just like the suicide notion, there are no bad theories. It's what you're here for."

She gave a wry smile. "To come up with off base ideas?"

"To contribute ideas that are different from mine. If we thought the same way, we'd probably miss out."

She shrugged. "Okay, here goes. What if she gave Lorraine the cross, one of the things she treasured most in life, because she was giving it to the person she loved?"

Gordie frowned. "You mean…"

"Yeah, I mean, as in a girlfriend."

"But she went out with Jamie. She went to dances with boys."

"Of course, she did. She couldn't acknowledge her feelings."

Gordie sat back. "Good Lord."

She expanded her idea. "It would explain both why she gave away a thing she loved, but as well, she may have felt that she wasn't being a good Catholic by even having these feelings."

"Hmm. As hard as it is to even imagine this scenario, let's go with it for a minute. It still leaves us with the fundamental question of who would be so enraged by the situation to warrant killing her?"

"Jamie? Same scenario as before but different motive."

He nodded. "It's possible. I would go back to the dad. He doesn't strike me as a man who would be very understanding if he found out his daughter was batting for the other side."

She frowned. "There's no way it would be the object of Sarah's affections, would it?"

"God, no. I can't see it. If it were true, that Sarah was in love with Lorraine, which seems a huge stretch to me, I doubt if Lorraine was even aware. The way she talked, she didn't seem to be concealing something that big."

"I agree."

"The problem is, even if you're right, and quite honestly I don't think so, but even if you are, what difference does it make? We have the same suspects, just an alternative motive."

Albright shook her head. "I suppose you're right."

Gordie pointed to Albright's notebook. "Okay, it's a line of questioning that I think is worth exploring, anyway. We need to circle back and talk to Sarah's mother about a few things. First, we were going to check about her computer. Is it the same one that was in the house when Sarah was still alive? If not, was the data transferred from the old one to the latest one? Next, check into her thinking about this new theory. Did Sarah ever seem to have any schoolgirl crushes on other girls? She was bullied when she was younger; dig into that a bit more. Why was that? It sounded like it stopped when she started hanging out with Mary-Catherine. Was there more to that friendship than we first thought? Also, check on the money angle regarding the dad. Remember, I wondered if he hit her up for money and she turned him down. Let's not forget that option. Did she have money in the bank when she disappeared? Or did she keep it under her mattress? Maybe she caught him searching her room. He's my first choice, even if I'm not clear on the motive. We also need to continue to follow up on tracking down the other two kids from that group and set up meetings with both of them."

"Is Donny still important based on what Gerard told us?"

"I think so. Every person has their own perspective, and I'd like to hear his first-hand. Also, maybe he noticed something that he never talked about to Gerard."

She made further notes.

"And I'm still keen to get those phone records for Mary-Catherine. Roxanne, you're doing great. I'll never just turn away an idea out of hand. I may not agree with you, but I'll tell you why. You make me think in ways that I normally don't do. That's a good thing."

She flushed. "Okay. Thanks."

Gordie stood and put both their cups on the tray to carry back to the counter. "Let's get back. I want to catch up with Norris and see what he's come up with."

They both had more energy in their step on the way back to the car.

As they left the outskirts of Port Mulroy on the way back to Gordie's house, Albright looked at the clock. "Darn. I meant to call Nana before this. She had a doctor's appointment this morning. Do you mind if I call now?"

Gordie shrugged. "Go ahead and try, but along here, you usually won't get any service. There are all kinds of gaps around this area with no service or one bar."

Albright gave the verbal instructions for 'phone' and 'Nana,' but the phone didn't connect. "Shoot. You must be right."

"Wait until we turn on to Isle Madame. You'll get through then."

"I'll drop you off and then try again. It can wait a few more minutes."

They continued to hone the list of questions for each of the interviews they wanted to have, including another follow-up with Jamie.

As they neared his home, Gordie proposed she go home instead of the office. "Make the calls from home. You've got a computer at home so you can check your email and do your Google searches to find Donna Wright from there just as easily as the office."

"That would be great. Okay, I'll do that."

"I'm going straight into the office and then we can connect at five o'clock to see where things stand."

She dropped him off and he went in the house to greet Taz while she parked in the driveway to make her call, before heading home.

***

Taz pushed up against him when he went into the house. "Oh, now Taz, don't get me covered in hair, my love. I still need to go into the office, and you know how Sarge feels about dog hair."

He stepped out into the backyard for a few moments to smoke a cigarette while Taz rolled in the grass. Gordie stood and watched the dog, but his mind was busy thinking about the ideas that Albright had thrown out.

He spoke aloud. "She comes up with some interesting ideas, Taz. I'm not sure they're going to get us anywhere but, I like that she comes up with them. Makes me think about possibilities that I wouldn't normally consider."

He finished his cigarette and they went inside.

Gordie set down the dish of dog food and as Taz ate, he turned on the kettle to make a coffee in his travel mug. He slapped together a cheese sandwich, which he ate standing at the counter. Ten minutes later he was ready to leave again.

He bent to scratch behind the silky white ears of his dog. "I'll see you later, my girl. If it's still bright enough when I get home, I'll take you for a proper walk."

His mind ricocheted with questions and thoughts as he drove to the office, sipping his coffee.

***

He knew he probably didn't need another coffee, but he stopped anyway to pick one up for himself and one for Norris.

He threw his jacket over the back of his chair, checked his email, and then stepped along to Norris' workstation. He set the coffee on the desk. "Okay Rob, what's new and exciting?"

Norris leaned back, linked his hands behind his neck and stretched. "What makes you think I've got anything?"

"Because you've been too quiet. If you were at a dead end, you'd be on the phone to me."

"You're so sharp, you'll cut yourself." Norris sat forward again. He picked up the file and some loose pages. "Let's go to a meeting room so we can spread out."

Norris picked up the coffee as well. "Thanks for this."

Gordie nodded and led the way to a meeting room and held the door open for Norris before taking a seat on the far side of the table.

"It's not a lot really, but we've definitely confirmed that the money was nothing legitimate. I talked to her work, and her parents. No one had any idea where it might have come from. If she'd won a lottery or whatever, she would have told everyone, her mother is sure."

"Well, it's good to have it confirmed, anyway."

"About 20 minutes ago your girl flipped me the phone records."

"My girl?"

"Albright."

"Unless you want her to start calling you *my boy*, I'd suggest you think again about how you refer to her."

Norris held up his hands. "Okay, okay. Pardon me."

"Anything of interest in the phone records?"

"I just took a first sweep through it, but there are a couple of interesting calls. One was to Sarah's old home number."

Gordie slapped his hand on the table. "I knew it. She was calling the father to let him know she knew it was him."

"Not so fast. There were a couple other interesting calls. One to Jamie as well and then there are a bunch back and forth with her mother of course and one to the church."

"The call to Jamie. When was that?"

Norris studied the page that had various coloured highlighted lines. "He's orange. Let's see. That was the day before she was hit. The one to Sarah's house was the day the news came out with Sarah's identification."

Gordie sighed. "Dammit. It could have been either of them."

"I didn't call either of those two. I figured you might want to set up proper interviews, but I called the church to find out why Mary-Catherine called there."

"And?"

"Father John was busy, but I spoke with the Parish Secretary, Mrs. Adams. She remembers the call and from what she recalls, Father John said that Mary-Catherine wanted to ask about whether or not there'd be a funeral."

"Makes sense."

"Mrs. Adams also thought Mary-Catherine might have wanted

Father Peter's phone number because Father John asked her for the number."

"Well, again, I can understand that. It would have been a shock to hear the news, and Mary-Catherine might have wanted to connect with Father Peter who had known her. He might even do the funeral, I guess."

Norris slid the page over to Gordie. "This one's interesting. In blue. You see it there twice. First on the day before she deposited the money and then again, the day before she was killed. I called it and the number is out of service. Looks like a pre-paid that was used and tossed."

Gordie widened his eyes. "Now we're really talking pre-meditation. Mary-Catherine calls the person she knows or suspects and he says, 'I'll call you back'. The guy picks up a disposable phone and calls her back to set up a meeting. They connect and he gives her a down payment on the blackmail money. Then they talk again and make a date to meet. Out on that quiet road. She's standing there waiting, and that's it. He runs her down."

"It was still risky. Hitting her with the car is extreme, but as we know, not guaranteed. Did he go visit her in hospital to try to finish the job?"

Gordie frowned. "Jesus. Do we know for sure she died of her injuries?"

"I'm pretty sure, but I think it's worth checking into CCTV at the hospital to see what visitors Mary-Catherine had."

"Absolutely. Is there any way to track down the pre-paid phone?"

"Not really. They're sold in batches to places like Walmart or wherever. Even the grocery stores sell them these days, and that's assuming it wasn't something he picked up off one of those internet buy-and-sell sites."

"Right. Well, get on to the hospital. Maybe check with the parents as well. They might even know who came to visit. It sounds like one of them was by her bedside the whole time she was in a coma."

Norris looked at his watch. "I'll give the parents a call now and follow up with the hospital tomorrow."

"I've got some interviews I'm hoping to set up for tomorrow, including both Jamie and the father, but as well the other girl that was part of that youth group. Nothing might come of it, but I want to cover all the bases."

"Right. So, will you be in the office tomorrow?"

"I'll let you know once we've got things set up. Right now, I'm planning on it. It's time to brief the team again."

Norris left and Gordie went back to his desk to call Albright to see what she'd come up with.

He sat down at his computer and saw there was a note there from Albright.

Spoke to Alice briefly. She seemed a bit out of it (Pills? Booze?). I didn't get into the whole theory we spoke about but did ask about the computer. It's a new computer, but she's got the old one around still. She didn't have the info transferred over. I said I'd go by tomorrow to pick it up. I also asked about the bullying business. Sounds like, (according to Alice) it was just because Sarah was very shy when she was in her early teens. She had braces on her teeth and that didn't help, but once she became friends with Mary-Catherine, she gained in confidence and it seemed to just go away. Re: the dad wanting money – he did pester Sarah for money, but she didn't keep enough around to let him get his hands on it. She banked most of her pay and just took out small amounts at a time. Her bank account had a few hundred in it when she left (Alice saw the statements). Alice is now moving forward to get access to the account.

You probably know I got the phone records for Mary-Catherine and I flipped them over to Det. Norris.

Had an email from Donny and I'm setting up an interview. Still working on tracking down Donna Wright.

R.

Gordie typed a note in response.

Good work. Are you OK to go see Alice on your own or do you want to meet somewhere?

He got an answer right away.

I'm fine. Meanwhile, since my first note I found her! Donna Wright lives in Creignish and is now Donna Peddipas. Do you want to go see her? If yes, what works for you?

Gordie grinned. He felt the threads coming together. *Tomorrow morning, if possible. I'm going to see Jamie in the afternoon, but would like to talk to Donna first.*

Right. Stand by. I'm calling her now.

Gordie hoped Jamie would see him in the afternoon. *Should I just show up or call first?* He shook his head. *Better call.*

He dug out the number from the file. "Jamie? This is Detective Gordie MacLean. I have a few more questions for you and plan to come by to see you tomorrow mid-afternoon. Will you be home?"

Jamie's voice was sullen. "I don't get home from work until four tomorrow."

"Then we'll make it for four."

"I don't get what you can possibly ask me more than you already have. I've told you everything I know. Why don't you save yourself the trip and just ask whatever it is now?"

"I like to be face to face, Jamie. I'll see you at four tomorrow." Gordie disconnected.

This is how it worked. Step by step.

Ping! An email from Albright:

Spoke with Donna. Didn't seem too surprised to hear from me! She'll be at home at ten tomorrow morning. Here's the address.

Gordie did a Google Map search and saw that it was a rural address right on Route 19 north of Creignish, but not as far as Judique. He wrote it down and tucked it into his top pocket for tomorrow.

Great stuff. I'll connect with you after I see her. Going home now.

Gordie logged off, stretched, and pulled his jacket from the back of his chair. He knew they didn't have any more answers today than he did yesterday, but he felt like they were making progress. He decided he better just see if Arsenault was in his office and give him a quick update before tomorrow's group briefing.

When he walked down the hall, he heard voices. He gritted his teeth when he discovered Rob Norris relaxing in a chair, having a chat with Sergeant Arsenault.

Gordie tapped on the doorframe. "Am I disturbing you?"

Gordie looked at his sergeant but saw from the corner of his eye that Norris folded his arms in a defensive move.

"No, come in. I saw Norris walk by and asked him to bring me up to speed."

"Right. That saves me from telling you anything about the Cameron case, unless he's also briefed you on the Sarah Campbell case as well?"

Arsenault pointed to the other chair. "Don't get yourself in knots, MacLean. Norris just answered my questions so sit down and give me your report."

"You'll know about the phone records for Mary-Catherine." Gordie kept his voice flat, trying not to betray his anger at finding that Norris had already briefed their boss.

"Yes. I assume you'll be pursuing further enquiries based on that?"

"Albright and I have interviews set up for tomorrow. She's also managed to track down the other boy from the youth group along with a girl. We'll be talking to them to see if they know anything about her movements and friends." Gordie left the briefing at that.

Arsenault nodded. "Succinct as always, MacLean."

Gordie stood. "I'll give a full briefing tomorrow morning to the team, but if you have any other questions now for me?"

Arsenault shook his head.

Norris rose as well. "I was just on my way as well. I'll walk out with you, MacLean."

Gordie nodded to his boss and walked out, not waiting for Norris. He heard the other detective give a cheerful good night to their sergeant, and then he trotted down the hall to catch up with Gordie.

"MacLean, wait up."

Gordie marched out through the main doors and then stopped to light a cigarette. He inhaled deeply then turned to face Norris.

Norris held up his hands. "He called me in. I didn't go around to get a jump on your briefing."

"Right."

"Come on, Gordie. You know me. I just try to get along with everyone. I'm not trying to get on some fast track to a promotion or something."

Gordie took another deep draw, enjoying the feel of the smoke pulling into his lungs. He breathed out through his nose. "This is why I like to work alone. I know where I stand then."

"You know where you stand with me. We worked it out. You're in charge of the case, but if the damn boss calls me in to ask me what's new, then I need to give him something. I can't just say 'Ask MacLean, he's in charge.' It doesn't work like that. Not with Sarge."

Gordie felt his shoulders drop. He finished his cigarette, dropped it on the pavement and ground it out. He bent and picked up the butt and put it into the packet. "Okay. I get it. Maybe next time you can say, 'Let's see if MacLean is still here and we can go through it together.' Something like that. I don't like being blindsided."

Norris nodded. "Or I go out the back way."

Gordie cracked a smile. "Even better."

As Norris walked away, Gordie wondered how far he could trust the other detective.

CHAPTER 23

THE BRIEFING ROOM PULSED with too many bodies. Most had nothing to do with the case, but everyone was interested. They didn't often have murders, let alone two of them. Gordie went first and gave the highlights about the interviews conducted and who they were following up with further. He decided not to mention the lesbian theory since it was pure speculation, and it didn't make a difference to the list of suspects, anyway. Norris took them through what they knew about the money and what he was following up on. Everyone was absorbed, but no one had any insights to add. Arsenault sat in a chair at the front, with his legs stretched out and his arms crossed. Gordie was careful to stay well away from him, not completely confident that the legs weren't there with an intent to trip him.

Gordie closed the briefing, and he went back to his desk, followed by Norris who perched on the edge of the desk. Gordie checked his emails while Norris read from his notebook. "We should hear back later today about the burner phone. I've got Mike working on it. You never know, maybe the phones were all sold to some small place with CCTV."

Gordie closed his email and logged off. "That'd be nice, but we won't count on it."

"No. I'm heading out now as well to go to the hospital and look at their security recordings of the days Mary-Catherine was there. After that, I'm meeting the girl's parents. Do you want to connect later in Port Mulroy?"

"I'll give you a call. I have to get going. I'm going out to the other side of Creignish now."

Norris had turned to go back to his desk when Gordie spoke. "Give me a call first if you find anything, right?"

Norris turned back and nodded. "No problem."

Gordie left the building and forced his mind away from Norris and focussed on the interview ahead. *Donna, I hope you have something new to add.*

***

It had taken just under two hours to get there, but the drive was nice along Highway 30, which also went by the name of Cabot Trail Road as far as Margaree Forks before turning on to 19.

She came out of the house, a big two-storey that looked like it had once been a farm-house to which they had built an addition. The soft green siding was trimmed in white. Flower beds in front of the house showed signs of tulips pushing through the earth. She stood on the covered veranda waiting for him to walk from the car. He lit a cigarette and held up his hand in a wave to acknowledge her. "I'll just have a quick smoke. Go on inside if you're cold."

She shook her head. "It's nice to get some fresh air."

He smoked half the cigarette and then pinched it and replaced it back into the pack.

She put out her hand to shake his before he was at the top step. "Hi. I'm Donna."

"And I'm Detective Gordie MacLean. Thank you for taking the time to meet with me."

He followed her into the house, down a hall and into a large country kitchen. Donna went and clicked on the kettle. "Tea or instant coffee?"

"Whatever you're having, thank you."

She set a Brown Betty teapot beside the kettle and took two tea bags from a canister and laid them beside the pot. She carried two mugs to the table and took out the plastic jug of milk from the fridge. "Sugar?"

"No, thank you. Just milk. I put sugar in the coffee but not in tea. Don't know why that is, but there you are."

While they waited for the kettle to boil, Gordie admired the view from the sliding doors which led out to a large deck off the kitchen. "You have a nice spot here."

She smiled. "It's a bit out of the way, so we need to be organized with the shopping. Not many people just drop by, but we love it."

"Do you have children?"

"Not yet."

"It's a big house."

"It's been in my husband Sean's family for a long time. Luckily, his older brother lives in Halifax and wasn't interested in it, so when his mother wanted to sell, it was an easy transaction. We've done a lot of work to it over the past three years since we've had it. His mom lives in Creignish, sharing a house with her sister. She really never got used to living on her own after Sean's father died a few years ago."

The kettle boiled, and Donna brought the tea to the table and they sat across from each other.

She put some milk in each mug and then swirled the pot in small circles to steep the tea faster.

As she went through the mechanics of making and pouring the tea, Gordie studied Donna. She was slight with short cropped light brown hair, without a lot of concern about styling. *She's a woman who doesn't get too fussed over the opinion of others.*

Gordie took the cup of tea she slid towards him and took a sip. "Lovely, thanks."

"King Cole, made in the Atlantic provinces. Can't beat it."

He laughed. "You're absolutely right."

"Well, what can I do for you?"

"As Detective Albright mentioned, we are investigating the death of Sarah Campbell, so we're meeting with as many people that knew her as possible."

She looked at him over the rim of her mug. "I wasn't friends with her. Not really."

"You were in a youth group together, though. You would have had a fair amount of contact there, I think?"

She took a sip and put the mug down. "Yes, I remember her from that group, but she was closer to Mary-Catherine than to me."

"We know they were good friends, and we talked to Mary-Catherine a couple of times, but as I'm sure you know, Mary-Catherine was hit by a car and has now died of her injuries."

She nodded. "That was awful."

"I'm hoping that we can get to know more about Sarah's life and movements from what you may remember."

She sighed. "I didn't really know much about her life. I knew her before meeting her at the group. We went to the same school for just the last year. I used to go to a different school and then transferred in to the same one as her. I was in French immersion, but I really wasn't doing that great, so it seemed better if I went to an English school."

"And you got to know Sarah."

Donna shrugged. "Yes, but we didn't really hang out together."

"I understand."

"I went to the youth group more to please my mother than anything else. I had some friends she wasn't keen about so after I got into some trouble, we made a deal which had me going to the youth group."

Gordie nodded encouragingly.

"I wasn't really into all that discussion, but I didn't mind going out for the little day trips Father Peter sometimes took us on. Sarah seemed interested, though. She'd really get into it and she knew her bible a lot better than me. Better than any of us, I'd say." She smirked. "Of course, it may just have been that she was really inspired."

"What do you mean?"

Donna lifted a shoulder. "I think she was keen on Father Peter, even though that was a complete non-starter. I get it. He was cute, but I certainly wasn't going to waste my time on someone like that."

Gordie frowned. *This isn't getting me anywhere.* "Did you ever talk to her about boyfriends or maybe girlfriends?"

Donna had been taking a sip when he asked his question, and she started coughing and sputtering. "Girlfriend? You must be kidding. No. She wasn't boy-hungry like Mary-Catherine was, but there's no doubt in my mind that she liked boys. I remember when she went out with that Jamie guy for a while, but she had dumped him before she disappeared. I remember that."

"What about any other boys?"

Donna shook her head. "I never saw her with another boy." She drummed her fingers on the table. "Now that you mention it though, I do remember one time, pretty close to the time she left, or I should say disappeared, when I saw her go by in a car. I was walking, and the car was stopped at the lights right before you head out of town, by the butcher shop, you know?"

He nodded.

"She was in the passenger seat and had the window open so I could see her as plain as anything and I gave her a wave, but she completely ignored me. I know she saw me because before I waved, she was turned towards me."

Gordie felt the hair on his arms raise. "Did you notice who the driver was?"

"No, because I was just focussed on Sarah. I was really annoyed that she ignored me like that. It bugged me for a couple of days because I wondered what I had done to deserve it."

"Did you confront her about it?"

"I did, actually. I saw her outside the church before the next group meeting, so I went up to her. I don't know if confront is the right word. I asked her if I had done something to make her mad. At first it looked like she might deny the whole thing, but then she put her hand on my arm and apologized. She said it had nothing to do with me and please could we just forget the whole thing? So, I said sure. Once I knew it wasn't me, and she had said she was sorry, we just left it and I kind of forgot about the whole thing. We all have weird days, don't we?"

"Donna, I want you to really think back to that incident. Do you remember what sort of car it was?"

"I'm not great at cars. I remember it was dark, but that's all I can tell you."

"Dark. Like blue or black?"

She nodded.

"Donna, when Sarah disappeared, did the police question you? Did you mention this story to anyone?"

She frowned. "No, they didn't talk to me and I never volunteered anything because I didn't think it was important."

"What did you think had happened to her?"

"I thought she went to Halifax. She was smart, and I know she was fed up with her family situation. She sometimes alluded to her father in our group discussions. Like if we talked about forgiveness, she'd talk about how hard it was to forgive him his trespasses. I remember she said that once. So, yeah, I just thought she went off to find work somewhere else."

"Going back to the dark car. If you close your eyes and remember that day, can you give me any more information about the driver or the car?"

She closed her eyes. Gordie listened to the tick-tock of the grandfather clock in the dining room beside the kitchen. She opened her eyes. "No, I'm sorry. It's so long ago and really, if I think back to it, I just see Sarah."

"Did it seem like Sarah was enjoying herself when you first saw her as a passenger in that car? Or do you think she ignored you because she was stressed?"

"She was smiling. She looked happy, and then she turned away when she saw me. I think she was sorry that I had been there and seen her. I don't know why."

"Did you ever see that dark car again? Either with Sarah or without her?"

Donna frowned. "I feel like I did, but I don't know why or where. There was nothing special about it other than it seemed like it was old. Not an antique or anything, but my feeling of it is that there were some things about it that looked old-fashioned. I'm sorry. That's all I can tell you. I was a bit cool with her after that whole ignoring thing, and she was gone pretty soon after it, so I really just forgot all about it until now."

Gordie put his card on the table. "You've been very helpful. If anything else comes to you, however small it may seem, please call me or send me an email note."

She picked up the card and went to the fridge to stick it on the door with a magnet. "I will, but I honestly can't imagine what else I could tell you."

"You would have known Donny from the group as well. I haven't met him yet. Do you think there was any interest between them?"

"No, I can't imagine it. Donny and Gerard were buddies, and although Gerard was a bit like Sarah and sort of into the discussions, I think Donny was more like me. Just there, but not really engaged too much. I don't remember Sarah taking any real interest in either

Donny or Gerard, and vice versa. They didn't seem overly interested in her either. I mean, Donny was into his music and Gerard liked to tinker with things at the farm." She laughed. "I can't imagine that Sarah would be interested in any of that."

Gordie shook her hand. "Thank you again for meeting me. I appreciate it." He lit his half cigarette when he left and finished it before getting into his car.

On to meet Jamie again. What did he and Mary-Catherine have to talk about after Sarah's remains were discovered?

***

Once more Gordie sat on the hair-covered sofa with the dog sniffing him. He let his hand drop beside his knee to make it easy for the dog to push her nose against his skin. "Hi, Hilda. How's the girl?"

Jamie sat across from him with a scowl on his face, waiting for the questions to begin, so Gordie took back his hand, pulled his notebook and pen from his breast pocket and flipped open to a new page. "Jamie, I appreciate your ongoing cooperation with our investigation."

"Like I have a choice." He shrugged. "I just don't get what more I can tell you."

"You've probably heard that Sarah's friend Mary-Catherine Cameron was killed recently."

Jamie raised his eyebrows. "What does her car accident have to do with anything? I thought you were here about Sarah?"

"Because they were close friends, we're asking everyone who knew both of them further questions."

"Such as?"

"Such as what you and Mary-Catherine had to talk about on," Gordie looked at the date of the phone call, "on May 14th."

Jamie frowned. "She called me after the news of Sarah was in the papers. I don't even know how she got my number, but she called out of the blue. She just wanted to talk about Sarah, I guess."

"You knew who she was when she called?"

"Sure, I knew. When Sarah and I were together, we spent a lot of time hanging out all together."

"Was she asking anything in particular?"

He shook his head. "She wasn't really asking anything. Just, 'Did you see the papers? They found Sarah's body.' That kind of thing."

"What was your reaction to hearing from her?"

"It was pretty shocking to read about it, so I guess I was glad to talk to someone. I can't really talk to Linda much about her, you know? She gets in a bit of a snit whenever I bring Sarah's name up."

Gordie nodded. "So, you and Mary-Catherine talked about the discovery of Sarah's remains. What else?"

"Nothing, really. We did a little trip down memory lane, talking about some things we all did together like going to the dances and parties at the beach."

"Did she mention any specific things that may have happened shortly before Sarah disappeared? People she saw her with or places she may have gone?"

Jamie frowned, thinking back to the conversation. "I don't know. She mentioned Sarah's father, I think. She said something like, 'Remember how obnoxious her Dad was? I wonder how she ever put up with living there with him?'"

"And what did you say?"

Jamie shrugged. "I just agreed. I know I wasn't always perfect either, so I couldn't really say much." Jamie's eyes widened. "Jesus. You think Sarah's dad killed her?"

Gordie ignored the question. "Jamie, just for our records, where were you on the evening of May 15th? "

Jamie frowned. "What day was that?"

Gordie sighed. "The day after you spoke with Mary-Catherine. The day she was hit by a car."

Jamie's face paled. "Good God. I had nothing to do with that. I thought it was an accident."

"Can you please just answer the question?"

Jamie picked his phone up from the coffee table and tapped into it. "Wednesday night." He looked up with a grin. "We're in the middle of an eight-week cribbage tournament at the Legion, so that's where I was. Both Linda and me. That's where we were."

Gordie made a note. "Is there anything else you can tell me about your phone conversation with Mary-Catherine? Did she seem nervous or really sad or what? What was your sense of her state of mind?"

Jamie relaxed back in his chair once he provided his alibi for the night Mary-Catherine was run down. He made a wry face. "I'm not great at figuring women out. If I had to guess, I'd say she seemed weirdly excited. For the first couple of minutes, she was all crying and sniffing, but she got past that pretty quick. Oh yeah, she talked about a funeral too. She wondered if Father Peter would come back from Antigonish to officiate. I just said I didn't know." He shrugged. "I'm not much of a church-goer, so I don't know the rules for that sort of thing."

Gordie nodded. "That's helpful. Thank you, Jamie."

As Gordie stood, Hilda leaned against him, so he bent down to give her a scratch under the chin.

Jamie stood as well. "Is that it now? No more questions?"

Gordie smiled. "There are always more questions, Jamie." He left, leaving Jamie with a scowl on his face.

CHAPTER 24

GORDIE DROVE TO THE main Tim Horton's in town. There were always more seats available there than in the smaller one. Before getting out of the car, he called Albright.

"Roxanne. Where are you?"

"I'm just leaving the Campbell's place."

"Did you find anything useful?"

"Mmm. Maybe. Where are you?"

"Sitting in the parking lot of Timmy's on Main."

"Okay. I'll be there in ten minutes."

"I'll see if Norris wants to join us."

"Right. See you shortly."

Gordie dialed again. "Norris? It's MacLean. Where are you?"

"In the security office at the hospital, looking at CCTV."

"I'm meeting Albright at Timmy's on Main. If you finish in the next half hour, come and join us."

"You buying?"

"Depends on what you've got for me." Gordie disengaged before Norris could respond.

Gordie went into the coffee shop and used the facilities. He bought himself a small coffee, knowing that he'd be getting more when the others got there. He took the table in the furthest corner, away from the front door and the tall windows where most people liked to sit. He flipped open his notebook. He liked to summarize what he learned from each interview with a few bullets.

* Alibi – probably solid. Check to make sure.

* M-C excited? Knew she could blackmail someone?

* Talked about Bill Campbell.

* Talked about the funeral. Hoping to see someone there?

He looked up as the door opened. "Albright. Over here."

She came over and pointed to his half-empty cup. "Ready for something else?"

He stood up. "You sit down. I'll get it. What are you having?"

She slid into the bench seat. "Thanks. I'll have an old-fashioned plain donut and a steeped tea."

He nodded. "Milk, no sugar." He took his cup, knowing they'd top it up for him at no cost.

He got himself an oatcake with a pat of butter on the side to go with his warmed-up coffee and brought it all back on a tray.

He sat down and buttered the oatcake. "What have you got?"

"Alice was there, Bill wasn't."

"Perfect."

She nodded. "Alice had dug out the old computer. I can see why she got a new one. The screen has blue wavy lines on it, and it looks likes it's ready to crash at any moment. It took forever to boot up."

Gordie saw her nibbling on her bottom lip. "Okay, don't be coy. What did you find?"

"Photos. Sarah had her own file folder with photos."

"Ah. That *is* good. Did Alice let you take the computer?"

She nodded. "Yup. She said that she took copies of all the pictures that she cared about and had printed some and had some on a disc, so she was fine for me to take it. I've got it in the car. I figured the tech guys could grab everything and save it to an external drive before the darned thing dies on us."

"Good. Well done."

"Did you ask Alice about Mary-Catherine calling the house?"

"I did, but she said she knew nothing about it. It must have been when she wasn't home."

"Hmm. That's interesting. We know that Mary-Catherine called, so she must have spoken to Bill, and Bill didn't see fit to mention it to Alice."

"I know. Intriguing, isn't it? I asked Alice where she and Bill were on May 15th and Alice said that she was home watching television and Bill was at the pub."

"Does she know who he was with?"

"Apparently not."

"So, we need to talk to Bill again."

"I left my card and asked Alice to tell Bill to give me a call."

"Okay. We'll see if he does. Otherwise, we'll track him down. I'd like to look him in the eye when he answers our questions."

Albright broke a piece from her donut and raised her eyebrows. "What about you?"

Gordie reviewed his interview with Jamie as Albright ate her donut and drank her tea. He was just going through the points he had made in his notebook when Norris walked in and joined them.

Gordie stood. "What'll you have?"

Norris glanced over to the glass case which held the pastries. "A large double-double and a cruller. Thanks, Gordie."

Gordie heard Albright ask: "is this your lunch?" and Norris' answering laugh.

When he returned with Norris' order, Albright and Norris both had their notebooks open already.

Gordie sat down and opened his own again. "Can you talk and eat at the same time, Rob?"

Norris took a slurp of coffee to wash down the bite of donut. "Of course." He read from his notes. "CCTV revealed nothing of interest." He looked up. "I went through every day between the victim's admittance and when she died. No one of any interest. Just her family and medical staff."

Gordie nodded. "You're sure the medical staff were all in fact employees?"

"Yeah. I saw them coming and going over the course of the days. No strangers at all."

"Okay. It was a long shot. The person who did this would have really had to have nerve to try anything in the hospital. I'll bet they heaved a sigh of relief when the news came out that she died of her injuries."

Norris nodded. "Bastard. The family's really broken up."

Albright shook her head. "Were they a close family?"

"Seems to be. The brother lives out west, but they spoke regularly on the phone, and Mary-Catherine went to see the parents every week. Took her laundry, had Sunday dinner, that sort of thing."

She continued. "Does that mean they talked together a lot? Do they know anything that might lead us to who did this?"

He shook his head. "She said nothing to the parents about coming into any money and didn't talk about Sarah more than one would expect. The brother is still here though, and he apparently spoke with her the day before she died."

Gordie nudged Norris. "And?"

Norris took another bite of his cruller to make them wait.

"Don't be such a drama-queen. What did he say?"

Norris swallowed and wiped his lips with his knuckle. "He told me *they* talked about Sarah. He knew her fairly well because the girls and he and his friends often hung out together, so it was natural that she would talk to him after they found Sarah. Mary-Catherine asked him about the car."

Norris waited for their reaction.

Gordie looked at Albright, frowned, and turned back to Norris. "The car?"

"You know. The dark car that supposedly picked Sarah up on the day she disappeared."

Gordie felt his heart begin to race. "Does he know who it belongs to?"

"Sadly, no."

Albright groaned. "For God's sake."

"Does he remember it though?"

"No."

"But Mary-Catherine did?"

"Yes. That's the thing. It's key. We know now that it wasn't some random car. Mary-Catherine knew it was important."

Gordie flipped open his book. "I knew that already."

Now it was Norris and Albright's turn to stare.

He continued. "I met with Donna Wright today, or should I say Donna Peddipas? She also mentioned the car. The interesting thing here is that Donna saw Sarah in this dark car before the day she disappeared."

There was silence as that sunk in.

Albright was the first to speak. "Not a stranger picking her up hitchhiking. then. It was someone she knew." She slapped her hand on the table. "I knew it."

Gordie smiled. "It's good to have it validated, though."

Norris nodded towards Gordie's book. "What else did she say?"

"She didn't see the driver, and it seemed as though Sarah regretted that she'd been spotted. She didn't wave back, which pissed Donna off. Next time they saw each other at the youth group Sarah apologized but didn't give any explanation."

Albright bit her lip. "Could she give a better description of the car? Or maybe a license number?"

"You must be kidding. No, and no. The only thing she could add was that it seemed like an older style car. The style seemed old-fashioned but not an antique."

Albright drummed her fingers on the table, a habit she seemed to have when she was excited. "So, Sarah didn't want to be seen. It must be a married man. We're not back to the store manager, are we?"

Norris sighed. "This doesn't get me much further. A car that was old ten years ago isn't around now anymore. It must be someone we haven't even considered yet because you've checked the car that everyone drove back then, right?"

Gordie nodded. "Yes. We did. And it couldn't be a rental. They always look shiny and new. I know. It doesn't get us much further, but we can rule out stranger-murder. It was someone Sarah knew and someone who Mary-Catherine was able to track down. Someone who knows their way around here well enough to either suggest or at least agree to meet Mary-Catherine on a deserted stretch of road."

Albright looked at her notes. "I have her computer."

Norris' eyes widened. "You do?"

"I picked it up from Sarah's mother today. I don't think there's much in the way of documents, like a journal or whatever, but there's a folder of photos, so that might give us something."

Gordie gathered the cups and plates, piling them on a tray. "I want to head home. I need to walk and get some thinking time in. Albright, will you take the computer down to the office? Maybe by tomorrow they'll be able to give us a thumb drive with the photos for us to sort through. Norris, did you have someone go door-to- door along that stretch of road to make sure we haven't missed any witnesses?"

"We did, but there were a couple of places with no one home. I'll go back over that and see where the gaps are."

Gordie nodded. "Spread the net wide." He pointed to Albright.

"I recall what you were saying about riding your bike as a kid and your aunt knowing all about your movements before you even got back to the house." He looked back at Norris. "Someone's seen something. I want to know what." Gordie put his notebook away. "All right. We'll regroup tomorrow morning in the office. And I'll call Sarge this afternoon to give him the latest findings."

Gordie spoke to Sergeant Arsenault on the phone as he drove and gave him the summary of all the day's work.

The sergeant's voice was gruff. "Are you actually getting anywhere with all this running around, MacLean?"

Gordie tried to keep the sigh out of his voice. "Yes, Sergeant. I believe we are. Tomorrow should be revealing when we go through those photos."

"I sure as hell hope so. Two killings and nothing to show for it. The press is continually calling me for news."

"Tell them to have some patience, Sergeant."

Sergeant Arsenault disengaged without another word.

I guess he didn't like that advice.

Gordie needed to think through all the threads. He'd pick up the dog and go for a walk. *Just don't sit down at home, or you won't get up again.*

He'd no sooner had that thought and the phone rang. He saw on the display that it was V. Hunt. *Vanessa.*

He pushed the green button on his steering wheel. "Detective MacLean speaking."

Her voice was tentative. "Gordie? It's Vanessa Hunt. Are you all right to talk for a moment?"

"Certainly. Is anything wrong?"

"No, nothing at all. It's just that when I read about that girl Mary-Catherine being killed in a hit and run, I thought about you and how much pressure you must be under." There was a pause and through the car speaker he heard her breathe.

"Yes, it's been a hell of a week."

"I thought that with everything going on, you may appreciate a home-cooked meal. I'm making a stuffed pork tenderloin tonight, which is way too much for me on my own. You may not have time to actually join me for supper, but I'd be happy to package some dinner up and if you are in the area, you could pick it up and take it home to reheat."

Gordie did a quick assessment of himself. Somehow the tiredness had drained away. "Vanessa, that's very thoughtful. Do you know, that may be exactly what I need. I'm on my way home and I need to work for a couple of hours, but I'd like nothing better than to come over for supper."

"Are you sure you can spare the time? The last thing I want to do is add pressure to your day."

"A home-cooked dinner is exactly the tonic I need, as long as I'm not eating it on my own."

He heard the smile in her voice. "What time works for you then?"

"Seven o'clock?"

"Perfect. I'll see you then."

"Gordie – bring Taz. I have a massive bone I've been saving for her."

Gordie put his foot down on the gas. His stomach had butter-flies, and he wasn't sure if it was because he felt like he was playing hooky, taking an evening away from the case, or from excitement.

***

The next morning after the briefing, Gordie and Albright sat in front of Gordie's nineteen-inch monitor to look at the photos that the technicians had saved to a USB flash drive. Slowly they clicked through the photos one by one. They saw Sarah in a few, her auburn hair shining in the sun of summer afternoons long past. They recognized a much younger, fresh-faced Mary-Catherine laughing and clowning for the camera. Photos of Alice, serious and frowning in the kitchen stirring a pot, Jamie flexing muscles and a host of others with young people they didn't know slowly paraded past in a kaleidoscope of colour. Nothing seemed out of the ordinary for a teenager's photo collection. No one person took centre-stage or seemed more important than others. They came to a series obviously taken at one of the youth group outings. In the background, a lighthouse stood, with cattle lying in the grass in the foreground.

Gordie peered at the photo of the lighthouse. "Where is this? Do you know?"

Albright shook her head. "Google 'lighthouses in Cape Breton'"

He minimized the photo to a quarter of his screen and started clicking through photos of lighthouses. "There. That's it. Cheticamp."

He closed the website and enlarged the photo again, clicking through to the next one. A smiling Father Peter with his arms folded and hair blowing in his face stood beside another man with his thumbs hooked into the front pockets of his jeans. His dark hair was cropped short, and he looked tidy beside the wind-blown priest. Gordie glanced at Albright. "Do you recognize him?"

"Nope. I haven't seen him in any other photos either."

Gordie sent the photo to the printer and then kept scrolling through. More photos of the same place. Gordie recognized Gerard leaning against the white wall of the lighthouse, sun sparkling off the deep blue of the water in the background. There was one with Gerard and another boy doing handstands on a patch of grass between the lighthouse and what looked like an old house. "Think that's Donny?"

Albright squinted at the photo. "It's hard to say. It's pretty far away and I've only seen pictures of him on his website."

Gordie sent this one to the printer as well. "Take these with you when you meet with Donny. See if he can tell you who they are. Especially that older man with Father Peter."

There were a couple more with Mary-Catherine and then one last one with the two girls linking arms with Father Peter.

Albright sat back. "No picture of a dark, older model car."

"No. I guess that was too much to hope for."

Gordie stretched. "You're meeting with Donny this afternoon, right?"

"Yes, I'll have to leave shortly. Did you want to go with me?"

"No, you're doing a fine job. Can you also swing past the church again to talk to Father John and confirm what he talked to Mary-Catherine about?"

Albright made a note. "Sounds good. I'll give you a call later."

"I'm going to track down the missing Bill Campbell. Obviously, he hasn't called you, so I'll run him to ground. Before I go, I'll check in with Norris to see how the door-to-door is going."

Gordie found Norris in the briefing room. He had pinned up an aerial map of the road on which Mary-Catherine had been hit. He had red 'x's marked on certain houses.

Gordie stood next to him and studied the map. "A red x means you've spoken to the residents with nothing gained?"

"Yup."

"Looks like a lot of x's."

"I'm just waiting to hear back on these two." He pointed to the two houses near the end of the road where it merged on to the highway. "Hard to imagine they would have seen much. It's a way from the scene. It's why we haven't really pursued it before now." He held up his hand before Gordie said anything. "But we need to check with everyone. I know, I know."

Gordie nodded. "I'm heading out to speak with Bill Campbell again. I want to ask him about the phone call and press him a little further about the night Sarah died."

Norris shook his head. "Full marks for persistence, anyway. Hard to imagine he's going to cough anything up if he hasn't already."

Gordie shrugged. "Find the right pressure point, and the strongest will crumble."

"If you say so."

***

As he drove, he thought about Bill Campbell. *It's great to say just apply pressure, but what can I pressure him with? God, I'd love to catch the bastard out on something.*

Gordie pulled into the driveway of the Campbell home and Alice answered the door. If having closure with the discovery of Sarah's remains had helped her at all, it wasn't obvious. Her hair was lank and a stain on her black t-shirt, which may have been egg yolk, looked days old.

Gordie nodded. "Good afternoon, Alice. Is Bill home?"

She sighed. It seemed as though she didn't have the energy to even talk to him. "He's not home."

Gordie looked at his watch. "He's finished work by now though, isn't he?"

She nodded. "He'll be at the Legion, I guess."

That suited Gordie. "I'll track him down there then. Can I ask you one question first?"

Alice shrugged. "What is it?"

"Have you noticed any large sums of money leaving your bank account recently? Money to which your husband may have had access?"

Alice scowled. "We aren't the kind of people that have large sums of money lying around. We're waiting for some money to come in from a small life insurance policy that Mr. MacIsaac tells me is coming our way now that we have confirmation that Sarah's really dead. I didn't even know there was such a thing, but seemingly it's part of her benefits. Imagine. We'll be getting ten grand because Sarah was murdered." Her eyes filled with tears.

"But you haven't received the money yet?"

"No. They're going to call when the cheque is ready and then we can pick it up."

"All right, thank you, Alice. Sorry to disturb you."

He got back in the car and drove the few minutes to the Legion. He was tempted to walk to enjoy the spring afternoon, but thought he may not feel so light-hearted after the coming interview.

There was a long concrete ramp that led into the main entrance. They had built the building with older people and veterans in mind. He walked into the low red brick building and stood for a moment to allow his eyes to adjust to the gloom inside. It was a long room with a bar at one end. In one corner a small stage stood waiting for a band. This room would be hopping on a night when they hosted a dance, but now it was quiet. There were three men playing darts and a man and woman sitting at one of the small square tables near the bar. Gordie almost missed him. Bill Campbell sat on a stool at the end of the bar. His head rested on his hand, propped up by his elbow on the bar. A half-empty glass of beer rested in front of him and as Gordie watched, Bill straightened, lifted the glass and drained it.

Gordie walked purposefully towards Bill and he felt all eyes turn to watch his progress through the room. Bill tapped the rim of his glass and slurred an order for the bartender to put another beer in. The bartender watched Gordie approach and nodded when Gordie held up a hand in a silent gesture to stay Bill's order.

Bill saw Gordie, and he frowned. "What do you want?"

Gordie addressed the bartender. "Is there anywhere quiet here that I can have a little chat with Mr. Campbell?"

The bartender pointed to a door halfway along the side. "You can use the kitchen. The door's not locked." Apparently, the man didn't need to see Gordie's badge to know he was someone official, despite the casual clothes.

"Come on, Bill. I won't keep you away from your drinking for long."

He looked like he might protest, but then he muttered a curse under his breath and stood up. He held on to the edge of the bar for a minute, and when he had his balance, he walked towards the kitchen door.

Gordie closed the door behind them, and they sat across from each other at a large table in the middle of the kitchen.

Campbell folded his arms across his chest and stretched out his legs under the table. His chin sank towards his chest and he peered at Gordie through bloodshot eyes.

Gordie pulled out his notebook. "Bill, do you remember Mary-Catherine Cameron?"

Campbell frowned as he processed the question. "Who?"

I should just take him along and throw him in the drunk tank for a while. If it wasn't such a long drive, I would. He'd probably puke in my car before I got him there.

"Mary-Catherine Cameron."

Campbell blinked a few times and then Gordie could see recognition dawning in the man's eyes. He straightened and leaned forward, resting both arms on the table. "Is that Sarah's friend?"

"Was. Yes, she *was* Sarah's friend."

Campbell waved his hand before letting it flop back to the table. "Yeah, all right. Was. Obviously. Sarah's been dead for ten years, so they aren't friends anymore."

"Mary-Catherine isn't anyone's friend anymore, Bill. She was killed in a hit and run." He leaned forward, his face close to Campbell's. "What do you know about that, Bill?"

Campbell blinked rapidly and shifted away, pressing his back into his chair. "Nothing. Jesus. Why would I know anything about that?"

"Why? Let me tell you. We know...," he repeated it, "we *know* that you spoke with the girl on May 8th."

Campbell flushed. "I remember now. She phoned me. She wanted to talk about Sarah. She..." His voice cracked and his red eyes became even darker. He wiped his hand across them.

"She what, Bill?"

His voice was loud and angry. "She was saying crazy things."

Crazy things? Gordie felt a shift in the tone. *Damn. I should have taken him to the station.*

Gordie pulled out his phone and lay it on the table between them. He opened the record function and pushed the red button.

"Mr. William Campbell, I'm going to record our conversation. I want to give you the following warning: You need not say anything. You have nothing to hope from any promise or favour and nothing to fear from any threat whether or not you say anything. Anything you do or say may be used as evidence."

At the formal words, Campbell's mouth dropped open, and he licked his lips. His forehead beaded with sweat.

Gordie nodded towards him. "I just want to make sure that I don't misunderstand what you are telling me. Please go ahead. You were saying that Mary-Catherine Cameron called you on the eighth of May to talk about Sarah, but she was saying crazy things. Please tell me more about that. What kind of things did she say?"

Campbell closed his eyes. His body slumped in the chair. As if a switch had been flipped, he went from belligerent to maudlin. Tears slipped from his closed eyes. He took a breath. His voice was monotone. "First she asked if my wife was home. When I said no, I thought she'd go away, but she seemed glad. I didn't understand. It's like she wanted to torture me."

"Torture you how, Bill?"

"She said that the last few weeks of Sarah's life, she'd been really unhappy, and she asked if I even knew that? I said that we weren't close, so if things were bothering her, I didn't know about it."

Gordie frowned. "That doesn't sound too crazy, Bill. Did she say why Sarah had been unhappy?"

Campbell stared at Gordie, his eyes a red, wet mess. His nose started to run as well. Gordie stood up and gathered a handful of paper napkins from the counter and gave them to Campbell, who blew his nose noisily.

"What else did she say, Bill?"

Gordie had to lean forward to hear Campbell's words. "She said that Sarah—" he looked at Gordie with a lost look. "She said that Sarah was pregnant."

"Pregnant? Did you believe her?" *Dear God, is this what happened? Did her own father make her pregnant?*

"I didn't want to. Sarah was a good girl. She was a good Catholic." He sniffled, tears trickling down cheeks that were criss-crossed with broken red blood vessels.

Gordie tried to keep his voice level. "Bill. Did you make your daughter pregnant?"

Campbell stared, his face blanching from brick-red to wax-white. He stood, weaving momentarily, and then turned abruptly and rushed to the sink and vomited, the acrid, beery stench filling the room. He ran the coldwater tap, first to rinse out his mouth and then to clear the sink. He splashed water on his face and dried it with more paper napkins. When he turned back to Gordie, his voice was quiet. "I'm a lot of things, man, but not that. Never, never that."

He slumped back down into the chair. He crossed his arms on the table and hung his head down, staring at the table. "I'm not guilty of that. Not of that, but yes. I am guilty." And then he put his head on his arms and cried.

CHAPTER 26

DETECTIVE ROXANNE ALBRIGHT WASN'T sure if she preferred being on her own or working together with Gordie. She liked doing the interviews together with Detective MacLean, or Gordie as he insisted, because she always learned something. He had a quiet way that was deceptively astute, and he had a remarkable memory. She wrote everything down in her notebook because otherwise she would forget, but he seemed to pull out salient tidbits without effort. On the other hand, she liked to prove herself. She wanted to move up the ranks, and she knew that being tied to MacLean for any length of time wouldn't do her career any good. Secretly she hoped she would be the one to come up with the breakthrough that would solve this case. Her first murder. It would make her name and put her on the ladder.

So, she met with Donny Boudreau on her own, missing and not missing MacLean's presence.

They met at his sister's house in Hureauville. The scattering of homes that made up the community followed the path of the river, each driveway leading off from Lower River Road.

He was alone in the house, his sister gone for the day with the children and his brother-in-law at work. Donny's freckled face was in a permanent flush as he explained all this as if to convince Roxanne that he wasn't simply squatting in this large empty house.

She smiled at him. "Would it be too much trouble to ask for a cup of tea, Donny? It's a long drive from Sydney to here."

He leapt up from the table. "Yes, of course. I should have asked. I'm so sorry."

As he hustled around, putting on the kettle, putting out two mugs with a tea bag in each, he kept up a running commentary. "I live in the basement here. It helps them with the expenses, and it got me out of my mother's house. I know I should get a place of my own, but it suits me, you know? And we often have gigs on the weekend, so we'd be travelling together anyway, you know?" He seemed to run out of steam then and stood silently waiting for the kettle to boil. He put a saucer for the tea bags, the carton of milk and a sugar bowl on the table.

Roxanne pulled out her notebook and the printed photos but left them folded in half for the moment. "Donny, you aren't in any trouble here. We just want to ask you what you remember from the days before Sarah disappeared. You were friends and we're talking to all her friends."

He sat with his hands wrapped around his mug. "Sure, sure. I get it, but I didn't know her very well. I doubt I can really tell you anything."

Roxanne thought about their previous interviews. "Tell me a little about your friendship. Did you talk to her regularly at the youth group?"

He shrugged. "Yeah, I guess so. I don't remember having any great discussions or anything. Mostly I just wanted to get out of the house, so the group was a place to go. But I didn't *not* talk to her, you know? I mean I didn't dislike her or anything." He blushed even more deeply as if he suddenly thought he might be considered a suspect.

"Yes, I understand. Okay, it sounds like you didn't seek her out to talk to her, but when you did, you got along. Would that be fair?"

"Exactly."

"Did you ever see her with other friends that were not in the group? Maybe someone dropping her off or picking her up afterwards?"

"Nope."

Roxanne stifled a sigh. "What did you think happened to her when she suddenly stopped coming to the group?"

He lifted one shoulder. "I didn't think much about it, really. I think it was a couple of meetings before I even realized she wasn't around and that was only because everyone else was talking about it."

Roxanne tried a different approach. "You play the fiddle, I believe and your sister the piano. Is that right?"

Donny nodded.

"Do you play a lot of the local dances, like in the Port Mulroy or Creignish Legions?"

Again, the nod. "Those are mostly where we play. We can do country western, step dancing. That kind of thing." His voice became more animated as he spoke of his music.

"And you were already playing back then, weren't you?"

"Yes."

"Did Sarah and Mary-Catherine Cameron ever go to dances where you were playing?"

"Yeah, I remember seeing them there."

"And I bet you see a lot from your place on stage, don't you?"

A shrug.

"Do you remember anyone in particular being interested in Sarah at the dances?"

"It was a long time ago."

Roxanne bit her lip. "Yes, it was, but I'm asking you to really think for a minute. Was there anyone at all?"

He drank his tea. "I remember one guy."

"Did you know him?"

"His name was Jamie."

"That was her old boyfriend. Was this after they broke up?"

Shrug. "I don't know. That's the only guy I remember in particular. Mostly she danced with anyone who'd ask her and sometimes her and Mary-Catherine just danced together."

Roxanne unfolded the printouts. "Take a look at these pictures, Donny. This one with you and Gerard. Do you remember that day?"

A smile. "I remember. We had a laugh that day. The weather was good. It wasn't super religious like when we went to a shrine or whatever." He picked up the photo and studied it. He shook his head. "I couldn't do a handstand now."

"Where was this place?"

"Cheticamp."

It was good to have it confirmed. "You're sure? As you said, it was a long time ago."

"I've been there since. See this building here?" He pointed to the building beside the lighthouse.

"Yes, what about it?"

He grinned, and his cheeks pinked. "It used to be where the lighthouse keeper and his family lived. Now it's supposed to be an equipment lock-up or something, but the lock was broken years ago and kids use it as a make-out spot. I haven't been there in years, but there used to even be a couple of beds still in the bedrooms. No one really emptied the house out when the last keeper left or died." He slid the photo back to her. "It's gross, when I think of it now."

Roxanne made a note in her book and then slid the other photo over to Donny. "Who is this man? It looks like he was there on the trip with you."

Donny picked up the photo and frowned, and then his face

cleared, and he laid the sheet down again. "I remember him now. He was another priest. Father Peter and he shared a house I think, but I don't know his name now. I think Father Peter brought him along to help supervise or something. I don't really know why he was there. He spent more time talking to the girls than to Gerard and me."

Roxanne felt sweat prickle under her arms.

"Okay, Donny. Thank you for your help and the tea." She laid her card on the table. "If anything else occurs to you, please call me."

He walked her to the door and closed it behind her with, Roxanne was sure, relief.

CHAPTER 27

GORDIE CHECKED TO MAKE sure the phone was still recording as he stood staring down at Bill Campbell sobbing into his folded arms. He let Campbell get past the worst of the first frenzy while he walked over and picked up the last of the small stack of paper napkins. He placed them on the table beside the crying father.

The movement seemed to break the crying jag, and he slowly straightened. He picked up three or four napkins and wiped his face and then used the last few to blow his nose. He gathered the sodden napkins in a bundle and stood up, walked over to the garbage can and disposed of them before coming back to sit down again across from Gordie. He nodded, as if to say, 'I'm ready now.'

Gordie had his notebook open and his pen in hand. "Mr. Campbell, you just said something very important. You said that you were guilty. I need to hear more about that."

Campbell blinked. "Could I get a beer first?"

"No."

Campbell sighed. "I'm guilty of causing all this to happen." He fluttered his hand before letting it fall back to the table.

"I need more than that, Mr. Campbell. I need to hear exactly. What specifically have you done?"

Campbell seemed lost in his own thoughts.

Gordie became impatient, a little afraid his phone would run out of charge. "Mr. Campbell. Please focus. Did you kill Sarah?"

Campbell sucked in his breath. "Good God, no."

Gordie frowned. "So, what are you talking about? Did you kill Mary-Catherine?"

"Why the hell would I do that?"

Gordie heard his own voice rise. "What is it, Mr. Campbell? What did you mean when you said you were guilty?"

"I mean that I've been a terrible father. A rotten husband. I didn't mean to be. All those years ago when Alice said she was pregnant, I was thrilled. She was beautiful then. Alice did some amateur modelling, even. I couldn't believe my luck that she was going to be my wife and that together we were having a child. I vowed to be the best father ever."

Gordie sighed. "Are you guilty of any actual crimes, Mr. Campbell?"

The man across the table looked like he had aged in the last hour. His eyes were rheumy, and his skin was sallow. "Isn't it a crime to cause your daughter to hate you? Because she couldn't come to me with her problems, all this happened. She was out there trying to deal with things herself and she should have been at home where the three of us could have figured it out together. It's a crime against nature for a parent and child to be so against each other."

Gordie pushed the 'stop' button on his phone.

Oblivious, Campbell went on. "It was the drink. I never drank like this when I was young, but it just got the better of me over the years and now I can't do without it."

"Why did Mary-Catherine call you, Bill?"

It took some effort for Campbell to recall where they had left off with their conversation. "I don't really know. Maybe just to taunt me. She hated me because of how it was between Sarah and me. I thought she wanted me to pay for what had happened. And I will pay. For the rest of my life, I'll pay."

Gordie tried again. "But aside from telling you that Sarah had been pregnant, did she say or ask anything else? Did she ask you for money?"

Campbell frowned. "Money? Like a loan, you mean? Good luck with that. We can barely make the mortgage. No, she didn't ask for money." He paused. "Funny enough, now that you mention it, it did seem like she was trying to get information from me, but I can't imagine what."

"What makes you say that?"

"The way she was talking to me was almost like questions instead of telling me. When she told me about Sarah, she said 'Did you know she was pregnant?' She didn't say 'Sarah was pregnant.' And then she asked me if I knew who the father was."

"What did you say?"

"I was so angry. I told her I didn't believe her, and I hung up the phone."

"But you do believe it."

He shrugged. "Why would she lie?"

"Who do you think the father might be?"

He glowered. "That Jamie fella. There was no one else."

"Just for the record, where were you the night that Mary-Catherine was struck by a car?"

"When was that again?"

"Wednesday, the 16th of May. Just about three weeks ago."

"Wednesdays are cribbage night here. I don't play but I come and watch and have a couple of beers, so I was here." He closed his eyes briefly and then continued. "I remember it now because I wanted to drag that Jamie MacNeil outside and thump him, but I never saw him without his girlfriend. Even so, I almost said something, but there were too many people. I didn't want everyone to know Sarah was pregnant."

Gordie made a note. It would be easy to confirm that. He put his notebook and phone away. "That's all for now. I suggest you go home now, Bill and get cleaned up."

Campbell pushed himself to his feet and took a deep breath. "I've had my last beer."

"I hope for your sake, and Alice's sake, that's true. Get the help you need, Bill."

Gordie turned and let himself out of the kitchen and with a nod to the barman left the building, not waiting to watch if Campbell followed or stopped at the bar.

CHAPTER 28

WHEN ROXANNE LEFT DONNY'S house, she tried to phone Gordie, but the phone wouldn't connect. *Damn, no service. I'll call when I'm done at the church.*

She had called before leaving the office to confirm that Father John would be in and available to talk to her. At the time she thought it would be a quick conversation about what Mary-Catherine wanted on the phone. Now there was a whole new line of questioning. The other priest. The one who had taken off to Alberta.

As she drove, she imagined herself flying to Alberta to confront the man, to bring him home in handcuffs. Of course, she knew that would never happen. The Mounties would be called in to follow up with him, but she might start with a phone interview.

Roxanne pulled into the familiar parking lot. The heavy wooden front doors of the church were locked, so she followed the concrete walkway around to the back. There was a relatively new, newer than the church itself, wooden vestibule built on the back, leading to a simple white entry door. She stopped for a moment before entering, to admire the view. Beyond the old cemetery and the decaying, falling-down cedar-rail fence, the sun shone on the water in the distance. Roxanne enjoyed the feeling of the sun on her face before stepping into the shadow of the covered porch. The door was unlocked, and she let herself in. Steps led up to a short hallway and from an open office door she heard the soft sound of classical music. She called out before arriving at the office, so as not to startle the priest. "Father John?"

"In here."

As before, Roxanne went through the empty front office, where she imagined the parish secretary usually sat, and into Father John's office.

He rose to walk over to the radio and clicked it off. "Good afternoon, Detective. Please sit. On your own today?"

When they were both sitting Roxanne opened her notebook. "Yes, sometimes it's more efficient to share out the work."

"Of course. I'd like to share out more of mine, but my secretary is only here two days a week."

And that answers my question about where she is.

"I won't keep you long, Father. I just want to follow up on the call that you had with Mary-Catherine Cameron. She called you here. Do you remember that?"

He steepled his hands in the way Roxanne remembered. "Yes, of course. Such a terrible business. She called me and then a week later she was dead. It was a shock."

Roxanne nodded sympathetically. "What did you talk about?"

"Not much of anything, really. She asked if we'd be having a funeral for Sarah Campbell, and I said that I imagined we would, but it would be up to the family and I hadn't heard from them yet. She asked me if Father Peter would be there to officiate, and I told her that it was unlikely. According to church guidelines, the funeral should be celebrated in the parish of the deceased. That means that the parish priest," he smiled for a second, the gap between his teeth making the grin endearing, "meaning me, should officiate. Of course, that wouldn't mean that Father Peter couldn't participate in some way if he and the family should so choose."

"What was her reaction to that?"

Father John frowned. "To be honest, it didn't seem to bother her, and my sense was that she was more interested in seeing or speaking with Father Peter than in the actual arrangements for the funeral."

Roxanne made a note. "Go on. What else did you talk about?"

"I remember she was quiet, and I thought she might be upset and trying to collect herself. That often happens with the bereaved, and I just let her take her time. Then she asked me if she could call Father Peter. She didn't seem to know that he was just in Antigonish, only that he wasn't here anymore."

"I said of course, and she asked me if I had his number. I called out to Mrs. Adams to ask her for the number. She wrote it down and I read it out to Mary-Catherine. She thanked me and that was it. We said goodbye."

"Did you call Father Peter to let him know that the girl would be calling him?"

He shook his head. "No. I didn't see any reason to. We aren't talking about a stalker here. Simply a girl looking for comfort at the loss of her friend. Although we now know that Sarah died many years ago, the loss was fresh, as though it just happened. I thought it was perfectly understandable that Mary-Catherine would seek out solace from Father Peter, whom she knows."

"Thank you. I have one more question." Roxanne pulled out the folded photo of the other priest from the back of her notebook. "Do you know this man?"

Father John squinted at the photo. "Isn't that Father Duncan Landry?"

"Who is Father Duncan Landry?"

"Father Duncan was the parish priest in Creignish. He left soon after I arrived here from Ottawa. I believe he's in Edmonton now.

I'm afraid I'm not very good at keeping in touch with people. There doesn't seem to be enough time."

"Can you tell me why Father Duncan left?"

He frowned again. "Where is this leading? Is there something I should know? Perhaps I should be referring you to our Diocese."

She gave a reassuring smile. "We are just doing all the due diligence, Father. I'm not aware of anything amiss with Father Duncan. This photo was taken on an outing with the youth group that Father Peter ran, and where Sarah was present. We've talked to everyone else who was on that outing except for Father Duncan. It's just a matter of closing off any possible threads of information. She may have said something to him, or he may have seen something that could help us in our investigation."

His face cleared. "I know he is from out west, and Father Duncan was interested in going back there. That's really all I can tell you."

"Would you have a phone number for him, Father?"

Father John sighed and stood up. He walked to the outer office, and she heard him opening and closing drawers. Returning to her, he waved a yellow sticky note. "Here you go. This is for the parish."

She stood and walked over to pull it off his finger. She stuck it on the page with her notes from this interview, closed her book, snapping the elastic band that held it closed, and tucked it back into her pocket. "Thank you for your time, Father."

He nodded. "I hope it's been helpful."

She left the same way she entered. Along the hall, down the short flight of steps and out through the covered porch into the spring sunshine. She closed her eyes for a moment against the bright light and heard seagulls crying.

CHAPTER 29

ORDIE WAS DRAINED. HE had been so sure that
it was over. Bill Campbell was about to confess. He had
known all along it was Campbell. Now he realized he had
wanted it to be Campbell so intensely, that he had been too ready to
leap to that conclusion.

He sat in his car and called Albright. "Roxanne. Where are you?"

"I'm just leaving the church."

"How did it go with Donny?"

She told him what she had discovered and then about her conversation with Father John.

He heard the excitement in her voice and tried to settle her
enthusiasm. "We don't know that Father Duncan is in any way connected. He went on a day trip. That's all we know, but yes, certainly
it's worth following up further."

He needed time to think and wanted to cut short his conversation with the keen young detective. "Look, go home now and type
up your interview notes to present at tomorrow's briefing. I'm going
to touch base with Norris and then I'm heading home as well."

He didn't give her time to ask about his interview with Campbell. He disengaged and then called Norris. "How's the house-to-house going? Anything worthwhile?"

"I think so. The last house on the road, the one closest to where it joins the highway?"

"What about it?"

"The people have been away in Cuba. They left at six in the morning of the 16th so they didn't hear about the hit and run until they got home and even then, didn't think much of it."

"The 16th and Mary-Catherine was struck on the night of the 15th. Tell me someone saw something."

"The husband drove past there on the way home that evening. He remembers her car pulled over, and she was standing out on the edge of the road, maybe on her phone, maybe not. It was dusk, so he doesn't know."

"And?"

"And after he drove past, he saw in the rear-view that the car behind him had his signal light on. The car was still a ways back but this fella was sure he would pull over and he was glad because he was feeling guilty, thinking he should have stopped to ask if she needed help. There's a big bend in the road there though and he didn't see anything else."

"Can he describe the car?"

"He only saw it for a second and it was in the rear-view, at dusk, so let's not get excited."

"But?"

"But he is a bit of a car aficionado and thought it might be an old Nissan. He once owned a Stanza, and he thought it looked pretty much the same. It was dark and had a square boxy nose, those were his words, and narrow headlights."

Gordie leaned his head back against the headrest. "An old Nissan. How old?"

"He wouldn't say, but he said his was a 1992 Stanza, and that was the last year they made them here in North America."

"Is it really possible we're still looking for the same car? Let's say it was a '92 Stanza. That's almost a 30-year-old car." He shook his head. "It can't be."

"I know. Surely anyone driving a car like that around here would be known."

Gordie massaged his temple. "Okay. That's great work, Rob. You and your team did well to track this guy down. Go on home and we'll go over it all again in the morning at the briefing."

As much as he didn't feel like it, he made one more call.

Gordie was glad to get Sergeant Arsenault's voicemail. "It's MacLean here. We've had further interviews and at tomorrow's briefing we'll cover the details, but we're continuing to eliminate suspects and we've gathered a few new important facts that will help narrow the field further."

Gordie knew that wasn't quite accurate. Far from narrowing the field, they now had Father Duncan to add to the list and more importantly, they needed to track down the owner of an old Nissan. Assuming the car enthusiast was right.

***

The next morning Gordie took the time for a walk with Taz before leaving for work. The wind off the North Atlantic was crisp, causing his white hair and Taz's matching silky locks to stream behind them.

Gordie's words to his dog were shredded before they even reached her ears. "Where do we go from here, eh Taz? That's the question."

Tears streaming, he turned around, the wind at his back making the return walk easier. Taz kept turning, preferring the wind in her face with all the smells it carried.

Gordie went home, changed into work clothes and wet down his hair so it didn't look quite so Einstein, and was on his way. After the walk, and talk with his dog, his mind was clear, and he was ready to give direction to his team.

After a brief stop to pick up coffee at Tim Horton's, he used the drive to review the points he wanted to summarize in the briefing. He would have Norris and Albright give their own updates, but he'd chat with each of them ahead of time to ensure the focus was on the right things.

***

He was at the office early and took time to add sticky notes to the wall. One had the word Pregnant on it. Another one said Nissan Stanza. And Father Duncan. These would serve as reminders after the briefing for anyone who wanted to stand in front of the wall and mull over the findings. He added the printouts of some of the photos from Sarah's computer, including the one showing the lighthouse and old keeper's house beside it.

Gordie talked to both Albright and Norris when they got in, so they were ready when the rest of the team from the Major Crime unit assembled in the meeting room.

Gordie started. "We've been busy re-interviewing people who knew Sarah, and also those who knew Mary-Catherine Cameron. They need to be the same set of people because we are convinced that the cases are connected."

I spoke with Sarah's father, Bill Campbell again. We know from phone records that Mary-Catherine phoned him shortly before she was struck in the hit and run. Under pressure he told me what the substance of the call was about." All eyes were on him. "According to Mary-Catherine, Sarah was pregnant when she was killed."

There was an audible murmur around the room.

"Based on the conversation as Bill Campbell related it, I believe Mary-Catherine was probing Sarah's father to see what he knew about it. I think she was trying to figure out who the father was, and she considered the possibility that it was Bill Campbell."

The murmur grew louder. He heard some curse words as people considered this abhorrent idea.

Sergeant Arsenault had lost his usual sneer. "Is it possible?"

Gordie shook his head. "I thought it was certainly possible at first but by the end of the interview, I no longer believe that."

Like at a tennis match, the eyes of the audience swivelled back and forth between Gordie and Arsenault. "He had a meltdown while we talked. When I asked him point-blank that very question, he threw up."

"That could be guilt."

"I agree, but the further I probed, the less it seemed likely. He feels extreme guilt all right, but it's more of a 'I let my wife and daughter down' nature versus 'I killed that mouthy kid' nature."

"You aren't letting your gut dictate your conclusions are you, MacLean?"

"Sergeant, if I went strictly by my instinct, Bill Campbell would be locked up right now."

"Well, carry on then."

One of the other detectives called out. "Are you back to the boyfriend then?"

Gordie nodded. "It's an avenue we need to pursue, but he seems to have a solid alibi for the night that Mary-Catherine was killed. Also, they had broken up quite a while prior to Sarah's death, so I believe that if she had gotten pregnant while they were still together, more people would have been aware of her pregnancy. Furthermore, I think that Jamie would have been thrilled if Sarah was carrying his child and would have used it as leverage to get back together with her. Having said all that, we will go back to him and to check that alibi."

Gordie gestured to Albright to take over from him.

She had her notebook open. "I spoke with the last member of the youth group, Donny Boudreau. He wasn't close to Sarah but certainly remembered her. He didn't really have anything to add to our knowledge of Sarah, her movements or her friends. What he did add, though was the identification of this man." She held up her copy of the printout of Father Duncan. "This is Father Duncan Landry. He was the parish priest in Creignish at the time of Sarah's disappearance and he had more contact with her than we first realized. He shared a house with Father Peter West who was the leader of the youth group. We know of at least one occasion when he went along on a day trip with the group. He was transferred to Edmonton so we will contact him to find out what he might be able to add to the picture. According to Donny, Father Duncan and Sarah sat together on the bus for much of the drive so he may know something more about her friends or life." She glanced at Gordie who nodded. He had given her strict instructions not to implicate him any further than simply as a witness. Not at this point.

Norris took her place and held up a photo of a 1992 black Nissan Stanza. "We believe we are looking for this make and model of car. The door-to-door from the area where Mary-Catherine Cameron was killed has unearthed a man who saw a car like this on the night she was hit. Although we can't be positive, the witness has some knowledge of cars and seemed fairly confident it was this sort of car. What makes this very interesting is that it matches the description of the vehicle that Sarah Campbell was seen getting into the night she disappeared."

In the silence that followed, Sergeant Arsenault gave a sceptical snort. "Are you saying you think the same vehicle was used in both crimes?"

"Yes, Sergeant."

"Ten years apart?"

"I know it's a stretch, but that's what it looks like."

"It beggars belief."

Norris' voice was calm. "Well, it's a path we think worth looking at."

Gordie got back up. "So that's what we've got at the moment. Next steps are to follow up on Jamie MacNeil's alibi for the night Mary-Catherine was killed and then speak to him again to gauge his reaction to the news that Sarah may have been pregnant. As well, do some hunting into old Nissan Stanzas that are still on the road around here. Albright will track down Father Duncan to have a quiet conversation. The other piece I want to go back to is the money. Campbell said something useful when I asked him if Mary-Catherine asked him for money. He said 'she'd be lucky' and I think that's a good point. We need to see who amongst our circle of suspects was in a position to give Mary-Catherine Cameron five thousand dollars at short notice. That's it for now. We're making progress." He glanced over at Arsenault. "I feel it in my gut."

Many of the detectives chuckled as they filed from the room.

CHAPTER 30

GORDIE MET WITH ALBRIGHT and Norris after the briefing in front of the wall. "Roxanne, you'll give Father Duncan a call. You know what to ask?"

She nodded. "No problem, Boss."

He grimaced. "Right. Norris, you'll need to keep digging into this car. I think that more people will know something of this car. It's unique. It's old, but still driving around. So far, the focus has been on the road where Mary-Catherine was struck, but what about in Port Mulroy? The car must have had damage, and even if the driver hasn't brought it in for repair, they may have taken it somewhere over the years to keep it running all this time." Gordie tapped the picture of the car. "Someone's seen the damn car. Let's find them."

Norris made a note in his book. "They may be cautious and not go local, but we'll start calling around further afield. Antigonish, Truro, Halifax even. But you're right. We know that Donna saw Sarah in that car right in Port Mulroy, so we'll start with local. mechanics in Port Mulroy, Sydney, wherever."

"Good. After Albright talks to Father Duncan, let's get back together to address the money question." He turned to her. "See if you can figure out if he's got the cash to give five K up without anyone noticing."

Norris frowned. "But was he in Port Mulroy when Mary-Catherine was run down?"

"Good question."

Albright nodded.

Gordie shrugged. "Even if he wasn't, it doesn't take him out of the frame. You know there are people who will do just about anything for the right price."

"But they needed access to the old car."

Gordie nodded. "True. It all comes back to the car."

Gordie looked at Albright. "You're quiet."

She tapped the photo of Father Duncan with the lighthouse in the background. "I'm wondering why they even went there for a day trip. I can see if they went to Saint Peter's Church in Cheticamp. That's beautiful. But why here?"

The three stood staring at the photo until she spoke again. "Donny said that he found out later it was a real make-out place. I wonder if Sarah knew that already and if the place had special meaning to her."

Gordie tilted his head. "You think she had some influence on choosing the destination?"

"I don't know. I just think it's an odd place to take a church youth group."

Gordie nodded. "There's another question to ask Father Duncan, or perhaps I'll call Father Peter. Yes, that makes more sense. He was in charge of the group. I'll call him. Good question, Roxanne."

Gordie turned away from the wall of photos and sticky notes. "Let's get to it." He looked at his watch. "Timmy's on Main Street in Port Mulroy at five o'clock?"

The others agreed, and they got ready to chip away on their separate tasks.

***

Gordie was thoughtful as he drove. *The money. That and the car. What a stroke of luck that the car is unique. If it actually is. We could be chasing our tails on that one, but it seems worth chasing.*

Gordie was tired. *God, I'd love to see if Vanessa's home later. Maybe pick up a pizza, and Taz and head over there. Funny how, although her home is a crime scene, still it's one of the most restful places I know.* He tried to put her to the back of his mind and concentrated on the interviews ahead. First, he'd go to the Legion to confirm Jamie's alibi for the night Mary-Catherine was struck down. Next, over to find Jamie and see his reaction to the news that Sarah was likely pregnant. After that, a call to Father Peter to see what had inspired the day out at the lighthouse at Cheticamp.

As he drove, he called John Allen at the lab. "Hey John, MacLean here. Listen, there's some new information that leads us to believe that Sarah was pregnant. Is there anything you can tell forensically to confirm or deny that?"

There was a silence as he considered the questions. "No. If she had given birth, I'd be able to tell from the bones, but pregnant? 'Fraid not."

Gordie sighed. "It was a long shot, but I thought I'd try. Thanks anyway."

"Good luck. If there's anything else, don't be afraid to call."

Gordie smiled as he disengaged. "As if."

For the love of God, Mary-Catherine. Why didn't you tell us what was really going on? You thought you could make money from your friend's death. That's pathetic, but I should have been more tough with you. You were hiding something, and I knew it. Dammit, I should have pushed you. If only I had, you wouldn't have died. Gordie felt his heart racing as he thought about what he should have done instead of what he actually did. He knew this was masochistic, but he couldn't help himself.

He shook his head and turned up the radio when one of his

favourite Celtic songs came on. *I can't dwell on it. Just move forward.* He was actually surprised that Sergeant Arsenault hadn't given him grief over this point. Maybe he didn't understand the full scope of Mary-Catherine's death and that he, Gordie MacLean could have, should have, prevented it.

Gordie turned his focus to Jamie. He really didn't believe that the boy was the father of Sarah's baby, or that he even knew about it. *No, Sarah had hidden this secret. Why? Because the father of the unborn child was married. Had to be. It would explain things. The secrecy in the car, the fact that no one knew about who she was seeing. Even her best friend didn't know, although she did know that Sarah had been pregnant. Did that make sense? Would a girl tell her friend that she was pregnant without revealing the identity of the father? Maybe.*

Gordie had wanted to go directly to the Royal Canadian Legion to confirm Jaimie's alibi for the night Mary-Catherine was struck, but it didn't open until three, so he came here to Jamie's instead. He pulled into the now familiar drive of the clay- coloured mobile home. *This kind of place would drive me crazy. No privacy, no space to breathe.* He knew that for many people it was the only path to homeownership, and in the grey drizzly morning, he saw signs of tulips and daffodils pushing through small flower beds in front of some of the homes.

The door opened, and Hilda bounded out to greet Gordie like a long-lost best friend. He bent down and murmured to her as he grabbed her collar to ensure the dog came back into the house with him.

Jamie nodded. "Thanks. She doesn't usually take off, but you never know."

Gordie released the dog into the house and straightened. "Hi, Jamie. This shouldn't take long."

Jamie nodded and stood leaning against the kitchen counter. There was no offer of tea or to take a seat in the living room. Gordie slid his hands into his jacket pockets. He didn't take his notebook out. This question only needed his eyes on Jamie's reaction.

"We heard that Sarah was pregnant. Did you know?"

His face paled. "Jesus. No, I didn't know." He moved from standing at the counter to sit at the small round kitchen table.

"Were you the father, Jamie?"

"God, no. For one thing we always used protection and for another, she dumped me months before she disappeared. I told you that. She would have been, like eight months or something by August, if it had been mine."

"You sure you didn't have a one-night 'break up sex' thing with her?"

He frowned. "I promise you, I didn't. I'm not saying I wouldn't have, but she was not, and I mean *not* interested." He sighed. "In the beginning we talked about having kids. We both wanted them. She really did and I bet if I hadn't insisted on using protection, she probably would have gotten pregnant quite happily. I think she believed she would do a much better job of being a parent than what her parents did. She couldn't wait, but there was no way I was ready." He paused, his shoulders slumped, and his voice grew quiet. "And she was right. She would have been a great mother. I know she would have."

Gordie was sure he was telling the truth. "All right. Thank you, Jamie. I'm going to ask you again. Who might the father have been? You followed her around for a bit, you shared some of the same acquaintances. Who could it have been?"

The young man frowned and rubbed his forehead. "I don't know. Honestly, I never saw her with any one guy. Sure, I saw her at a couple dances, but it never seemed to me that she was interested in anyone. Maybe she was paranoid that I'd get jealous, and she was extra cautious, but I just don't know. I'd tell you."

Gordie nodded. "I'll leave you now. If you come up with an idea, however unlikely, let me know."

***

He was still a few minutes early, so Gordie stood under the overhang by the front door having a smoke. As he stood, watching the rain drip down from the roof edge, he enjoyed the freshness of the air with its promise of new beginnings.

He was just about finished his cigarette when the bartender he had met previously drove in and parked at the far end of the lot. He walked briskly through the rain, but didn't have an umbrella or a hood, not seeming to care about getting water down his neck.

Gordie nodded as the man joined him under the covered concrete front entry. "We met briefly a few days ago. I'm Detective Gordie MacLean."

The man lit up his own cigarette and offered one to Gordie, who pointed to the butt in the bucket of sand and shook his head. "Just had one, thanks."

The man, who looked to be in his early sixties with a short salt-and-pepper brush cut squinted through a cloud of smoke. "You're back again, then. Bill Campbell won't be here for another couple hours, if he comes at all. I haven't seen him since you were here last. What did you do to him to scare him away?"

Gordie gave a small smile. *There may be hope for Campbell yet.* "I'm sure you know there's nothing I could say to keep him away. That's his choice."

The man held out his hand. "Syd Armstrong. You're right. Let's hope it sticks. So, why are you here, then?"

"To talk to you."

Armstrong finished his cigarette and buried the butt in the sand. He pulled out his keys and unlocked the double-locked door. "You better come in, then."

Gordie followed Armstrong as he flipped light switches on his way to the bar.

He shrugged off his jacket at the chrome coat rack pushed against the wall beside the door to the kitchen and hung it up. He then pulled out a bar stool and sat down. "You have my undivided attention. What can I do for you? Is this about Sarah?"

Gordie raised his eyebrows. "Did you know Sarah?"

"Sure. Bill and I used to ride the school bus together although he was a few years behind me. We aren't friends as such, but I knew the whole family. Alice was a real looker once." He chuckled. "There was more than one of us jealous of him. But Sarah? I knew her to see her, to wave hello. If she came in here for a dance or cards when I was home on leave, we'd chat."

"On leave from what?"

"Twenty-five years in the Navy. Sarah disappeared while I was away. Posted to Esquimalt B.C. at the time, but I heard about it from my folks who still lived here then. We all figured she ran away to get away from a bad family situation." He shook his head. "Never imagined she was murdered. So sad."

"You're retired now?"

"Yup. Five years ago. I have a nice pension and I work here 25 hours a week. Every day from 3 to 8 pm five days a week and a bit more if one of the others can't make it for their shift. I like being back home. My mom's still alive and living in an assisted living place in Sydney and my brother lives in Truro."

Gordie nodded. "It sounds like you know the people who come here and notice what they're up to."

Armstrong grinned a smoke-stained smile. "The lot of a bartender. I like it. People are friendly and there's always something to watch and think about from my spot behind the bar."

Gordie pulled a photo out of his inner pocket. "Do you know this guy?"

He frowned. "Sure, that's the MacNeil boy. He hasn't done anything has he? I figured him for a good one."

"So, you know him. Good." Gordie pulled out his phone and opened the calendar to show the month of May. "I know you only work until eight, but were you here the evening of May 15th?"

Armstrong got off his stool and walked over to where his jacket hung. From the inside pocket he pulled out a small calendar book and returned with it. "What day did you say?"

"May 15th."

He nodded. "Oh, I remember that night. Cribbage tournament night. I was here until ten because the guy who takes over from me had a birthday thing for someone, so I covered a couple hours for him. It was busy at first, but once people settle down, they're focussed on the game."

"Was Jamie MacNeil here? Can you remember?"

Armstrong closed his eyes and then opened them pointing to a table by the window. "He and the wife sat there."

Gordie smiled. "I don't think she's his wife."

Armstrong shrugged. "To me, if someone is part of a couple, she's the wife until they break up. Could be weeks, could be forever."

"Fair enough. You're sure he didn't leave for a period of time?"

"I'm sure. A player going missing would create a stir."

Gordie stood. "That's all I need. Thank you for your help."

"You aren't going to tell me what it's all about?"

"Not now. Maybe when this is all behind us, I'll come in for a drink."

Armstrong nodded. "Sounds good. I better get at it, then. The thirsty hordes will be arriving any time now."

As Gordie walked back to his car, he mentally put a line through Jamie's name. *That's another one off the list. Our pool is getting smaller. Am I missing someone?*

He got back in the car and looked up the number for Father Peter. Why did they go to the lighthouse that day?

CHAPTER 31

ROXANNE SAT AT HER desk with a fresh page open in her notebook. First, she called the Archdiocese of Edmonton where Father Duncan was now working. They gave her the number for the church in Hinton which was his actual parish. Upon calling there, she discovered that he was on his way to Jasper, about an hour away, to officiate over a funeral, as the parish priest there was down with the flu. Reluctantly the parish secretary gave up Father Duncan's cell phone number, warning Roxanne that she'd be better off simply to leave a message in Jasper to have him call at his convenience. "There are a lot of places where there isn't any cell service."

Roxanne responded with a sympathetic tone. "It's the same around here. Lots of places with no service, but I'll give it a try just the same."

She dialed the number, and in one of those quirks of mobile phone usage, she got through after one ring and the reception was as clear as if he were just down the road.

"Father Duncan Landry here."

"Father Duncan, this is Detective Roxanne Albright calling from the Cape Breton Police Service."

"Cape Breton. My goodness. It's nice to hear your accent. I have to warn you, Detective that I could lose you at any time, so apologies ahead of time if that happens."

"I understand. Let's get right to it then while I have you, and if I do lose you, can you please call me back when you have service again?"

"Very good. Go ahead. What's happened?" His voice was suddenly alarmed. "Has someone I know died?"

Interesting that this would be his first thought. "There is no emergency. We are working on an investigation that you may help us with. Do you know the name Sarah Campbell?"

"Ah, Sarah. Yes of course I remember her, and I read in the paper that her remains have been discovered. So very sad. Such a lovely, friendly girl."

"Father Duncan, you'll recall then that Sarah was a member of a youth group that your housemate, Father Peter ran."

"I do, of course."

There was some crackling noises and Roxanne was afraid she was losing him, but then he came back again. He was saying "I went along a couple of times on field trips and remember her as a bright, interesting girl."

"It's about those field trips I want to talk to you. Where did you go?"

"I went along on two of them as far as I recall. Once we went to the Guadalupe Shrine. Beautiful peaceful little spot with gardens and a shrine. We had a picnic and discussed missions. Very nice. It's not often you get young people willing to talk about those things these days." His voice was warm with the memory.

"Where else did you go?"

"We went to some lighthouse once. I'm sorry, I can't recall the exact one now. It was a long time ago."

"Why did you go there, Father? It doesn't seem like a very holy place to take a Church youth group."

"I agree. It was rather an unusual choice. I think Father Peter just liked to take the group out. Part of the point of the whole thing was just to get the kids talking. I remember having a great chat with one of the boys about farm machinery. He was quite enthusiastic about fixing things as I recall."

That must have been Gerard. "I see. I understand you spent the drive sitting beside Sarah. Do you remember that?"

"Vaguely. I couldn't tell you now what we talked about, if that's what you're asking."

"Did you ever go anywhere with her when it wasn't a group outing, Father?"

His voice was hesitant now. "Are you asking me if I was ever alone with Sarah?"

"I am. Perhaps she came to you for help with a problem? She had a troubling home life I believe."

"No, Detective. I was only along on those couple of occasions to help Father Peter. The kids were his parishioners, not mine. If Sarah was troubled and wanted someone to talk to, it wouldn't be me. It *wasn't* me."

Roxanne switched topics. "All right, thank you. We're just trying to investigate every avenue to see if someone can shed more light on why she was killed. Father, did you know anyone who had an old black car, maybe a 1992 Nissan Stanza or something that looked similar?"

The air was filled with static again, and his voice faded in and out, but Roxanne heard him laugh. "That old thing? Sure. Boys and their toys. I can't believe..."

She lost him completely. "Damn, damn, damn." She looked at her watch. He should be arriving within the next 45 minutes. She'd wait here at her desk until he called back. She couldn't take the chance that he might call her only for her to be in an area with no service.

***

Gordie sat in the car with the windows down and called Father Peter. He was pleasantly surprised to reach him on the first attempt.

"Father Peter, this is Detective MacLean."

Gordie heard a barely stifled sigh. "What can I do for you, Detective?"

"We've been going through our notes as we continue to put together the events leading up to Sarah's death. You told us you sometimes took your youth group out for short day trips."

"That's right."

"There was at least one occasion when you took them to the lighthouse near Cheticamp. Do you remember that?"

"Yes, now that you remind me of it, I remember that. What about it?"

"Why there, Father? It doesn't seem to have any religious significance that I can find, so why there?"

"From what I recall, one of the kids mentioned it as a beautiful spot. It can't always be about shrines, Detective. Nature provides plenty of opportunity to meditate on spiritual things."

"I agree with you there, Father. I'm a great advocate for finding tranquility in nature. It just seemed like an unusual choice. Do you remember who suggested it?"

His voice was clipped with irritation. "No. It was a long time ago."

"True. I was also curious why you invited your housemate, Father Duncan along on that particular day."

"Good Lord, Detective. I have no idea. Maybe he was at loose ends that day. I remember it being a particularly nice afternoon so maybe he just wanted to come with us. What does it matter?"

"Do you think it was his idea to come along?"

There was a short pause before Father Peter responded. "I don't know. Again, why does it matter?"

"Did Father Duncan show any special interest in the kids?"

"The kids, as in Sarah?"

"Yes, Sarah."

The irritation in Father Peter's voice obvious now. "No. No special interest in anyone. He hardly even knew any of them. His parish was in Creignish, and while he may have seen some of them around, I don't believe he knew any of them personally. What are you suggesting?"

"I'm not suggesting anything. We've seen some photos of that particular outing and saw that he was there. Naturally I wanted to understand how that came about."

"Photos?"

"Yes, from Sarah's old computer."

"I see. Well, there's nothing more to it than an afternoon out to enjoy the area, as the photos probably showed you."

Gordie chuckled. "I heard that particular place is a real make-out place for kids. Did you know that?"

Again, a pause. "No, I certainly did not. I wouldn't have taken them there if I had known."

Gordie felt something lurking in the spaces between the words, but he knew he wouldn't get anything further right now.

"Thank you for your time, Father Peter. I just wanted to hear your take on that day out."

Father Peter's voice was raised. "My *take*? What does that mean?"

"I'm sorry. I didn't mean anything by it. Detective Albright is speaking to Father Duncan right now, so it's always helpful to us to get two…perspectives… on an event."

"Are you accusing Father Duncan of some kind of wrongdoing? I'm sure you can't have any evidence of that, since I am confident that he is completely blameless."

"We aren't accusing him of anything. I just find his departure from the area interesting in terms of the timing. It was very close to the time that Sarah disappeared, wasn't it?"

Gordie was sure he heard the other man licking his lips before answering. "That may be, but it is purely coincidental."

"Thank you, Father. You've been very helpful. Goodbye."

Gordie disengaged and put his phone back into his pocket. He didn't have the date that Father Duncan left, but given Father Peter's response, he was going to look it up.

He looked at his watch. Still a bit early to meet the others. He had about half an hour to spare. Maybe he could help Norris. He pulled out his phone again.

"Norris? MacLean here."

"How's she cuttin'?"

Gordie shook his head. "You get to be more of a Newfoundlander every day. I'm done with my calls. Any local mechanic you want me to visit?"

"There's one guy. He's got his own business out of his home. We heard he specializes in old cars because his brother runs a junkyard."

"Give me the address." Gordie pinned the phone between his ear and shoulder and pulled out his notebook and pen.

Norris gave him the directions. "Thanks for this. I was just going to try to call him, but I know how you like to cast your eagle eye on things in person."

"No problem. See you soon." Gordie punched the address into the GPS. He might run a bit late for his meeting, but Albright and Norris could enjoy their coffee while they waited for him.

He headed north on Route 19 in the direction of Creignish.

CHAPTER 32

HALF AN HOUR AFTER she'd lost contact with him, Father Duncan called Roxanne back. He'd finished what he started to tell her and then he had to run to prepare for the funeral.

She had sat for a moment debating about whether to call Gordie right away, but she knew he was involved in his own interviews and she didn't want to distract him. At least, that's what she told herself when she stood up and grabbed her jacket to head out.

Now, as she drove, she chewed on her lip. *Maybe I should call him. He'll be really pissed if I do anything to mess this up. Maybe there's nothing to see after all this time.* She gave her head a mental shake. *I'll just do a quick reconnaissance and then I'll give him the full report at five o'clock when I see him.*

Roxanne felt her stomach churning. So close. They were getting so close to catching a killer. If the car was still there, she wouldn't touch it. She'd go and meet Gordie and let him take over. They'd get it picked up by the forensics team.

She turned up the music to distract her from her thoughts, but when the news came on, she realized she had been driving in a fog with no idea of what had been playing on the radio.

Roxanne passed through St. Peters, Louisdale and Port Mulroy proper. She slowed down then to search and saw the turnoff to Parish Lane. *Where it all began. No, where it all ended.* A little further she saw it. A small lane on the left, heading west towards the water. There were some new houses here now. Property close to the water was becoming more desirable. The old farms were crumbling and falling to pieces, and like a phoenix, grand new houses were rising.

She pulled over. Here. The farmhouse itself, set back from the road a hundred feet was still intact but slowly falling in on itself. The boards, that had once been white, were now blackened with age and mould. There were still curtains in the upstairs windows, but the front door was pried open and hanging on one hinge. It was once someone's pride and joy, and not that long ago. Ten years ago, this house had still housed people, but when the widow who owned it had died, it was abandoned.

Roxane got out of the car and took a couple of photos. The roof was still in good shape. The building wasn't beyond hope yet, but Roxanne knew no one would take the trouble to fix it up. Soon, no doubt, the property would finally be sold and the house and barn bulldozed down.

She walked up the driveway, whose gravel was still in surprisingly good condition, crunching underfoot. Small spruce trees and alders sprung up amidst the stone, but it was still driveable. There were large clumps of wild roses flourishing along the driveway.

The barn was hidden behind the house, almost invisible from the road. Only the top of the rusted metal roof revealed that the building was there. The driveway looped around to the back and Roxanne walked along the overgrown drive, looking closely at the house to ensure there were no spying eyes watching her progress.

When she came around the back of the house, she stopped and sucked in her breath. There was a car parked in the patch of brown weeds in front of the barn. The building itself seemed in better shape than the house. A set of corrugated tin sliding doors hung over a wide opening, closed and concealing the interior of the barn. There was a window that held a rotting piece of chipboard hanging from one corner. Possibly the window had been boarded up at some time and either with the assistance of time or a pry-bar, had been pulled away. The glass remaining in the decaying frame was broken and jagged. Roxanne knew it was time to back away and get help. She hadn't expected anyone to be here. Just as she made up her mind to retreat, she heard him behind her.

"You shouldn't have come here, Detective."

Roxanne stood still, feeling the pressure of the muzzle in her back. *Can I get the gun away from him if I turn fast enough?*

The moment passed. He was fully in charge. "I'm reaching into your pocket to remove your Taser and your phone. If you move in any way, I'm afraid this gun will go off, so be a good girl and don't move."

She stood still and allowed him to reach into her jacket pocket, quivering with rage at the invasion.

"Walk on to the barn. You're here for the car, aren't you? Well, you might as well go and see it."

He clasped the neck of her jacket to ensure she didn't run. With one hand holding her firmly and the other pressing the gun into her back they made their way to the barn in an oddly intimate tango-like dance step. Their two right legs stepped and then their two left.

"Go around to the right. There's a man-door there that's unlocked."

She still hadn't said anything; her brain frozen. She licked her dry lips. "What are you going to do?"

"I don't have a lot of choice, do I?"

"Of course, you do. Sarah may have been an accident. I don't know, but this? Killing a police officer? You're too good for that."

They reached the side of the weathered grey barn and she pushed open the chipped and rotting wooden door. Roxanne stumbled as she stepped over the raised door frame, but he gripped her jacket tightly and she stayed upright. Roxanne blinked in the sudden darkness inside, the only light coming from the uncovered window. He shoved her forward to a bench built against the wall near the door.

"Sit down and don't move. Don't talk. I need to think."

She sat down, and in the dusty gloom, her eyes now adjusted, she saw him. He wasn't dressed in his dapper sport jacket, nor was he wearing his dog-collar. Father Peter looked like any man in his early forties, except he was perhaps better looking than some.

He leaned against the black Nissan parked in the barn. On the far side of the building were pieces of debris from the abandoned farm. Rusting machinery, broken chairs, an old stove and a couple of broken, rotting bales of hay lined the far wall. Desperately, Roxanne scanned for something she could use as a weapon, but even if she could make it that distance, there was nothing that looked useful.

Roxanne sucked in her breath. Peter seemed to come to a decision and straightened up, his eyes sorrowful.

***

Gordie pulled into the mechanic's yard. There were several cars in varying stages of disrepair parked beside the large garage and he wondered if they were waiting for, or the providers of, spare parts.

A man in his fifties wearing a ball cap and blue coveralls stood hunched over the engine of a boat-sized white Pontiac Bonneville. He looked up as Gordie got out of his car. The mechanic pulled a greasy rag from his back pocket and wiped his hands before coming around from the front of the car in the garage out into the afternoon light.

"Can I help you?"

Gordie pulled out his identification. "Detective Gordie MacLean."

The man nodded. "Dennis LeBlanc. What can I do for you?"

Gordie pulled out the printout of the Nissan Stanza. "Ever work on this car?"

Dennis came closer and peered at the picture and then shrugged. "Worked on just about everything over the years. Why? You have one that needs work?"

"We're looking for a car like this. We believe someone's got one and we're hoping you've been helping to keep it on the road."

The man frowned. "You have a VIN number?"

"No. We can't find one registered to anyone locally, so it might not actually be this exact make and model but one that looks similar. Ring any bells?"

LeBlanc considered the question and folded his arms across his chest. "Maybe."

Gordie felt his heart speed up. "Don't be coy. What can you tell me?"

LeBlanc unfolded his arms and pulled off his ball cap. He ran his hand through his wiry red hair and then replaced the cap. "It's been quite a while since I saw it, so it might have gone to the scrapyard by now for all I know."

"Go on."

"There was an old lady," Dennis waved his hand vaguely back in the direction of Port Mulroy "who used to have one. Hardly used it, because it belonged to her husband and he died about 15 years ago, and although she had a license, she didn't really like to drive."

Damn. An old lady? Are we chasing our tails here? Maybe she hit Mary-Catherine by accident. "Does she still have it?"

"Doubt it." He gave a slow smile. "She died."

Gordie sighed. "Oh, for God's sake. When?"

"'Bout eight years ago, give or take."

"Do you know who inherited the car? A son? Maybe a grandson?"

"They never had kids."

This was like pulling teeth. "OK, no kids. So, do you know who inherited the car? It went to *someone.*"

"I couldn't really say. You'd probably want to check with Mrs. Scott's executor."

Gordie fought to keep the exasperation from his voice. "Do you know who that is?"

Dennis nodded. "I heard that Father John over at Our Lady of Mercy looked after things when Mrs. Scott died. She didn't have any people to do for her."

Gordie nodded. "And you haven't seen this car recently?"

"No, no, can't say I have."

"Thank you. You've been helpful."

Dennis nodded and turned away to return to the Bonneville while Gordie went back to his car to make a phone call to Father John. Damn him. Why wouldn't he have mentioned the car before now? As he waited for the priest to answer the phone, Gordie's mind churned. *Mrs. Scott, Mrs. Scott. Why was that name familiar? Was that the old lady that owned the house before Vanessa? God almighty, have we come full circle and it was someone who belonged to that woman?*

He almost gave up hope when the phone was answered. Gordie heard the huffing of a man who had run for the phone and as Father John was still gasping out "Our Lady of Mercy, Father John Sullivan speaking."

"Detective MacLean here, Father. I need to ask you about an estate for which you were the executor a number of years ago. Name of Mrs. Scott. Do you remember it?"

"Yes, of course. What about it?"

"Father, she owned a car. A black Nissan Stanza. We've been searching for that car. Who inherited the vehicle, Father?"

Gordie listened to the panting as Father John tried to compose himself. "There was no car."

Gordie frowned. "I've just heard from a mechanic out here by Creignish that Mrs. Scott once owned a car like the one we've been looking for. What happened to it?"

"I'm telling you Detective, that when I took this over, there was no car. There's an old house with an out-building and about five acres of land, but that's it."

"You say you took it over. What does that mean?"

"Mrs. Scott left everything she had, in other words the house, to the church. That was shortly before I got here and so Father Peter was looking after it with a local lawyer, but when I came and Father Peter moved to Antigonish, it landed on my desk. I went out there once to look at it and quite honestly, I'm not sure we'll ever sell it. The church considered renting out the house, which is why I went out there with Father Peter to look at it, but it was in a deplorable condition and it would have been more costly to make the repairs than we would have ever made in rent."

"Is the house on Parish Lane?"

Father John's voice was puzzled. "What? No. It's beyond the church, on the way to Creignish."

Gordie sighed. "It's just abandoned land then up for sale?"

"Yes, pretty much. I suspect even the sign has fallen down by now. I really should go out there one of these days to have a look. It's such an out of the way spot. I can't imagine what the Diocese was thinking to imagine I might want to live there." The priest had caught his breath again. "How Father Peter and Father Duncan managed all those years is beyond me, but of course Mrs. Scott was alive then, so it probably was fine at that time."

"Wait. Are you saying that this property is the house that Fathers Peter and Duncan shared?"

"It is. That's what I've just said."

"Father, where is this place? I might take a look at it, if that's all right with you."

He scribbled down the directions and then hung up. Gordie looked at his watch. *Damn. Five-ten already.*

He called Roxanne's number and frowned when it went to voice-mail. He then called Norris and smiled when he heard the grumpy tone of the detective's voice. "Where the hell is everyone?"

"I'm just finishing up at the mechanic's. Sorry I'm late. I'm on my way now. Isn't Albright there with you?"

"No. I've been sitting here on my own for twenty minutes and I'm ready to pack it in."

Gordie looked at his watch again. "That's strange. She's usually early. Did she call?"

"Nope. I tried calling her, but it went straight to voicemail."

"Me too. She must be in a dead zone. I'm on my way now. I shouldn't be more than twenty minutes or so. Can you wait that long?"

He heard the sigh. "Yeah, all right. Will it be worth my while?"

"It will. Listen, do me a favour and call whoever's on the desk and find out what time Albright left. I hope she hasn't broken down somewhere."

"Okay. See you soon."

Gordie saw Dennis LeBlanc watching him. *Probably wondering what the heck I'm doing sitting here all this time.* He gave the mechanic a wave and pulled out of the yard. *Would have been nice to find this property since I'm out this way, but it's getting dark, anyway. Best leave it until tomorrow.* With that thought, he put his foot down and accelerated south on Route 19.

CHAPTER 33

IT WAS MORE LIKE half an hour before Gordie reached Norris. When he walked in, he felt a prickle on the back of his neck to see Rob Norris sitting alone reading a newspaper. When Norris looked up and saw Gordie, he flung aside the paper. "It's about bloody time. I can tell you the latest score of every pee-wee hockey game around the Island by now."

"Any word from Albright?"

"Nothing, and the desk told me she left about one o'clock."

"She should have been here by now. Let me think. She was going to call Father Duncan, and then she was coming here to meet with us. That's right, isn't it? She wasn't going anywhere else, was she?"

Norris shrugged. "She's your protegé, not mine."

"Yeah, yeah, I know." He tried her number again but hung up without leaving another message when it went to voicemail.

While Gordie made the call, Norris got up and got them each a coffee. He put it down in front of Gordie. "I'm sure she's fine. Like you said, she probably broke down somewhere with no service."

Gordie tore open two packets of sugar and dumped them into his cup. "I don't know. Her vehicle isn't old. It seems unlikely."

Norris took a sip of his own. "Speaking of vehicles. Tell me what you found while we're waiting."

Gordie went through his conversations with LeBlanc and Father John for Norris.

Norris set his cup down. "You figure the car is still sitting there at that property? Maybe some local kid has discovered it and got it running?"

"I don't know. I doubt it's a local kid. It's just too much of a coincidence that it was owned by the woman who looked after Father Duncan and Father Peter."

"So tomorrow we go out there to see what we can see?"

Gordie nodded. "Right now, I need to figure out what's going on with Albright. There aren't many stretches between here and Sydney where there's no service." He drained his cup. "You go on home. I'm going to drive down and look for her car."

Norris frowned. "That doesn't make sense. I live down that way, anyway. I'll head out now and look. If I get as far as Sydney Forks and don't see her, then we know she hasn't broken down because between there and Sydney the cell service is good, and she would have called." Norris rose. "Look, I'm sure she'll turn up. I'll call you in an hour and a half if not sooner, and if you hear from her, give me a shout."

Gordie nodded. "Thanks. I'll talk to you later." He sat for a moment after Rob Norris had left while he considered what to do and then went back to his car.

He took a deep breath and then called his sergeant. For a change, he was glad when the phone was picked up right away. Gordie would have hated even more if he'd had to call his boss at home.

"Sergeant, MacLean here. We may have a problem."

The response was sharp. "What sort of problem?"

"Detective Albright may be missing."

For the space of a heartbeat, there was no response, and then Arsenault's voice was quiet. The usual edge of sarcasm was missing. "What do you mean?"

"She was scheduled to meet Norris and me at five o'clock, but she hasn't shown and she's not answering her phone. Norris checked with the desk and they said she left there at about one."

"She was to meet you in Port Mulroy?"

"Yes. Norris left here a few minutes ago and is on his way home. There's only one road she would have taken, so he's on the lookout for her car. He's going to call me when he gets to Sydney Forks unless he finds her, or her car, before that."

"How the hell did you lose her, MacLean?"

Gordie had expected more bluff-and-bluster, but he understood his sergeant's heart wasn't in it. First, they had to find her. Recriminations would come later.

"She was going to track down Father Duncan, the priest who went out west. After that she was going to head straight for Port Mulroy. I thought it was straightforward."

"She took a page from your book in other words and went off somewhere without telling anyone."

Gordie sighed. "Looks that way. Listen, I want to call Albright's grandmother, just in case she's tucked up at home after getting the flu. Or maybe, Albright called her to say what time she'd be home for supper, or something, anything to give us a starting point. The number should be on Albright's next-of-kin form.

Gordie heard Sergeant Arsenault typing as he accessed the personnel records. "Right, here's the number. 828-1920."

"Got it. Thanks."

"Look, try not to alarm the old lady too much." His voice softened. "And MacLean, call me after you've spoken to her. We may need to call in more support. Let me know how I can help."

Gordie clenched his teeth at Arsenault's warning, but closed his eyes as the tone changed. His boss was right, of course. He didn't want to alarm the woman, but he needed to do something. He couldn't just sit here waiting as Norris drove home.

Gordie heard a television playing in the background, and Helen Albright's cheerful voice, a smile embedded in the 'hello?'

"Mrs. Albright, this is Detective MacLean."

Immediately her voice dropped, and he heard her quick footsteps cross the wooden floor to turn down the television. "Yes, Detective." There was a quaver in her voice. "Has something happened?"

He put on his most calming, positive voice. "No, not at all. You'll remember that I am Roxanne's partner?"

"Yes, of course. Her boss."

Gordie winced. "We keep missing each other this afternoon and now I suspect she's in an area with no cell service at the moment, so I just wanted to check if you've heard from your granddaughter this afternoon?"

The quaver was more pronounced now. She was gulping back tears. "I haven't heard from her all day. Not since she left this morning. What's happened to her, Detective?"

"I'm sure there's absolutely nothing wrong. Please don't be alarmed." Even as he said the words, he knew that she would, of course be alarmed and there was nothing he could do to change that. "Thank you, Mrs. Albright. I'll let you get back to getting your dinner ready. If she does come in, or you hear from her, please ask her to give me a quick call."

"I will. Please Detective, if *you* hear from her, will you ask her to call *me*?"

"First thing, Mrs. Albright. First thing. And if it seems like it might run late, I will personally call you, all right?"

"I'd appreciate that. Thank you."

He hung up, wishing he hadn't had to do that, but she would have started worrying soon no matter what, as the hour grew later, and her granddaughter didn't arrive home for her dinner.

He called Arsenault back. "No luck, Sergeant. The grandmother hasn't spoken to her since she left home this morning."

"I went down and looked at her desk. She's got a pad of paper there where she's written down a couple of phone numbers. She's made circles around one, so I'm guessing it's the one that worked best for her. An Alberta number. Do you want it, or do you want me to call?"

Gordie blinked at Arsenault's helpfulness. "I'll call. It must be Father Duncan's number."

Arsenault read it out and then continued. "I called Norris. He's well on the way and nothing so far. MacLean, I'm going to call the Mounties. We can cancel them when we find her, but right now, we might as well get as many eyes out there looking as possible."

"I agree, Sergeant. I'll call you back after I've spoken with Father Duncan."

CHAPTER 34

G ORDIE HATED THE IDEA of calling Father Duncan. If this man was somehow connected to what had happened to Sarah, Mary-Catherine and now Roxanne, the last thing Gordie wanted to do was alert him that he had the advantage over the police. The number he dialed had a 403 prefix so although it was an Alberta area code, Gordie knew that didn't mean that the man wasn't right here in Nova Scotia now. He may in fact have Roxanne captive. Gordie wished they could just ping cell phones and get instant results the way the American cop shows did so he could easily locate both Father Duncan and in fact, Roxanne. Sadly, his resources didn't stretch to that kind of technology. He put his reservations out of his mind. He had to take the risk.

Father Duncan answered on the second ring. "Father Duncan Landry."

"Detective MacLean of the Cape Breton Police Service here, Father."

"Good heavens. I just spoke with your colleague a few hours ago. Do you have more questions for me?"

"Where are you right now, Father?"

"As Detective Albright no doubt told you, I've been at a funeral in Jasper and I'm just now getting ready to head back to Hinton. Why?"

The man didn't sound stressed or tense. "I just wanted to ensure you were somewhere you could take my call safely."

"No problem. Go ahead. How can I help you? I thought I told Detective Albright everything I could think of."

"I'm just following up to confirm some matters. I'm going to record this call, Father. Is that all right with you?"

Gordie heard the puzzled tone. "Sure. Go ahead."

He pushed the record button before continuing. Gordie took a breath and a guess. "When you spoke with my colleague, she asked you about the black car."

"Yes, Mrs. Scott's old car."

Gordie felt his heart pound. "Yes, that's the one. I want to capture this on tape, so can you please repeat what you said earlier?"

His voice was hesitant now. "There isn't much to tell, but all right. As I mentioned, I know that Mrs. Scott, my old landlady, had a black Nissan. She didn't like to drive. It actually belonged to her deceased husband, so Peter would often drive her around for her shopping or if she wanted to visit someone. He owned a clunker of a car and although he kept it running, he liked the Scott car better. That's what he called it. The Scott car." Gordie heard Father Duncan chuckle. "He was passionate about cars and would tinker away with it to keep it tuned up and only took it to a mechanic when it needed some part. He did his own oil changes, though and other basic maintenance. Is this what you're looking for?"

Gordie tried to keep the impatience out of his voice. "Yes, thank you. What happened to the car after Mrs. Scott died, Father?"

"That was after I left so I'm afraid I'm not sure what happened, eventually. I suppose Peter sold it, but I don't know that for certain. I never really thought about it again after I left to come out west."

"Is it possible he simply kept it?"

"It's possible but I don't know why he would. He's got a car of his own now, I believe. You have to understand, I didn't keep in touch with Peter after I left. My father died and my focus was caught up with my family and my new parish once I moved here, so you should just give Peter a call."

"You left right around the time Sarah Campbell went missing, didn't you?"

"Yes. I do remember that happening and talking to Peter about it, but he didn't seem overly worried. He believed she had left a troubled home life to start again." Father Duncan made a *tutting* sound with his tongue. "Terrible when one thinks of it now we know the poor girl was murdered. I must call Peter to see how he's faring." Almost as an afterthought, he added "Did the detective find the car, then? I had a sense she was heading out to the old Scott place to have a look around."

Dammit, dammit, dammit. "Thank you, Father Duncan. You've been very helpful. I'll let you get on with your drive home now."

"Oh. All right. Anytime."

Gordie disengaged and stopped recording. *Not him. Not Father Duncan.*

Gordie dialed Sergeant Arsenault again and at the same time, cranked on the engine. "Arsenault."

He was almost shouting as he wheeled his car out of the parking lot. "She's at the old Scott place. The place where Father Duncan and Father Peter lived when they shared a house. I drove right past on the way back to Port Mulroy. "

"Where? Where is this place? I'll get the Mounties over there."

Gordie gave the directions, his voice clipped and tight.

"Wait for backup, MacLean. Do you hear me? If you get there first, wait for backup!"

MacLean pushed the button on his steering wheel to cut the phone and gave all his attention to speeding back up the road he had driven only a couple of hours previously. It was drizzling now, the road shiny and treacherous. Gordie put the wipers on and with every swipe back and forth they seemed to say *too late, too late, too late.*

***

Father Peter straightened up, and keeping the gun trained on Roxanne, walked to a tarpaulin partway along the wall. He pulled it aside and lifted a battery-powered lantern that had been hidden underneath. He set it on a low shelf and clicked it on. Roxanne blinked in the sudden light. His eyes narrowed with determination; he took a step towards Roxanne. She held up her hands as if to ward him off.

"Why, Father Peter? What's this all about? What happened all those years ago?"

He stopped and blinked. "What does it matter now?"

"It matters to me. If you're going to kill me, I'd like to understand why."

He sighed and glanced upwards. Roxanne wondered if he was having a silent conversation with Sarah or God. Or was he simply remembering?

He shook his head. "What happened? I let sin get the better of me. It didn't start out like that." He looked at Roxanne, pleading for understanding. "She had a rotten home life. Her father a drunk, her mother fooling around."

Roxanne gasped. "So, Sarah knew about her mother?"

"She knew. I can't remember how, but she knew. It tormented her because she wanted her mother to be happy, but in the Roman Catholic faith, marriage is something worth fighting for. Sarah looked tough to some people, but I know she was torn between her faith and what she thought was best for her mother. That's how it started. We talked. She wanted guidance."

Roxanne nodded. "Something changed." *Keep him talking. It's a start.*

The hand holding the gun dropped a little as his arm relaxed. "Yes. Everything changed. One afternoon she stayed late as she sometimes did, just so we could talk. We were in my office. She cried. I held her. It was a natural, comforting thing to do."

"And then hormones kicked in."

"Yes." He closed his eyes for a second and Roxanne tensed. *Can I run for it?* He opened his eyes again, staring off above her head. "Yes. We both felt it. I didn't force myself on her. We just couldn't resist. Neither of us could resist."

Roxanne nodded again. "I understand. We're still just human, Father. Even you." She kept her voice low and sympathetic.

"If it was a one-off, I would agree, but it was just the start. After that, we looked for ways to be together. We couldn't be in my office again." He shook his head. "What an insane risk that was. Anyone could have walked in."

Roxanne looked around. "Did you start coming here?"

"A couple of times, but even this was dangerous. People knew me. No, mostly we went to the lighthouse."

Roxanne blinked. "Yes, of course. The lighthouse. Was that 'your place' even before you went on the group trip?"

He heaved another sigh. "It was Sarah's idea. She loved it there and pleaded with me, so we went there once with the group. Nothing happened while we were all there, of course, but she loved the intrigue of it. I didn't. Once was enough."

"And then everything started to go wrong, didn't it?"

He frowned. "Started? It was wrong from the beginning. She was like a drug to me. I was obsessed. The devil was having his way with me." He stepped back and slumped against the car again. "But yes. A bad situation got even worse."

"She told you she was pregnant."

Peter's eyes widened. "How did you know?"

"Did you argue?"

He closed his eyes. "She told me when we were up at the lighthouse one day. I thought I was going to be sick. It was like she had thrown ice water over me. Just like that, it was over for me. I was horrified." He looked at Roxanne. "She told me she was on the pill. She lied to me. She wanted to get pregnant, and she was so happy when it happened." He gave a short bark of laughter. "Sarah thought I'd be happy too. She said I could be a mechanic." He shook his head. "The deluded girl thought I'd give up my life to be a mechanic."

"Is that when you killed her? Were you enraged?"

"No. I was," he hesitated, searching for the right word "stupefied. I tried to explain I couldn't just walk away. This is my calling. I had been tempted, and I had failed the test, but that didn't mean I was prepared to throw it all away."

"How did she react?"

"I believe she thought she could change my mind. That I'd see reason in time."

He hung his head. "All the way home I tried to make her understand. At one point, God help me, I offered to pay for an abortion. She was shocked. I was shocked at myself. Then I offered to send her to Toronto to stay with a cousin of mine until the baby was born and put up for adoption."

"She got all quiet then. I think she was starting to understand that this wasn't going to lead to happy families with us. She said she needed time to think, so I asked her not to talk about it to anyone. She said she wouldn't, and we made a date for her to come see me in a couple of days."

"A couple of days being August 17th?"

He nodded. "I picked her up near work."

Roxanne nodded to the car. "In this car?"

"Yes, I always used this car. I didn't want people seeing us in my car."

"You picked her up. Then what?"

"She wanted to go to the lighthouse, but I was done with that. I took her to my office. It was after hours. No one was likely to come in, but I wanted to get on to a different footing. Somehow maybe I thought I could go back in time." He shrugged. "Crazy, I know. I thought we could just dissolve this relationship somehow, so I wanted to make it as professional as possible." He closed his eyes again.

By now the gun hung limply in his hand by his side, and still Roxanne didn't dare make a move. There were several feet between them. She'd never make it to him before he raised the gun again.

He opened his eyes and blinked. "I know it sounds foolish now, but I wasn't very experienced with women. I was out of my depth."

Her voice was soft. "It didn't go as planned, did it?"

He pursed his lips. "No. We argued some more. Just going back and forth. She really wanted the baby and then she said she was done talking. Done with me. Done with God, even." He stopped talking as he remembered the scene.

Roxanne twitched. *She gave her cross to Lorraine because she was done with God.* The inexperienced detective's muscles tensed, ready to leap and wrestle Peter for the gun, but still she hesitated, and he continued with the tale.

"She left. I watched her for a minute as she walked down the hall. She was so pretty in her red and white dress. She went down the steps and outside. I followed her. Just to plead one more time. I went out behind her and she had stopped. She didn't turn to look at me. I told her I'd even pay support if necessary, but she had to leave. That was the deal. She had to go away. She listened, without ever looking at me, and then she said she didn't care what I thought. It was her decision."

Roxanne waited, seeing the image of the beautiful girl in her mind, poised to begin a whole new life.

His voice was low, his breath ragged. "It's like I wasn't even in control of my own actions. I was in some kind of daze. I picked up a piece of wood. We were having a little enclosure built around the back door, so there was wood lying all around. I picked it up and swung it." He choked on the words. "It was awful. So much blood. I never imagined there could be so much blood. I stood there for a minute and then I went into a panic." He looked up again at Roxanne. "Anyone could have come. I just picked her up and put her out of sight in the back enclosure while I tried to think. It was already late, and I went to wash up and have a brandy and by then it was pretty much dark. I backed up the car, the Scott car, as close to the walkway as I could get it and then I carried Sarah out and put her in the trunk. It was unbelievable, really. No one came by, not even when I was burying her. I kept expecting someone to drive by and say, *Hey Father, what are you up to?* But no one did."

"Why there? Why did you pick that garden?"

"It was close by. I couldn't bear to drive around with Sarah in the trunk for any longer than necessary. I knew the house. It belonged to a parishioner, a close friend of Mrs. Scott's. I often drove Mrs. Scott there, so if anyone saw the car, they wouldn't think twice. The lady was elderly and went to bed very early. A couple of days earlier, I had been doing some gardening in that spot already, so it was simple to dig there. I didn't really think it through. It was the first thing that came to mind."

Roxanne waited. Perhaps it was nearly over. Maybe he would simply hand over the gun.

He blinked as if to drive away the mental pictures and then focussed on Roxanne. "So now you know." He straightened.

"What about Mary-Catherine Cameron? What happened there?"

He frowned. "That was different. She wasn't an innocent."

"She knew it was you and she contacted you, didn't she?"

"She suspected it was me. Even all those years ago, I would see her watching us at the group meetings. She was too sharp for her own good, that one. I asked Sarah once if she had told Mary-Catherine, but she swore she hadn't, but I could tell she knew something."

"She phoned you and wanted money."

He nodded. "I gave her some, but I knew even as I handed it over that it wouldn't be the end, and just as I expected, once I gave it to her, she told me that was a down payment. She wanted another five thousand. I thought it was all behind me. I've lived a good life since that awful time."

"But then Sarah's body was discovered."

He nodded. "Such a nightmare. I should have known that no amount of good work could make up for that wrong. She rose from the grave to accuse me."

"But it wasn't Sarah accusing you, was it?"

"No. It was that girl. She called me and at first it seemed that she just wanted to talk about Sarah and her funeral, but then she started making little suggestions about how I had been such a special friend. When I didn't react, she finally came right out with it. She said she knew that Sarah had been pregnant. I was shocked. I didn't think Sarah had told anyone."

Roxanne nodded. "I don't actually believe that Sarah told her who the father was, even though she may have told her about the pregnancy."

He gave a little 'huh' of surprise. "She made it sound like Sarah had told her and that she had some sort of evidence like a diary."

"I think that's unlikely."

Father Peter wiped his brow with his free hand. "I could have just denied it all."

"Instead of running Mary-Catherine down, you mean?"

He chewed on his lip. "What a mess. It just gets worse and worse."

"Father, it's over now. We know everything. You might as well give me the gun now."

He raised his hand again. "It isn't over. No one knows I'm here and obviously no one knows you are either."

"You're wrong. My partner is on the way with backup."

His face flushed. "Liar. I've had enough of liars." He straightened again and stepped towards her. "Get down on your knees facing the wall."

Her heart beat madly. *Damn it. I should have just kept him talking.* "No, Father. Don't make things even worse."

He gritted his teeth. "What's one more body? Down. Get down on your knees."

Shaking, she slowly slid off the bench and down on her knees. She shuffled around to face the wall. She heard him pop open the trunk of the car. Images raced through her mind. *Drop and roll. Do a head butt to his crotch if he gets close enough.* As ideas flashed and were abandoned, she felt him behind her.

Roxanne tensed and cried out when she felt a jolt to the back of her neck. She fell face forward into the dirt and mouldy hay of the barn floor, her body cramping in a massive spasm as the electricity from the Taser coursed through her. She was helpless to fight him as Peter lifted her and placed her in the trunk of the car. Roxanne groaned. Her muscles ached, but she was slowly regaining control. She twitched and tried to lift her arms to prevent the trunk from closing but didn't have the strength and coordination. With a hard metallic *thunk*, the lid came down, enclosing her in darkness.

She heard him just above her, saying a prayer and she vaguely recognized one of the psalms. "O loving and kind God, have mercy. Have pity upon me and take away the awful stain of my transgression."

Roxanne swallowed and called out, her voice raspy and dry. "It's not too late. Let me out. You know if you go ahead with this, you're going against God's will. Don't do it."

The prayer stopped and after a brief silence, she heard his voice again, close to the lid of the trunk. "It'll be over soon. Say *your* prayers, Detective. There's an old logging road near here that leads down to an overhang and a drop straight into St. George's Bay. Drowning isn't a bad way to die, I believe."

CHAPTER 35

GORDIE WENT PAST THE cut-off the first time and had to turn to go back. There were no other cars on the road, making the U-turn easy, but the lack of lights made the way even darker. He was careful not to go too far on to the shoulder in case he went into the soft ground beside the road. He couldn't afford to get stuck in the mud out here.

He crept along the road, the passenger window down and his high-brightness flashlight trained along the side of the road.

He found the turn and turned off the flashlight. There. Albright's car parked blocking the entrance to the driveway reflected his head-lights. He parked behind it and got out of the car, closing his door softly. He stood listening. Nearby he heard the waves of St. George's Bay hitting rocks. Shoosh, shoosh, shoosh. He heard the crying of seagulls and chirping of pond frogs, but that was all. The old house was in darkness.

Where are you? Dammit Roxanne, what were you thinking coming out here on your own? At the back of his mind, he recognized that similar words had been thrown at him in the past. He edged forward, holding his hand on the Taser in his pocket. It was his only weapon, and he hoped that the Mounties would get there soon to back him up. *If only she's still here. If they're gone, we're lost.* The driveway was long and Gordie's instinct was to run, feeling that every moment counted, and at the same time knowing that he needed to fight the impulse and continue with stealth to move around to the back of the house. If there were any motion-sensor lights on the house or barn, he'd be in trouble. He peered through the darkness and rain, walking on the grass rather than the gravel. Gordie reached the house and pressed himself against the weathered board siding. He slid along the side, stopping to listen every few steps. Nothing. He reached the corner and saw the barn. Light filtered out from a partially covered window, dulled by the greasy rain.

Gordie knew he should back off and wait for backup. It was still quiet, even the seagulls muffled in the rain. He made up his mind and after one more careful look at the barn doors sprinted across the open farmyard to the safety of the barn wall. He stumbled in the darkness over a pile of lumber, rotted and half hidden by weeds and brown grass. His back stiffened, and he froze, listening to hear if he had attracted any attention.

Gordie crept to the window and took a fast look inside before pulling back again. He frowned. Father Peter was there, but Gordie hadn't seen Albright. *Where are you?* He chewed his lip for a moment, thinking about what he'd seen. Father Peter hunched over the closed trunk of the car, hands resting flat against the trunk lid. *She's in the bloody trunk.* He felt his gorge rise in rage. *If she's dead, so are you, Father.*

In the dark night he saw flashing lights approaching. Gordie sprinted back to the shelter of the house. He ran down the driveway, racing to reach the RCMP cars now pulled over on the side of the road.

His breath gasping, he reached the first officer. "Kill the lights!"

Immediately the officer did, and the second car followed his lead.

Gordie stood with his hands on his knees, catching his breath. He straightened. These were men that Gordie knew well as they were from the local detachment and had supported Gordie many times.

"What's happening here, MacLean?"

"Hostage taking. There's a man in the barn who's taken Detective Albright. I'm pretty sure he's got her in the trunk of a car we've been looking for. He's either planning to just leave her there and maybe burn the place down or take her away somewhere. Either way, it's going down soon. Let's get these cars moved further away, so he doesn't see us before we can surround him."

Gordie hustled to his own vehicle while the two Mounties moved their cars further along the road. *God love you, Roxanne, for parking in the driveway. He won't get around you. He may have your keys, but he'll need to get out of the car to move yours, or he'll try to drive around you. Either way, it'll slow him down.*

The Mounties had called for more backup and Gordie knew that the extra cars and people would soon attract attention, but at the moment it was still quiet, and they followed Gordie's directions. Fanning out on either side of Albright's car, they hunkered down, taking cover behind wild rose bushes. They were barely in place when Gordie heard the scrape of the old corrugated metal barn door being dragged open; the sound muffled by the rain. He hoped the others had heard it too and were poised and ready to move. He didn't dare flash his penlight to signal them in case Father Peter saw it.

The car started up; the engine missing twice before it started. Briefly Gordie wondered how the man planned to manage two cars, but the thought slid away as he saw the headlight come around the corner of the house. One light was broken and Gordie imagined they would find evidence on the damaged front to prove the car had struck Mary-Catherine.

Every muscle tensed as the car came down towards Albright's parked car. It slowed, then stopped. Father Peter put his car in park and got out. Gordie sensed, rather than heard him curse and take a step away from his car, leaving the door open. The interior light showed him clearly as he seemed to consider the problem of the obstacle.

"Now!" Gordie shouted. He leaped forward, taking grim pleasure in the shock on Father Peter's face. Peter made a lunge to jump back in the car, but Gordie was too quick and reached out to clutch at his jacket. By then the other two were there, the shine of silver from their Smith and Wessons glinting dully.

"Down on the ground. Now, now! Do it. Hands behind your head."

Father Peter lay down, his hands laced on the back of his head.

Gordie reached into the car and took the keys, hustling to the trunk. His heart pounded as he unlocked and raised the lid.

He laughed when he heard Albright's grumble. "Took you long enough."

He helped her out and steadied her as her legs crumpled under her. She held on to the trunk for a moment. "I'm all right. I'm fine, just pins and needles in my legs from being squashed into the damn trunk."

He squeezed her shoulder. "What the hell were you thinking?"

She sighed as she straightened up. "I thought I'd just take a little look before I gave you a full report."

"You thought you'd be a hero, you mean."

She shrugged.

He shook his head. "I've been there. Come on. I'm taking you to the hospital to get checked out." He handed her his phone. "But first, call your Nana."

***

By the time Gordie pulled into his driveway many hours later, he was exhausted. Taz greeted him at the door, tail waving gracefully. He got a Heineken from the fridge and went out into the backyard with the dog. He talked to her quietly as he stood, drinking in the fresh spring night along with his beer.

"Taz, I screwed up." She turned her head to study him and then, satisfied he wasn't calling her, continued her patrol around the perimeter of the yard.

"I almost cost that girl her life. I started out all right. I took her along with me, let her take her turn, and listened to her ideas. She impressed me. Struck me as someone who could go ahead on her own with assignments, and I was right. She could and did."

He took a long pull at the beer. "Where I screwed up was that I forgot that we were partners. I was so bent on proving to Arsenault that I could do this, that I was happy to split the work and let her go off on her own. I knew we were making progress. Hell, I even suspected who we were after. He seemed too chummy with her, but I didn't say a word."

Gordie went back to the white plastic chair near the door, sat down and clamping the beer bottle between his knees, lit a cigarette. "Did I tell her my theory? Nope. I'm used to keeping my own council. Sure, I listened to what she had to say, but I didn't tell her what I was thinking. If I had, she probably would have talked to me before haring off on her own. I didn't create a working relationship where it was a natural give and take."

He sighed. "I should have been talking to her instead of you, Taz."

Hearing her name, Taz came over and rested her head on his knees. He caressed her, scratching behind her ears. "The case is solved Taz, but at what cost? She's fine, thank God, but it was too close a call. It might be the end of my career, Taz."

He ground out the cigarette in the small pail of sand he kept beside the chair, drained the bottle, and went inside to a restless night's sleep.

***

Gordie was surprised to see Roxanne at her desk first thing in the morning. "I thought you'd be taking it easy today."

"I'm fine." She grinned. "Can't let you take all the glory."

He shook his head. "Damn. Well, go make a start on getting the briefing room set up. I'll see if Sarge is in yet. I gave him the highlights last night, but I'm guessing he'll want a word or two."

Gordie walked down the hall to Sergeant Arsenault's office. The door was open, and his boss was tapping on his computer. He looked up and waved Gordie in and gestured for him to sit.

"Detective Albright is setting up the briefing room. I thought you might want a word before the briefing?"

Arsenault leaned forward, resting his forearms on his desk. "How do you feel the operation went, MacLean?"

Gordie swallowed. "I screwed up."

Arsenault nodded. "Go on."

"We didn't communicate properly. It almost cost the life of my partner."

Arsenault leaned back. "Damn right. Detective MacLean, you solved the case. I didn't think you could, but in your own plodding but persistent way, you did it and that's a good thing. I assigned you a partner though, and I expected that you, as senior man, would look out for her, and in that you failed."

Gordie nodded.

Arsenault studied Gordie in silence for a moment. "Well, if there's nothing else, go help your partner get ready for the briefing. The team will want to hear every gory detail."

Gordie rose and walked away in a daze. *Maybe he's not as bad as I thought.*

***

After a day of paperwork and phone calls with the RCMP who were embroiled in their own reports, they were free to enjoy their success. The team left the office early and drove the ten minutes to their favourite pub, *The Old Triangle*. They pushed several tables together and ordered platters of deep-fried seafood and chicken wings to go with the drinks. Gordie had one beer and nursed it while he, Norris and Albright took turns telling and re-telling pieces of the investigation.

When he slipped away, satisfied in the knowledge that Norris was taking Albright home with him to sleep in the spare room for the night after too many glasses of celebratory wine, he felt better than he had in a long time. While he enjoyed the camaraderie of his colleagues, there was someone's company he would prefer.

He phoned as he drove. When she picked up, he was suddenly tongue-tied. "Hi, Vanessa. It's Gordie."

Her voice was warm, and he heard the smile. "Gordie. I'm so glad to hear from you. I've heard nothing else on the news but about you and the arrest you made last night."

"I'm sorry it's been a while since I called, but as you can guess, I've been tied up."

Her voice was serious, even though he'd been hoping for a chuckle. "I can only imagine what you've been going through. Are you nearby? Would you like a cup of tea?"

"I'm on the way home from the office. I'm still a good hour away, but I'd like that, if it won't be too late for you?"

"Why don't you stop and pick up Taz on your way and then come over? It won't be too late…whatever time it is."

Gordie hung up, feeling as if his quiet life may be in for a change in the future.

The End

WITH THANKS

Thank you to Dr. Christopher Kyle, Chair and Associate Professor, Forensic Sciences at Trent University, Peterborough, Ontario – my professor of *Introduction to Forensic Science*, and gracious resource for my questions with this book.

Thank you to my beta readers Erma Hamilton and Irene Stern; two strangers who signed up to read my very rough manuscript and left me encouraged. Thanks also to my beta reader and first editor, Jimmy Carton, and the members of various facebook support groups who answered numerous questions and provided insight and feedback.

With huge gratitude to Dave Wickenden who did a manuscript review and mentored me. As well, more thanks to Sharron Elkouby who has been editing and proofreading my writing now for more than 30 years!

Thanks to my writing soulmates of both the Writers Community of Durham Region and the Sudbury Writers Guild.

Last but not least, with thanks to The Writers Union of Canada for financial support by way of a grant. I'm proud to be a member!